CH

My Darling Dorothy

My Darling Dorothy

JO VIRDEN

Plainview Publications

My Darling Dorothy
Published by Plainview Publications
Arvada, CO

Library of Congress Control Number: 2016936882
Virden, Jo, Author
My Darling Dorothy
Jo Virden

ISBN: 978-0-9974308-0-6

FICTION / Romance / Historical

QUANTITY PURCHASES: Schools, companies, professional groups, clubs, and other organizations may qualify for special terms when ordering quantities of this title. For information, email info@plainviewpublications.com.

To my Mom and Dad
Wilmer and Dorothy Smith
And to
Lloyd Grever

Author's Note

A few facts regarding *My Darling Dorothy* need to be made clear:

- While authentic letters provided the inspiration for the novel, it is important to remember that *My Darling Dorothy* is a work of fiction.
- Letters from Tommie and Smitty include the original misspellings and grammatical errors in order to stay true to their identities at the time.
- All of the stamps, postmarks and postcards are authentic and taken from the original letters.

Part 1

HONOLULU HAWAII
SEP 13
1 - PM
1941

BUY
DEFENSE SAVINGS
BONDS AND STAMPS

1

Summer 2012

Jo opened the top box with trepidation.

She pulled out a grocery list written on the back of an empty used envelope. "Mom!" she yelled, looking skyward. "Really? Did you ever throw *anything* away?"

"Precious junk," her mom's term for the five boxes gathering dust in the corner of the basement, awaited Jo's scrutiny.

Thirty-gallon, extra-sturdy trash bags sat at the ready. Jo's practical side begged her to slip the boxes, unopened, into the bags, climb the stairs, go directly to the Dumpster, throw them in, close the lid, and walk away. Yet her inner hoarder, finely tuned through a childhood of watching her parents save everything from broken potty chairs to faded plastic flowers, wangled its way into her thoughts.

What if there is something important or valuable in

all this junk? Jo thought as she shuffled through the box's contents—a 1957 program from Fred Johnson's funeral; a birthday card from her sister, sent in 1932; a letter from Jo's great-grandfather to her great-grandmother written in 1896; and *la pièce de résistance*, a department store receipt from 1975. Any sensible person would have stopped right there, but her inner hoarder reared its messy head. *There must be some reason she kept this stuff. I need to dig deeper.*

To appease her more pragmatic side, Jo began to create piles of birthday cards, Christmas cards, and letters, and in honor of her mom, a pile Jo labeled "Miscellaneous Precious Junk." She pulled out another handful of items. A large group of letters wrapped in a blue ribbon caught her eye. She thumbed through them. The envelopes all bore the same handwriting. Her inner hoarder beamed with the satisfaction of victory.

Now we're talking.

Jo opened a letter. The first page, a rather boring account of the day in the life of a soldier, seemed innocent enough. She quickly lost interest and jumped to the second page:

> I wish my year was over. It's kinda fun to lay around and build air castles and then let them burst. I still have hopes of not having to go over the pond and blow Hitler off the map. But maby I can be lucky. Who knows? We are sure going to have fun when I get out, ain't we? I've got it all figured out; where, when and how.
>
> Maby you think I'm foolish, I don't know

and you may think I'm kidding myself, but I'm not, because when you hear I'm heading home, get ready. That day I land in Nebraska is our wedding day, rain, snow or shine.

The way my brother wrote in his last letter he figures on getting married this summer if they don't call him to the army too soon. If they do he plans to get married before he goes. I think he's foolish. I would much rather do it our way, go to army first & get married afterwards. Then, if we get in war & get blowed to bits wont leave a widow. Don't you think that's best?

Well darling, I've been pondering over this piece of paper for an hour and just can't seem to think of any more to say. Take good care of yourself. I think about you lots, only wish I could be closer than 1200 miles from you. Remember, I am still looking forward to those pictures you promised me and some more of those nice letters. Bye now

Loads of Love and Kisses,
Tommie

Tommie? She glanced at the date again: May, 1941. Eighteen months before her parents were married. *Who is Tommie?*

Winter 1926

Jack looked away, unable to tolerate the lifeless, hollow eyes of his six-year-old sister, Annie. He knew she was still alive because her body shook in violent spasms as feverish chills consumed her. Not a trace of color remained in her face.

"Jack, get me another quilt from upstairs," his mother ordered, an edge of panic in her voice. "I can't get her to stop shaking."

Outside, the unyielding Nebraska wind howled, and snow beat against the front door in a horizontal pattern. An eight-foot drift covered the front window. Jack figured it might just keep the place warmer. He moved closer to the kitchen stove, the only heat source in the drafty, ramshackle farmhouse, opened the door to the wood box, and tossed in the last of the corn cobs, trying not to think about what would happen when they were gone. He took the stairs two at a time, yanked the last blanket off Annie's bed, and rushed back to the stove, where he warmed it before placing it on her trembling body.

His pa had left hours ago in pursuit of Doc Olson, who lived in Beaver City, twenty miles to the south. Now, Jack worried that his pa might be stuck in the blizzard somewhere, or worse. He looked at his ma, and a sense of helplessness welled up inside him like the snowdrifts mounting outside the front door.

I'm the man here. I gotta do something! Anything!

"Ma, I gotta go find some more wood for the stove. We're out of cobs. Maybe I can chop a branch off the old elm tree. They're hangin' pretty low with all the snow. I'll be back as soon as I can."

"You stay right here, Jack Smith. You're not goin' anywhere!" his mother admonished. He didn't look back, opened the front door, and began digging his way through a solid wall of snow with a nearby broom handle. All the while, his mother screamed in anguish for him to stay, not to leave her there alone with Annie.

Once outside, he grabbed the ax from the front porch and headed in the direction of the elm tree in the front yard. He knew it was there, had always been there, even though all he could see right then was a wall of white. He closed his eyes and began walking in the direction that he was sure would lead him to the tree, waving his arms in all directions in the hopes he would stumble into one of the low-lying branches. It worked. He began chopping at the tree with more strength than a ten-year-old should have, but a child filled with the mission of saving his ma and baby sister renders even a scrawny kid into a valiant hero. He swung, he chopped, he yanked, he tugged until the limb gave way. Branch in hand, he closed his eyes, pictured the front porch, and dragged the large piece of wood behind him.

His mother watched from the front window for any sign of her little boy while she held Annie close to her chest, hoping to maintain her body temperature. She screamed when she saw him trudging past the house. He made an about-face at the sound of her voice, realizing his error, and heaved the bulky limb onto the porch.

His mother opened the front door. "Come in now and warm up, son," she pleaded. "You can watch Annie, and I'll chop the wood. You've done enough, Jack. Please come in."

If he had had his druthers, he would have preferred the bitter cold to looking at Annie one more minute, but he could hear the panic in his mother's voice and he relented.

The year was 1926, three years before the Great Depression. Jack's family would barely notice when it started in 1929. They often wondered what all the fuss was about. No money? No food? Hard times? Jack dreamed of a time when maybe those things wouldn't define his life.

Little Annie lived through the blizzard. Her pa arrived with Doc Olson the next morning, but by then she had turned the corner between becoming another victim of the flu epidemic and having a chance at adulthood.

The harshness of that winter haunted Jack for the rest of his life. When he wasn't trying to find enough wood to warm the house, he was trying to find one more turnip in the garden, maybe even a leftover potato to feed the four of them. His pa brought home all manner of wild game, and they ate it with pleasure; raccoon or coyote, it didn't matter to them.

A ten-year-old shouldn't have to worry about whether a sibling would live or die or where the family would find fuel for the fire, let alone food to fill their bellies. He shouldn't have to, but Jack did. He began looking over his shoulder, wondering when the next disaster would occur, what he could do to prevent it, and how he could help his pa more than he already had.

His only relief from worrying came when he sneaked away, hiding behind the chicken coop to smoke a cigarette stolen from his cousin. He would take a drag, lean his head against the coop, and dream.

A RED 1926 Indian Scout motorcycle stood in the driveway. He jumped on, started it up, and savored the roar of the engine. He knew from a magazine he had read that the Pacific Ocean was next to California and that, if he headed due west, he would run into it sooner or later. He took off toward the setting sun and drove until he could hear the sound of the ocean waves lapping the shore. Or at least he imagined what they might sound like. He figured it must be similar to the Platte River when it was flooding.

A different sound began wriggling its

way into his dream. What was it? A voice maybe? A man's voice?

"OH SHIT, IT'S Pa!" he mumbled as he jumped to his feet, stomped out the cigarette, and ran in the direction of his pa's voice. "Comin', Pa!"

"Goddamit, boy! Where the hell you been?" George, Jack's father, stood barely 5 feet 4 inches, the same height as Jack, but he commanded center stage anyplace he occupied.

"We got a field to plow and cows to milk before day's end. So getta move on!"

"Yes, sir," Jack answered, making sure he stayed out of range of his father's reach. A swat upside the head or across the behind was George's favorite way of emphasizing any order he gave.

"I'll do the milkin', Pa," Jack volunteered, knowing he would have ample time to climb back onto the Indian Scout and maybe this time make it to the ocean.

3

March 15, 1934

Beaver City, Nebraska

Sixteen-year-old Dorothy Ayers stifled the urge to leap from her chair and open the casket. Perhaps the anguish that permeated every cell in her body would vanish if only she could see her mother's face one last time. Her twelve-year-old brother, Walter, sat to her right. Each sob emanating from his small frame shook his entire body. It required all her father's attention to console him. Walter's slight stutter and resulting timidity had worsened since their mother's death. Dorothy sensed his increasing vulnerability, and her heart ached for him. Was she strong enough to take their mother's place, giving him the comfort and support he needed? Her mother had been the one who had held the family together, consoling and defending them whenever their father became too overbearing. What would happen now?

Desperate to help him, Dorothy placed her hand on Walter's back and began patting him. His sobbing subsided. As far as Walter was concerned, his sister had a magic touch, brimming with a soothing tenderness that brought him peace. It had worked on Walter for as long as he could remember. He always knew he could count on his big sister to support him when their father became upset because of something that Walter had done that wasn't good enough or hadn't been completed quickly enough.

As Walter calmed, Dorothy turned to her left and looked into the eyes of her twenty-nine-year-old sister, Helen, her second mother. She found relief in those eyes, which were just as clear and blue as her mother's—a stark contrast to Dorothy's deep brown eyes, a match to her father's.

Helen promised she would stay for two weeks before making the long trek back to Superior. It'll feel good to have her three little ones running around. I hope Pa holds his temper with them.

Pa. Who is going to keep him from being so strict all the time? Mama always softened him, almost like magic. Now, it's just me and Pa and Walter. Mama, why did you have to go?

Dorothy long before had learned the ins and outs of cleaning a house, canning green beans, and doing the laundry. Her mother had insisted upon that. Just two weeks ago they had baked bread together.

"Feel the dough in your hands," her mother had told her. "You can tell from the feel when you've kneaded it enough."

Dorothy had continued to push the dough forward, turn it, and then push it forward again while her mother had stood beside her, rubbing her back and correcting her in a soft, gentle voice. "Don't push quite so hard, and slow down just a little. That's it. Now you're cookin'."

The relentless March wind bellowed across the cemetery. Dead grass mixed with fine grains of dirt chafed against Dorothy's cheek. She covered her face with her hands and hunkered down in her chair.

I couldn't feel it, Mama. You can't leave yet. I can't feel the dough. There's so much more to learn. I don't know how to take care of Walter, or calm Pa down, and you promised me you would teach me how to make homemade ice cream this summer.

She gazed out at the crowd surrounding the gravesite. It seemed that the entire town of Beaver City had stopped what they were doing to attend the funeral—and why not? Her grandparents, great aunts and uncles, and cousins from both sides of the family made up half the population of this small rural town. Looking into their faces, she basked in the sweet comfort of being surrounded by loved ones—always available, always supportive.

Beaver City was a fine place to grow up. The county seat of Furnas County, it had a certain level of excitement about it. A Civil War statue commanded center stage in the town square; the statue was surrounded by a park filled with ancient elm trees, park benches, and picnic tables. A gazebo stood in one corner of the square, and bands played there every weekend during the summer. Downtown businesses lined the square: Kelley's Grocer, Warton's Department Store, the Agricultural

Adjustment Administration, Ayer's Grain and Seed, and Brewster's Jewelry Store. The movie theater, post office, library, and American Legion Hall completed the list. Fields of wheat and corn surrounded the town, and on summer evenings the pungent, grassy aroma of alfalfa filled the air as it was processed into pellets at the mill.

Every Saturday night the town transformed into a bustling, thriving hub filled with farm families who came to buy their week's supplies. Some took in a movie or a dance at the American Legion Hall. Others filled the afternoon and evening walking around the square and catching up on news and gossip.

Everyone who lived in Beaver City was either a farmer or someone who did business with a farmer. Frank Ayers, Dorothy's father, did both. He owned the town seed store along with a farm just six miles east on Highway 89. Living in town instead of on the farm suited Dorothy. She took pleasure in residing near other people and being able to walk downtown to go to a movie instead of having to beg a ride from her father.

Looking down the hill from her mother's gravesite, a subtle shift began in her perspective about the only home she had ever known—an oppressive, suffocating hopelessness. She wondered if any of her relatives had ever ventured beyond the confines of Nebraska. Heavy, gray clouds filled the blustery March sky and seeped into her soul.

Mama, you're the only one who ever understood me. Even Helen doesn't understand why I might want to leave Nebraska after high school, but you did. You listened to my dreams of seeing the world, and you told me to keep dreaming, and someday my dreams would come true.

She stared at her mother's casket as they lowered it into the ground. Anguish roiled in her gut. She had never felt so alone. Her mouth dropped open, and a primal, guttural sound began to emerge from deep within. People who were leaving stopped and stared. Her body leapt from the chair as if of its own volition.

"Mama! Don't leave! No, stop, don't cover her up. Not yet!"

Arms engulfed her, and everything faded into an indigo haze.

4

April 1936

Carol Brown, Dorothy's next-door neighbor and closest friend, stood beside the door on the Ayers' front porch, pulling at her auburn hair, trying to reposition the ever-rebellious curl on the right side of her forehead. A navy-blue scarf adorned her long neck. Her skirt-and-sweater set matched the scarf and emphasized her blue-gray eyes. As she raised her hand to knock, Dorothy appeared, opening the door with a dramatic flourish.

"Hi, Carol. What are you up to?" Dorothy said in a voice loud enough for her father, in the next room, to hear.

Carol winked. "Nothing much; thought I might take in a movie. Wanna go with me?" she responded in an elevated tone.

Dorothy winked back. "Oh, sure, Carol, I'd *love* to go to the movies with you."

Her father was sitting in the living room, reading his newspaper. "Pa, I'm leaving now," she mumbled as she opened the screen door.

"Not so fast, young lady." Frank sprang to his feet and reached the front door just as the two girls were rounding the corner, giggling, deep in conversation. "Come by the store and check in after the movie," he yelled down the street after them.

"I will, Pa! Don't I always check in?" Dorothy made a face at Carol. "He drives me crazy."

"Oh, I don't know. I always thought he was a great neighbor. That's what my folks say anyway."

"Sure, everybody likes Frank. He's Esther and James's son, and he's Ethel and Albert's son-in-law. He's a pillar of the community, just like all my folks. Half this town is related to me. Try being his daughter for a day, and then we'll see what you have to say. If he isn't spying on me, Grandma is, or Aunt Jessie, or Uncle Emmett."

Carol feigned support, having now endured this diatribe for the fourth time in seven days.

"Let's talk about something else, Dottie, like the dance. Will *he* be there?"

Dorothy giggled. "Annie said he would be there. Do you know her? She's his little sister."

"No, I was already out of high school before she ever started. The only reason I know *you* is because we're neighbors."

"And we grew up together."

"You made the cutest baby in my little doll buggy."

"Don't you ever get tired of that story?"

"You were just so darn cute. I was only four."

"Yes, I know, and I was one, and you thought I was a doll—a living, moving doll."

"Well, it's true, and I've loved you ever since. You're like the sister I never had, only better."

"By the way, Mom wanted me to make sure I thanked you for the green beans and the leftover roast. She always says your green beans are the best in town." Carol stared at the sidewalk as they strolled down the street. "Honestly, Dottie, I don't know what we'd do sometimes if it weren't for you and your pa. Times are pretty tough right now."

"It's the least I can do, sweetie. Pa probably wouldn't have a single shirt without a hole burned into it if you hadn't taught me how to use an iron, and Pa raves about my fried chicken. I have your ma to thank for that. Anyway, that's what being neighbors and friends is all about, right? We help each other; we take care of each other. It's as simple as that."

Dorothy changed the subject. "Can I ask you a personal question?"

"Sure, kiddo, you know you can ask me anything."

"Why are you still hangin' around Beaver City? You graduated three years ago. I can't for the life of me imagine sticking around this place after I graduate. One month from now, I'm leaving."

"I like it here. It's just the right size—not too big, not too small—and I like my job. Why *wouldn't* I want to stay here?" A sense of exasperation tinged the edge of Carol's words.

Dorothy stopped walking and put her arms around Carol.

"I'm sorry, sweetie. Sometimes I can be such a dolt! How is your pa, anyway? Is he getting better?"

Carol appreciated her friend's concern. She knew Dorothy meant well, and she knew Dorothy would always be there for her. "Don't be sorry. You keep me going when the going gets tough. Anyway, let's not talk about Pa right now."

Dorothy jumped behind Carol. "There he is! I have to put on my lipstick."

"Why don't you ever do that before you leave the house?"

"One word—'Pa.' Need I say more?" Dorothy applied her orchid-red lipstick with the skill of an artist.

"I'm always amazed at how you learned to do that without a mirror."

"I had to. There aren't any mirrors to use on the way to school." Dorothy adjusted her wire rim glasses. "How do I look?"

Carol studied the green dress with large white flowers that covered the skirt and emphasized Dorothy's petite figure. Her white pumps added two inches to her five-foot-one-inch frame and allowed her to come to Carol's shoulder. She sighed. "Even with glasses, you're still cute as a button, kiddo. Now, smile pretty, and let's see if he notices you this time."

As they approached the American Legion Hall, Annie ran down the sidewalk to meet them. She pushed Dorothy forward. "Come on. He's here. I'll introduce you."

"Wait a minute; wait a minute! I don't know if I'm ready."

Annie put her hand on her hip. Although she was two years younger than Dorothy, her demeanor bespoke a woman years older—confident, some said spunky, and maybe a little too bossy—but Dorothy loved her for those exact traits. "You're ready," Annie said. "If I don't introduce the two of you, it'll never happen. You failed me twice already. Just leave this up to me."

Before Dorothy could protest, Annie pushed her forward so that Dorothy stood squarely in front of Annie's brother. "Jack, this is Dorothy, the girl I've been telling you about. Isn't she as pretty as I said?"

Dorothy blushed. Jack took her hand. His six-foot frame towered over her. He smiled, exposing a slight gap between his two front teeth. A dead ringer for Errol Flynn, Jack had a sly grin that gave him a devil-may-care, irresistible magnetism. It brought his brown eyes alive with mischief. His demeanor and his reputation as the best dancer in Furnas County melted any reserve Dorothy may have had.

"Wanna dance, darlin'?"

Dorothy tried to breathe. "Sure." She looked over her shoulder at Carol. "Keep an eye out."

Carol followed them into the dance hall. "I've got my watch on. I'll let you know."

Annie looked at Carol. "What's that all about?"

"Her pa. He thinks she's at the movies. We have to make sure we walk by his store at the right time, or he'll get suspicious."

"I should have known. He's even stricter than *my* pa. She's taking a big chance. I hope she doesn't get caught."

Carol nodded toward Dorothy and Jack. "Me too, but even if she does, I don't think she'll care."

The band began to play "Tennessee Waltz." Jack ushered Dorothy onto the dance floor. "This is one of my favorites. I love to waltz. Do you?"

"Sure."

"Is that the only word you know? Are you shy or somethin'?"

"No, I'm just nervous. I haven't danced much. My pa doesn't allow it."

"Who's yer pa?"

"Frank Ayers. Ayer's Grain and Seed? You must know him."

"Oh, yeah, Mr. Ayers. One of those guys everybody likes. That's your pa?"

"That's him. He's nice enough, unless you're his daughter."

Jack grinned. "Guess I'd better be on my best behavior, huh?"

"That's OK. I mean—you don't have to—oh, never mind."

Jack studied her face. "Peaches. Your cheeks look like cute little peaches. I think that's what I'm gonna call you from now on. Peaches."

"Most people call me Dottie."

"I like Peaches, don't you?"

"Sure." Dorothy blushed. "You can call me whatever you like, Jack."

"Well, most people call me Smitty cuz my last name's Smith. Anyway, I like it. That's what you can call me."

Dorothy struggled to think of something interesting to say. "Annie goes to Beaver City High School, but you didn't, did you?"

"No, I went to school closer to the farm. I don't care much for school. I'm a farmer, so I stopped goin' when I finished tenth grade; had to help my pa. It got pretty rough goin' back in '34. That wasn't a good year for us."

"It wasn't my best year either. That's the year my ma died."

"Oh, sorry to hear that."

"Thanks. Why was it a bad year for you?"

Jack bristled. *Why the hell did I bring up '34? I sure as hell ain't gonna tell her our crop failed and we almost got evicted.*

"Jack?" Dorothy asked, with a growing uneasiness at Jack's prolonged silence.

"Sorry, Peaches, let's just say it's been hard times for a long, long time, and I'm ready for somethin' new."

"Don't be sorry. My pa and my brother are farmers, and I know how hard it's been on them. We wouldn't be doing well at all if it weren't for the store. Anyway, you deserve the best; you've worked hard for it I'm sure."

Jack looked down at the delightful young lady he held in his arms. He couldn't remember the last time he had felt so comfortable around a woman, which at once left him strangely uneasy. They fell into a pleasant silence as they sashayed around the dance floor.

"How old are you anyway?" asked Jack.

"I'm eighteen. I graduate in thirty-three days—not that I'm counting or anything. I'm just ready for school to be over and to get on with my life. Like you said, I'm ready for something new. How old are you?"

"I'm twenty, and I plan on leavin' here too. Maybe we can go together."

Dorothy's cheeks flushed a deeper shade of crimson. "Sure."

They fell silent as the song continued. Jack held her a little closer, and she didn't resist. They glided across the dance floor, their steps in perfect harmony. The song ended, and Jack led her to the sideline with his arm draped over her shoulder.

Dorothy tried to relax. "You're a great dancer."

Jack winked at her. "So are you, darlin'. Care for another round?"

"Sure."

Jack flashed what a lot of folks called his "shit-eating grin." It camouflaged his uncertainty. He brushed his hand across her forehead. "Think I mighta messed your hair up a little. I like women with messy brown hair. They're my favorite."

Dorothy's knees began to buckle. He guided her back onto the dance floor as the band began to play "Moonlight Serenade." Their bodies touched and he whispered into her ear. "So, if I ask you for a kiss, would you say, 'Sure'?"

Dorothy leaned back, easing Jack's embrace. "Sure, Jack—I mean, *no!* I mean, I'm not *that* kind of girl."

"Sorry, darlin'. I'm not used to girls like you—you know, nice girls."

Dorothy's cheeks now resembled two Red Delicious apples instead of peaches. Flustered, she wracked her brain for some witty response. "So, do you like farming?"

"I guess. I don't know how to do much else, unless you need your car fixed. I'm real good at that. I like motorcycles too. How about you?"

"I wouldn't know. I've never been on one."

They remained on the dance floor—in each other's

arms—for two more songs. Dorothy wasn't sure her feet were touching the floor. She relaxed into a pleasant, floating sensation as Smitty swung her around again and again. He wasn't quite sure what to make of this nice girl, so shy and so different from the women he thought he preferred.

Carol tapped Dorothy's shoulder, bursting her bubble. "Time to go, Dottie. Now! We're just a little late, but I got a little distracted." She smiled at a young man standing behind her.

Smitty interrupted. "Where you off to? Can I come along?"

Dorothy pushed Smitty away. "No! Sorry, Smitty, but my pa doesn't know I'm here. We have to walk by his store so he sees us and knows what I'm doing."

"Well, can I see you again sometime?"

"Sure. I'll be back after a while. I just have to walk by his store every now and then."

DOROTHY AND CAROL ran toward Ayer's Grain and Seed at the opposite end of the town square. They started walking at a leisurely pace when they reached the library in order to catch their breath before they passed the store, two buildings away.

Dorothy popped her head in the doorway. "Hi, Pa. How you doing?"

Frank looked at his watch and pressed his pipe against his right cheek. "Little late, aren't you? I think the movie got out fifteen minutes ago."

"There was an extra feature, that's all. It's such a beautiful evening. Carol and I are going to walk around the square a little longer."

"Well, I'm closing up the store. Not much business tonight. I'll see you at home at nine o'clock sharp."

"Yes, sir."

Carol and Dorothy continued their walk around the square. Frank locked the front door and started home. They waved at him from across the street. "See you later, Pa."

As soon as Frank was out of sight, the girls ran back toward the American Legion Hall, where Dorothy searched the dance floor for Smitty. She finally spotted him holding a tall blonde in his arms, gliding around the floor with the same ease and grace she had experienced. Smitty grinned at the woman the same way he had grinned at her. He held the woman close to him and whispered something in her ear. She laughed and laid her head on his shoulder.

Dismayed, Dorothy decided to leave the hall and ran straight into her father. "Pa! What are *you* doing here?"

"Better question is, what are you doing here?"

"I'm just looking around. A lot of my friends are here. *Their* parents allow them to come to a dance now and then."

"Well, that's nice, but I'm not *their* parents. I'm *your* pa. Now let's go!"

Dorothy put her hands on her hips, ready to defy his orders, but then changed her mind. "Come on, Carol. Let's go."

"Was it worth it?" Carol asked under her breath.

Dorothy winked at Carol. "Oh, yes," she grinned, "and I'll do it all over again if I ever get the chance."

DOROTHY STOOD BEHIND the cash register at Ayer's Grain and Seed. "There you go, Mr. Linder," she said as she placed assorted coins into his hand. "Sixty-five cents change. Tell your wife hello from me."

"Sure will, Dorothy. Nice to see ya."

She began to straighten up the back counter.

"Hello, Peaches. How ya doin'?"

Dorothy turned around, knocking an entire display of seed packets off the counter and onto the floor. She began hastily picking up the packets and attempted to put them back on the counter, all the while talking at a frenzied pace. Smitty stood by, grinning.

"Oh, hi, Smitty. I'm just picking up these seeds, helping Pa around the store. I usually do that on Saturdays because it's so busy, but today it isn't so bad. Can I help you?"

"Well, I guess you learned a few more words since a week ago, when all you could say was 'sure.' Hey, what happened to you anyway? I thought you said you were comin' back to the dance, but I never saw you again. I was pretty disappointed."

"I did come back, but you didn't look disappointed to me. You seemed pretty happy with that tall blonde."

"She's just an old friend."

"One of those not-so-nice girls you mentioned?"

Smitty grinned. "I didn't come in here to buy seed, Peaches. Annie told me you'd be here today. Any chance you'd consider goin' with me to the movies tonight?"

Dorothy tried to stifle the blush rising from her neck up to her face, but to no avail.

"Sure."

"Here we go. Cat got your tongue again?"

"No, I'm sorry. Sure, I can go. I just have to figure out how to handle my pa. I told you how he is. Maybe you could just pick me up at the theater. Can you check back in about an hour?"

Smitty stood silent, nodding his head toward something over Dorothy's right shoulder.

Frank clicked his pipe against his teeth.

Dorothy was certain she couldn't be any more embarrassed as a deep shade of magenta rose in her cheeks. "Pa, this is Jack Smith. He's George Smith's oldest boy. You know George. He asked me to go to the movies tonight."

"George asked you?"

"Pa! Smitty asked me."

"Well, who the dickens is Smitty?"

"This is Smitty. He's Jack Smith, but everybody calls him Smitty."

Smitty extended his hand to Frank. "How do you do, Mr. Ayers? Nice to meet you."

"Hello, son. I've seen you in here before, haven't I?"

"Yes, sir. I run errands for my pa all the time, sir."

"And you want to take my daughter to the movies?"

"Yes, sir."

Frank studied Smitty for a moment and then turned to Dorothy. "Did you get the bookkeeping done like I asked?"

"Of course, Pa. Right on time, just like always."

"Well, then, the movie starts at seven o'clock sharp and gets over at eight-thirty sharp..."

"Pa! I know when the movie starts and finishes, and I know when to get home."

Frank scrutinized his daughter and then cleared his throat. "I will expect you home at nine o'clock—and why are there seed packets all over the floor?"

"I'll pick them up, Pa. Just a little accident."

Frank nodded to Jack. "Did you need anything else, son?"

"No, sir. Got what I came for."

AT 6:40 SHARP, Jack knocked on the door of the Ayers's home. Dorothy answered, with Frank close behind. "You two have a good time, and I expect to see you back here at nine on the nose," Frank mandated, clicking his pipe against the face of his open pocket watch.

Dorothy ignored his edict. Frank stood sternly in the doorway.

"Yes, sir. She'll be back on time. I'll make sure of it, sir," Smitty replied meekly, attempting to ease the tension and get away as fast as he could.

Frank closed the door and peeked through the front window as the two headed down the porch stairs. Smitty rushed to open the passenger door on his Ford pickup.

"Sorry I don't have a fancy car, but this is all I can afford right now. Someday I'm gonna get me a motorcycle. They're the best. Do you know how fast one of 'em goes? I'm just gonna get on one and start down the road, and who knows where I'll end up. Maybe Colorado, or maybe even California. I've always wanted to see the ocean. It's kinda peculiar, ain't it? Here we are in Nebraska, never seen anything larger than a lake, and I been dreamin' about seein' the ocean since I was just a little guy."

Dorothy chimed in. "I've always wanted to see the ocean, too, and the desert and the mountains," she said. "I want to see it all, don't you?"

"Hell, yes! Oh, sorry, there I go again, but I do wanna see it all. You're the first woman I ever talked to who seems to understand that."

Dorothy beamed. "You called me a woman."

"Oh, is that rude? I mean you *are* a woman—or should I call you a lady?"

"Jack, I like that you think of me as a woman. My pa thinks of me as a little girl who can't take care of herself. He expects me to do his books every week, and I do, just like clockwork, and they're *always* accurate, *always*! I make his meals, clean his house, and I take care of Walter, too, but then I ask to go out, and you'd think I was twelve or something. He makes me so mad I could just spit."

"He just cares about you, Peaches. You shouldn't get mad at him."

"Well, I guess. Don't get me wrong—I do care about him, it's just..."

"I know. My pa is pretty strict, too, and you ain't never seen a bad temper till you meet my pa."

"Guess we have a lot in common, huh?"

Smitty parked the pickup in front of the theater. "Peaches, I've talked more to you in five minutes than I think I've ever talked to anyone." He slid across the seat and put his arm around Dorothy, taking her chin in his hand.

"I like talking to you, too, but remember who I am," she warned as she backed away and, in one fluid movement, slid across the seat, opened the door, and jumped out of the pickup. "You said it yourself." She winked, her grin looking every bit as mischievous as his. "I'm one of those nice girls."

5

May 1936

"Wanna dance, darlin'? They're playin' our song." Smitty held his hand out to Dorothy and steered her onto the dance floor. They began to sway in rhythm with "Tennessee Waltz." He took pleasure in the sensation of her breasts against his chest.

Dorothy lightly massaged the back of his neck, a habit that had developed over the past month. It had an almost magical effect on him as he relaxed into her embrace, and she relished the sensual pleasure of his response to her touch. "So you think this is our song, huh? What makes it our song?" she whispered, not wanting to disturb the intimacy of the moment.

"Well, it could be our song. It's the first one we ever danced to."

Dorothy blushed. "You remembered."

The song ended. He left his hand on her waist as they worked their way back to a table. "What time do you have to be home?"

"I'm staying out a little later to celebrate graduation. I made a deal with Pa." She furrowed her brow and mimicked her father's stern voice: "Ten on the nose, and not a minute later."

"Well, that's a whole hour from now. Wanna try just a little bit of wine to celebrate?"

Dorothy tilted her head and smiled up at Smitty. "Where is it?"

"Come on; let's get outta here. I'll show ya." They worked their way through the crowd and out the front door. "It's in my Ford. We'll go to this little place I know on the edge of town. It's more private there."

Smitty opened the door of his pickup, and Dorothy climbed in. They drove down Main Street in silence.

"Hey, Peaches, whatcha thinkin' about? I'll bet you're thinkin' about your pa, ain't ya? I don't blame you—he's kinda scary, even for me." He slammed on the brakes. "Maybe we shouldn't do this, ya know? Maybe it isn't such a good idea after all."

Dorothy leaned over and jammed her foot down hard on the accelerator. The pickup shot forward. Smitty gripped the steering wheel. "Guess you made up your mind, darlin'; let's go have some fun!"

Smitty turned onto a small dirt road that ran beside the cemetery. Branches from ancient elm trees scraped along the top of the old Ford. He pulled over and parked under one of them. "Here we are."

"Here we are? Sounds like you've been here before."

He put his arm on the back of the seat. "And what if I have—so what?" He leaned toward her, and she backed away. "Relax. I'm just gettin' the wine." His face softened, and his grin disappeared. "Hey, Dottie, I don't mean to be teasin' ya. I like you. You're different than those other girls."

Dorothy raised her eyebrows. "Different?"

"Oh, hell, don't ask me any more questions. Here, just take a sip of it. Not too much. I don't want yer pa comin' after me. Try it, darlin'. It's pretty good."

He handed Dorothy the wine. She tilted the bottle back, stopping the flow with her tongue. "It does taste pretty good." She took a drink and then giggled. "I can't believe I'm doing this. You are a bad influence, Mr. Smith. Hey, look at that— the moon is shining right through those trees. Isn't it beautiful?" She paused, waiting for Smitty's response. "Aren't you going to look at the moon?"

"No, I'm not. Your eyes are prettier than any old moon could ever be." He leaned down and gave Dorothy a sensual, unhurried kiss that took her breath away.

Her reserve dissolved into a puddle. "Thanks."

"For what?"

"For bringing me out here. For saying 'Tennessee Waltz' is our song. For dancing with me. For letting me taste your wine." She reached up and gave him a gentle kiss, one that lasted for only a moment—and yet it hit Smitty like a bolt of lightning surging from his lips down through his body to his toes.

He stopped himself. "I better take you home now, Peaches. Your pa will be worried."

They drove the one mile to Dorothy's house in silence. Repressed desire filled the space between them. They took their time climbing the steps to the front door. Frank came out to check the thermometer on the porch, his routine whenever Dorothy came home with a date. He took a puff of his pipe. "Gettin' a little chill in the air. Hello, Smitty. How are you?"

"I'm fine, sir, just fine." Smitty started to walk down the stairs.

"Pa! Do you mind?" The conviction in her voice surprised even Dorothy.

Frank checked his watch and clicked his pipe against his teeth. "See ya in five minutes, Dorothy." He headed back into the house.

Dorothy ran down the steps. "Smitty! Don't leave yet. He's gone. Just wait a minute. Do you care if I keep the label from the wine bottle?"

"Sure, why not? The only payment I need is another one of those sweet kisses of yours."

"I can't. Not here." But, in one smooth motion, Smitty embraced her, bent down and touched his lips to hers.

Frank stuck his head out the door. "Dorothy! I said five minutes."

Smitty shoved the label into her hand. "Here's the label. Don't let your pa see it."

She slipped the label into her skirt pocket and darted up the porch steps, past her father. "Good night, Pa." She continued her hurried retreat up the stairs to her bedroom, closing the door behind her. Opening the large mahogany hope chest at the foot of her bed, she pulled out a small box made of cherrywood with a rose carved on the top, a gift from her mother on her thirteenth birthday.

"What should I put in it?" Dorothy asked her mother.

"It's for special things that you want to keep forever, that mean more than what they're made of. They're keep-sakes, honey. You'll understand soon enough."

She opened the box and reviewed its contents: the memorial program from her mother's funeral, a dried rose from her first formal dance, and a tarnished locket from her father that had belonged to his mother. Then she took a pencil from her dresser, turned the wine label over, and, in elegant script, wrote on the back:

May 27, 1936.
Our first kiss.

She studied her writing for a moment, kissed the label, and put it into the box.

The next morning, Dorothy took her time getting dressed. She lifted the label out of the box and read the writing again. *It wasn't a dream.* A tingling sensation ran down her spine.

She flew down the stairs two at a time to the kitchen, where she took a cast-iron skillet out of its drawer and began to whistle as she removed bacon from the icebox and arranged it just so in the pan. Next, she measured three and a half scoops of coffee into the coffee pot, added water, and turned on the burner. She cracked eight eggs into a bowl and whipped them while the bacon sizzled and the coffee perked. It had taken awhile after her mother's death, but this was her kitchen now, with everything placed exactly where she wanted. In it she moved with grace and ease, dancing her own private waltz.

"Good m-mornin', Sis," said Walter as he entered the kitchen. "You s-s-sure sound h-happy today."

"Good morning, sweet brother. I *am* happy. Aren't you? It's a beautiful day. Look at that sky; it couldn't be any bluer. And look at those big puffy clouds. They look like cotton balls, don't they? Sit down and have some coffee while I finish the eggs."

"I s-saw you with that Smith b-boy. That's why yer s-s-so happy, ain't it?"

"Maybe. Now drink your coffee and mind your own business. Did you get the cows milked?"

"S-s-sure did. Pa'll b-be along any t-time now."

Dorothy heard the front door open. "We're in here, Pa. Breakfast is almost ready."

"Hey, Peaches, it's me," Smitty whispered. "Is yer pa around?"

"Smitty! No, Pa's not here, but he will be shortly."

"I just wanted to see you again. Can you go for a walk with me?"

"I can't. I'm fixing breakfast. Come on in and have some. I'm a pretty good cook. Bet you didn't know that about me, did you?"

"It does smell good, but what about yer pa?"

"I'm eighteen years old. I just graduated from high school. It's about time I stood up to Pa, don't you think?"

Frank opened the front door. "Isn't that Smitty's pickup out front?"

Dorothy put her hands on her hips. "Yes, it is. He's having breakfast with us, Pa. Isn't that nice? After breakfast we're going for a walk. Don't worry. I'll be at the store at eight, *as usual*. Now sit down, have some coffee, and make our guest welcome."

Frank stood in the kitchen doorway, surveying the scene before him. He sat down next to Smitty, looked at Walter, and then at Dorothy. He fetched his pipe from his pocket and began to fill its bowl with tobacco. "So, Smitty, has your pa planted his wheat yet?"

Dorothy whistled a merry tune while she tended the bacon, and the men carried on a conversation about rain and crops and cattle.

After breakfast Dorothy gathered the dishes in the sink and took Smitty by the hand. "Come on. It's a perfect morning for a walk. Leave your pickup here. You can walk me to the store."

Smitty attempted to appear calm. "Okay, Dottie—that is, if it's all right with you, sir."

Frank began to answer, but Dorothy interrupted him. "I'm the one who decides who gets to walk me to work. Let's go." With that, she walked out the front door before her bravado failed her. Smitty followed close behind, amazed and baffled.

"What got into you, woman? I've never seen you like that."

"Well, it's about time, don't you think?" She began to skip down the sidewalk. "Let's not go right to the store. I know this place, up on Carter Hill just outside of town. We can go there for just a minute. It's a great place to watch the clouds."

"To do what?"

"Watch clouds. You know, look at them, make things out of them." She looked up at the sky. "See, like that one right there. It looks like a big dragon. There's its mouth with smoke coming out. See it?"

"Well, I'll be darned. It *does* look like a dragon. Of all things. I never thought I'd be gawkin' at clouds, but here you are, and here I am, lookin' at clouds, for cryin' out loud."

"Come on, Smitty. It's right over here."

STANDING AT THE crest of Carter Hill, Dorothy pointed to a spot a few yards away. "Over there is best. There's a little grassy spot to lie down on. That way you can see the entire sky."

Smitty complied. He put his hands behind his head. "Now let me try my hand. See that cloud over there? It looks like a motorcycle—and look, there we are, me in the front, you in the sidecar, and we're takin' off for California. And, look there, we're at the ocean, and we're jumpin' in and swimmin' and havin' a great ole time."

"Jack Smith, you're making fun of me. I don't see any motorcycle."

Smitty rolled over and faced Dorothy. "I do. Every time I look at you I see the future. I don't have to look at clouds to see that, Peaches. I just look at you, and there it is." He began kissing her forehead, her cheek, and her mouth. He lingered there for a moment and then pulled away.

"Now you better get to work, or I'm gonna be in a heap of trouble, and so are you."

6

June 1936

Smitty parked the pickup in front of the theater. "Peaches, I've got somethin' to tell you, and I don't know how you're gonna take it."

Dorothy sat up straight. "Are you breaking up with me? We've only been together for two months. We don't even know each other yet."

"Shh, darlin', stop talkin' for just a minute. I'm not breakin' up with you." He stopped for a moment, started to speak, and then stopped again. "You are the best thing that ever happened to me. You listen to me; you understand me. I know it's only been two months, but I love you."

"You love me? I love you too. You get me all excited about traveling, about leaving this place." Her eyes narrowed. "But why do you look so sad?"

"I'm leavin'. I got a job on a combining crew. We leave in a week. We'll be gone for three months. We'll work our way from Kansas up to Montana. I have to go. It's the only way I can make real money. My family needs it. I was so afraid to tell you. Will you wait for me? Will you still love me when I get back?"

She fumbled in her purse for a handkerchief. "Smitty, I would wait for you forever if I had to. I'll be here. I promise."

"You won't leave? You said you'd leave as soon as you graduated."

She put her hands on either side of his face. "Look at me, Jack Smith. I'm not leaving. I'm staying right here. I'll be here when you get back. I promise."

DOROTHY TOOK A sip of her Coca-Cola. Carol sat across from her at the café slurping down a chocolate milkshake. "Do you think you could help me get a job at the Triple-A?"

"Of course I can, but I thought you were leaving town. What's up, *Peaches?*" Carol attempted a serious look.

"You know exactly what's up. He said he would write me, and he'll be back in the fall," said Dorothy, in a slightly defensive tone. "If I could, I would follow him all the way from Kansas to Montana. Maybe I should. I could get a job cooking for the crew or something."

"Be realistic, honey. You can't go off following some guy across the United States, let alone be a cook for a combining crew. Think about it—the only woman with a crew of young men who would be hungry for more than just food. Come work for Mr. Anderson at the Triple-A, at least for the summer. Who knows? You might even decide to stick around. Meet me at work in the morning. I'll introduce you."

"Thanks, Carol. You're the best. I'll be there with bells on."

MR. ANDERSON PEERED at Dorothy over his wire rim glasses and tugged at his vest, attempting to cover his portly abdomen. "You're Frank Ayres's little girl, aren't you?"

"Yes, sir. And I'm Carolyn's granddaughter, and Sara's niece, and..."

"Yes, there are a lot of you folks around town," Mr. Anderson interrupted. "Well, being Frank's daughter is good enough for me. He's a hardworking, honest man, and I'm sure his offspring are cut from the same cloth. You're hired if you're sure you can work with farmers. You know they can be stubborn and demanding at times, especially if they think you might have cheated them or their check is late."

"My father is a farmer. As a matter of fact, I come from a long line of farmers."

Mr. Anderson cleared his throat. "Yes, of course. Then you understand. Well, we need someone to assist Miss Brown measuring farm acreage and doing it accurately so we can pay the farmers what they're due to keep their land fallow. Carol here can teach you to use the planimeter. She's our best operator. She knows this business inside and out. She could probably run the place. Can you start tomorrow, Miss Ayers?"

"Yes, sir, but I only want to work until the fall."

"Summer is our busiest time, so we can use some extra hands. How does $2.50 sound for wages?"

"A day? I've never made that much money in my entire life!"

Mr. Anderson chuckled. "Yes. Does that suit you?"

Dorothy blinked. "Yes, sir. That sounds fine. Thank you so much. I'll do a good job for you. I promise. Thank you so much. I..."

He headed for his office, waving his hand at Dorothy. "That will be all, Miss Ayers. Welcome to the Agricultural Adjustment Administration. I'll see you in the morning."

Carol hugged Dorothy. "I can't believe we'll be working together. Go enjoy your last day of freedom. We can walk to work together tomorrow."

"Thank you so much, Carol. See you in the morning."

Dorothy left and walked directly to the post office. Two weeks seemed more like two months since Smitty had left town. She crossed all her fingers before opening the mailbox—the magic paid off. She tore open the envelope as she hurried out the front door, sat down on the post office steps, and began to read:

Belpre, Kansas
June 2Ø, 1936
My Darling Dorothy,

Well, I am in Kansas. I got here around three o'clock. I never had very much trouble, just had one flat tire, didn't lose much time, but I had to stop at every town and get water. It sure was hot down here today.

Boy, I sure got a sweet place to stay. Everything is modern. I wasn't here only about ten minutes till I was at work running a combine. They have a new Wallis tractor to pull it with rubber tires. I worked till about nine o'clock. Boy, was I ever hungry when we quit. I could of eat a skunk. We sure had a good supper though. Now I am too full. There are two other guys working here too, the misses has got one of them drying dishes. They have around 600 acres to cut. If they can cut night and day, they figured it would take around 15 days to cut it, but if it's damp it will take longer. I like it fine down here so far. Well, I think I better take a bath and get some rest so ta ta. xoxoxo

    Love,

    Smitty

Dorothy folded the letter. She wondered what it would be like to drive the 192 miles to Belpre, Kansas, and surprise Smitty some summer afternoon.

DOROTHY TIPTOED UP behind Smitty. "Surprise!"

"Peaches! Am I dreaming?"

"No, it's really me. I came to see you. I'm going to cook for the crew. You and I can be together all summer."

"I'm so glad you're here. Come on; let's go for a drive. I'll show you around."

They climbed into Smitty's pickup and

drove around the town, then out into the countryside to the farm where the combines stood ready for the next day's labor. Golden fields of wheat waved in the afternoon breeze on either side of the road.

"It's just as beautiful as you said it was," said Dorothy. "I could stay here forever."

Smitty stopped the pickup on the side of the road. "It's not half as beautiful as you. Come here."

"WHATCHA DOIN', SIS? P-p-pa's been l-lookin' all over for ya."

Dorothy's eyes widened as she fully returned to the present and saw her brother standing before her. "What? Who's looking for me?" What time is it?"

"It's dinnertime. Why else would P-Pa be lookin' for ya?"

"Oh, horsefeathers! Run on ahead, Walter. Tell him I'm at Kelley's getting some potatoes or something. I'll be right there."

Walter ran toward home. Dorothy sat for a moment longer, reveling in Smitty's embrace.

A CREATURE OF habit, Dorothy walked to her bedroom window to check the weather. *Beautiful morning. Gorgeous clouds, just the `way I like 'em, big and puffy.*

She opened her closet door and rifled through her clothes. She chose a moss-green suit with a slim knee-length skirt and fitted jacket with shoulder pads and placed it on her bed. She then fetched a teal-blue dress with polka dots and laid it beside the suit. Both colors drew attention to her small, oval-shaped brown eyes. She studied both outfits and quickly made her decision.

My first day at work. I feel like polka dots. Besides, it doesn't need ironing. I hate ironing, and I don't have time anyway.

She put the green suit away and sat at her vanity table in her slip. An expert at applying makeup, she started with a new kind of pancake foundation she had purchased from Warton's Department Store. Next, she picked up her brown eyebrow pencil. Following the advice offered in the latest issue of *McCall's*, she penciled in the lower part of the eyebrow rather than the upper, and finished with a sweep toward the top of her ear. She smiled with satisfaction at her work. *It's as close to Rita Hayworth eyebrows as I can get.* She dipped her index finger into her Vaseline jar, procuring the perfect amount to stroke onto her eyelashes. She used an upward motion to give them a luxurious curve—at least that's what her beauty guidebook had said would happen. The final touches came with pink rouge to her round cheeks and plush red lipstick to accentuate her full lips.

After dressing, she put on her glasses and scrutinized her choices in the full-length mirror, assuring herself she had achieved the look of a professional woman. *Look at me—a grown-up, a woman with a job—but can I do the job?*

She reviewed the last two years of burned dinners and the constant cleaning required with two farmers tromping around in muddy boots. She took a second look at her image, put her hands on her hips, and spoke to the woman she saw reflected in the mirror, "I can do this. I can do anything I set my mind to," she said out loud with aplomb. She looked heavenward. "But, Ma, please stay close today. With you by my side, I know I'll be fine," she whispered.

She ran downstairs. As she swung open the screen door, she yelled to her father and brother sitting in the kitchen, "There's fresh coffee in the pot and rolls in the oven. See you at four thirty."

Carol was waiting for her on the front porch. "Good morning, Miss Ayers," she said with a slightly exaggerated adult formality. "Ready for your first day at the Agricultural Adjustment Administration?"

"Why, yes, Miss Brown. Are you ready to train me? I promise to be your best student."

"I'm sure you will be. You'll probably outdo me in a couple of months."

"I hope so." They both chuckled.

"Heard from Smitty?"

"Yes, he's in Belpre, Kansas. I looked it up on a map. It's 192 miles from here. That's a long ways. He says it's beautiful, and he loves it a lot. I got so excited reading his letter. I even dreamed I went down there. How long do you think it would take to get there from here?"

"I have no idea, and don't even think about it. What would your pa say? No, you're going to stay right here and work at the Triple-A, and by the time Smitty gets home, you're going to be filthy rich."

Belpre, Kansas

Smitty opened his makeshift ledger and turned to an empty page. His bookkeeping methods were quite simple. He drew two lines on the page, creating three columns. At the top of the first column he wrote, "In." Over the second he wrote "Out," and in the final column "Balance." He stared at the empty columns for a moment and then turned the page. At the top, he wrote, "How much do I need?"

What do I need? I don't even know. What does it take to be married, to buy a motorcycle, and to take off and see the world? he thought. He laughed out loud as a sense of giddiness bubbled through his mind.

He knew for sure how much a motorcycle cost. He had already established that piece of information years ago. It didn't have to be new, but it did have to be red, and it did have to be an Indian Scout. That was nonnegotiable.

He figured all he needed to be married was a ring and maybe a sidecar for the motorcycle or maybe just a back seat. He'd seen that model once at a big show in Kearney.

So, a ring then. Nothing fancy, maybe a small diamond, but that's it.

He closed the ledger, realizing he had some investigating to do before he could possibly know how much he needed. He got up and started to leave the bunkhouse; then he stopped and chuckled as he pulled his week's salary out of his front pocket and reopened the ledger.

"Twelve hours a day, seven days a week, plus room and board," he mumbled, scribbling figures in the margin. Under the "In" column he wrote: $29.40.

"Not bad," he said with some pride. He put the 40 cents in his pocket for gas money while the rest went directly into an empty tobacco tin he kept for just this purpose. "Better 'n any bank!" was his motto. He snapped the tin shut and pulled his suitcase out from under the bunk, slipped the tin safely inside, and clapped his hands with satisfaction. His dream was under way.

He spent another two weeks in Belpre and then moved on with the crew to western Nebraska, across Wyoming, and finally into southern Montana. The tobacco tin bulged with his earnings, minus the occasional sum he sent home to his family. The thought of seeing his dear, darling Dorothy again kept him going from town to town, and by September he felt like a rich man, at least by his standards.

"WANNA DANCE, DARLIN'?"

Dorothy nearly jumped out of her chair. "You're here! You said you would call, and now here you are surprising the dickens out of me."

Smitty laughed, picked her up, and swung her around just as Mr. Anderson entered the room. "I wondered what all the commotion was. Welcome home, Smitty. Now, Miss Ayers, aren't you lucky you have only one hour and 20 minutes left to work?" His smile disappeared as he tapped the photos sitting on her desk.

"Yes sir, I am lucky. I'm probably the luckiest girl in Beaver City."

Mr. Anderson continued tapping the photos.

"I haven't been out to the farm yet, Peaches, so I'll go see ma and pa, and then I'll come back and pick you up, say in about one hour and twenty minutes?" He grinned at Mr. Anderson, winked at Dorothy, and walked out the door.

GEORGE LOOKED UP from repairing a wheel on a wagon long enough to recognize Smitty's pickup. "Good! Yer home. You can milk the cows while I finish fixin' this goddamned wheel. You didn't get here any too soon, either. Old man Sanders is threatenin' to evict us. We fell behind on the rent again. So help me God, if it ain't one thing, it's another. I don't know what the hell we're gonna do this time. We can't spare sellin' anything else; we just can't."

Smitty stood silently, taking in everything his pa was saying, mentally counting the money in the tobacco tin.

"It's OK, Pa. I can cover it. Did you get the money I sent last month?"

"Sure did, son, sure did. But then the windmill broke. We had one of them big ole dirt storms, and it tore the damned windmill right in half, like it was some kinda toy. Look, son, I can't take yer money no more."

"Pa! Stop right there. It's a loan, remember? It's temporary. This can't go on forever. Times are bound to get better, ain't they?"

George stopped pounding the wheel long enough to take a long look at his son. "Go milk those damned cows now before they start bellerin' at us!"

"Yes, sir." Head down, Smitty walked toward the barn as his dreams melted like ice cream under a hot July sun.

"WHAT'S WRONG, HONEY? You seemed so happy this afternoon, but now you're barely talking. What happened?"

"Nothin', Peaches. It's just my family, we..."

Dorothy pressed her fingers against his lips. "Say no more." Should she tell him that Annie had told her everything? "You are coming home with me. I'm going to fix you a big ole fried chicken dinner, and then we're going to go to the dance, and maybe tomorrow we'll talk, but right now, sweetie, right now we're celebrating you coming home. I love you, Smitty. That's all that counts."

Smitty couldn't help but grin. How did she do it? He could be so distraught, and she would start talking, and all of a sudden his dreams would start to revive themselves. Hope—that's what it was. She was always filled with hope, and he absorbed it like a starving ten-year-old.

8

Spring 1938

Dorothy opened her hope chest and withdrew a stack of letters, all from Smitty, with return addresses from towns all over Kansas, Nebraska, Wyoming, and Montana—all places *she* had never been. She separated the letters from the summer of 1936 and tied them into a neat stack with a yellow ribbon. The letters from the summer of 1937 she tied with a green ribbon.

As she began to return them carefully to the chest, she noticed the wine label tucked into an envelope. She pulled it out. Two years of watching him pack up and leave every summer; two years of counting the days until his return in the fall; two years since that first kiss. She looked out her bedroom window at the early morning sky, heavy with dreary rain clouds. Another summer of letters and waiting lay before her. With a deep sigh, she put the wine label away and began to dress for work.

FIFTEEN MILES TO the north, Smitty stood beside his father and Mr. Sanders, surveying a field of corn stubble. Enormous gusts kicked up exhausted soil mixed with bits of dried cornstalks and leftover kernels. Smitty took a handkerchief out of his pocket to protect his nose from the debris. "It's a deal," he said, shaking Mr. Sander's hand.

George looked up at his son. "It's damned hard work. Are you sure?"

"Pa, I started helping you when I was ten years old. I think I know all about hard work. I wanna be a farmer. Besides, I need the money."

"It's that Ayers girl you been sparkin', ain't it?" George asked, delighted with the possibility.

"I need to make some money. Let's just leave it at that."

DOROTHY LOOKED UP from her desk at the Triple-A office. She blinked at the sight of Smitty walking across the street toward her, a bouquet of flowers in his left hand. He opened the door of the office. "Can you go to lunch, Peaches?"

"Smitty, it's only ten in the morning." She looked around the office. All eyes were fixed on her. "Sure, sure I can. Just give me a minute. I'll be right back."

She walked into Mr. Anderson's office. "Sir, I need to mail some checks to farmers who didn't come in this week. I think I'll go do that right now."

Mr. Anderson leaned over in his chair, which gave him a perfect view of Smitty standing at the front door. "I see, Miss Ayers. Well, don't be gone too long."

"Thank you, sir. I'll only be thirty minutes or so."

She winked at Smitty. "All set. We have thirty minutes. Let's go."

Smitty opened the front door. "Let's go to the park. I've got some important stuff to tell you." He handed her the flowers. "These are for you, by the way."

Dorothy smelled the flowers and studied Smitty's face. "Did you give me the flowers because you're leaving today?"

Smitty sat down on the first available bench. "No, nothin' like that." He took the flowers, laid them aside, and took Dorothy's hands in his. "Sit down, Peaches. I got really good news." He paused. "I'm not leavin' this summer."

Dorothy blinked several times. "Did you just say you're not leaving? You're staying here for the summer, the entire summer? Are you leaving in the fall, then?"

"No, darlin', I'm stayin' right here. I'm rentin' some land to farm from Mr. Sanders. I'll be growin' my own crop—*my own corn*—like a regular farmer. I'll be busy as hell, but I'll be here, and we can see each other and be together. Honey, if the crop does well, we can start to make plans, like we always said we were going to. We can leave here, you and me. We can go see the world. It's a start anyway. Peaches, are you all right? Say somethin', would ya?"

Dorothy threw her arms around Smitty and tried to kiss him between sobs. "You're not leaving. You're not leaving," she repeated again and again.

When she stopped to catch her breath, he leaned down

and kissed her—a long, deep kiss given and returned with no care or attention to their surroundings. It didn't matter. He wasn't leaving. He had plans for them. They were going to leave this place and see the world together.

CLAY SOIL IS quite dense and thick and makes up a large part of Nebraska farmland. When wet, it becomes sticky, but when dry, it becomes rock hard and forms large clods. Smitty hated those clods. They slowed the already arduous process of plowing a field with a team of horses. Some clods were too difficult for the team to break up, and he had to lug them out of the way. Through it all, his focus remained on plowing the field, planting the corn, watching it grow, and dreaming of the day he could ask Dorothy to marry him.

Two months later, as he waited for the rain to come, one of those clods lay not in the field, but in his gut. This clod, made up of sacrifice and grueling labor, grew larger as another week passed without rain, then another and another. But that morning, as he gazed to the west, he saw what looked like a large thunderhead coming his way. "I think it's gonna rain today, Pa. Look at that dark cloud. It's headed right for us."

George threw his hat to the ground. "That ain't no rain cloud, son. It's those damned grasshoppers."

The swarming cloud moved closer, and Smitty gawked in horror at the sight of his cornfield disappearing in a cloud of hungry, voracious insects. "What do we do, Pa?"

George spat. "Ain't nothin' *to* do—just keep prayin' fer rain, and maybe replant. This is the part of farmin' you don't understand until you live through it. You just move on and hope for the best. That's all you can do."

SMITTY SURVEYED THE bed of his truck where his harvested corn lay, awaiting transport to town. The heavy clod he carried, now his constant companion, made it difficult for him to move. *Might as well get started.* He jumped into the cab of the truck and revved up the engine. *Ain't gonna find out what I made sittin' here.*

Arriving in town, he made a point of bypassing the Triple-A office. *Don't wanna see her until I have some news to tell her.* He passed Brewster's Jewelry Store. *Damn, I forgot to ask her what size ring she wears.*

He pulled his truck into the line at the entrance of the corn elevator and waited with the other farmers. He took his accounting book out of the glove box and reviewed his expenses for the third time in as many days. *I gotta make enough to buy the ring and cover expenses for next year's crop. If I go out with the combining crew next spring, I can maybe make enough for us to at least get started.*

His turn came. The manager weighed his corn. "OK, Smitty, here ya go." He handed Smitty a check.

"This is it?"

"That's it. You didn't expect much more than that, did ya, for this measly crop?"

"I worked my ass off for that corn, and this is all you're gonna give me?"

"'Fraid so, son."

Smitty pushed the accelerator of his truck to the floor,

spinning the tires and spitting gravel and dust into the manager's face. He kept driving until he reached the edge of town, where he stopped to take a second look at the check. He subtracted his expenses.

"Twenty-five cents. I made twenty-five damned cents!" He banged his fist against the steering wheel. The clod shattered into a thousand pieces and filled every cell in his body, leaving no room for dreams.

SMITTY TURNED THE pickup onto the dirt road—*their* dirt road—beside the cemetery. Dorothy giggled. "Where you goin'?"

He grinned at her like he always did, but his eyes belied his true feelings.

"Honey, what's wrong? I know something is wrong. Tell me."

He stopped the car, avoiding any eye contact. "I have to leave."

"You said you weren't going to leave. What happened?"

"I'm leavin', Peaches. I'm leavin' for good. I can't make a living here."

"When you say you're leaving for good, you mean *you and I* are leaving, right? What about your corn crop?"

He put his hands on her shoulders. "You aren't hearing me. I said *I* am leaving, not *us*. There's nothing for me here. I should never have even tried. This damned dried-up place can't grow anything. I have to make a living, Peaches, don't you get it? How can there be 'us' when I can't even make a living?"

"What do you mean there's nothing for you here? What about *me?* We can do it together. I have a job, remember? We can save money from my job and use that to leave."

Smitty started the pickup. "I have to take you home. It's over, Peaches. It's over."

Dorothy struggled to take it all in. The drive to her house seemed interminable. He stopped the pickup in front of her house and rushed to open her door, but she pushed it open herself and ran to the front porch.

He stood by the pickup door with the engine still running. "Wait! I'm sorry. I'm so sorry."

"Mark my words, Jack Smith. You will regret this day." She didn't care if her father could hear her, for nothing mattered now. "You should *never* leave me. You'll regret it."

"I'll write to you, Peaches. I promise."

"Why bother?" She ran into the house, slamming the door behind her.

Smitty jumped into his pickup and pushed the accelerator to the floor. *She's right. Why bother? Who needs any of it? No more nice girls. No more bullshit dreams. I'm stickin' to my guns. I'll see the world and find me a woman wherever I damned well please.*

9

Fall 1940
Washington State

The Great Depression held the country in its iron grip as people migrated from one area to another searching for *the* break, *the* job that would sustain them and provide even the smallest bit of hope. It didn't exist. But, people rationalized, it would be better in the next state or on the coast or away from the Dust Bowl, anywhere but where they found themselves, a place where hope remained as inaccessible as the next meal. Smitty fell into this assembly of drifters. He worked the wheat fields of Wyoming, then tried the fields of Montana, and then, on the advice of a cousin, he hopped a train and rode the rails to Washington state. Rumor had it that good jobs with good pay were plentiful there.

The promised work didn't materialize. One dead-end job led to another, and he fell into a routine of sorts: working all day in the apple orchards, then heading for his favorite bar or dance hall. He sat alone, pen and paper situated on the table before him. After a shot of whiskey, he picked up the pen. "My Darling Dorothy," he wrote. Another shot of whiskey followed, then another and another. He hummed "Tennessee Waltz" and stared at the paper. Eventually, a woman would saunter up and put her arm around him. "Hey, Smitty. Why don't you put that silly pen down and come dance with me?" After months of this same routine, he put the pen and paper down for good.

Whiskey and women, drawn to him like moths to a light, were the two constants that filled his time. They numbed the yearning for something better. Despite it all, one dream remained, unscathed by the harsh reality of a failed crop, two years of miserable, worthless jobs, and a lifetime of struggle. It sustained him, just as it had since childhood, and when he wasn't drinking or dancing, he spent long hours lounging on his bunk remembering every detail of that red Indian Scout motorcycle. And Dorothy? She became a murky dream. In fact, at times, he began to wonder if she had ever existed at all.

10

Beaver City

Dorothy checked the mail every day. Sometimes there would be a letter from Montana and, for a while, from Washington. She devoured them, reading for any sign that he might come home. Instead, his letters came less often, and when they did, they gave no hint of homesickness or of missing her. Finally, they stopped altogether.

One spring morning, two years after Smitty had left, Dorothy walked into Warton's Department Store. Annie spotted Dorothy coming toward her, too late to hide behind a nearby rack of dresses. Annie had successfully avoided her for several months, but now it appeared her luck had finally run out.

"Hi, Annie, long time no see. Where have you been anyway?"

Annie continued rummaging through the sale rack. "I've been around. Where have you been?"

"Just working away, as usual. Say, have you heard anything from you-know-who?"

Annie looked away, half hoping Dorothy would somehow vanish if she looked away long enough.

"Annie? Are you avoiding me?"

"Dottie, I..."

"No need to say more. I get it."

"Dottie, wait. I *have* heard from Jack. He's got a job picking apples, and this time it's lasted. They even said they could use him after picking season is done. The other news is that he has a girl. Her name is Lucky. He says she's..."

Dorothy saw Annie's lips moving, but she stopped hearing anything Annie said after "he has a girl."

Annie saw the devastation on Dorothy's face and reached out to comfort her. Dorothy mumbled something about being busy and needing to go to the grocery store and how nice it was to see her again. To Dorothy, the front door seemed miles away. She walked toward it, fumbled to find the handle and open it, and then ran down the sidewalk taking in deep breaths of the brisk spring air. Her thoughts tormented her as she continued running toward home. *It's over. He's never coming back. What's wrong with me? Why can't I let go?*

CAROL TOOK A sip of her cherry coke. "Don't you think it's time you started dating again? It's been two years, Dottie. Two years, and you said he has a girl. And how long has it been since you got a letter from him? Almost a year, right?"

Dorothy hunched her shoulders and sat back in the booth. "I just don't think I'm ready yet. He broke my heart."

"You've got to move on. It's time. I don't care if you aren't ready. There's a dance tomorrow night in Stamford. I've got a date with Jimmy—remember him? You can come with us—no, you *are* coming with us. I won't have it any other way."

"Fine! I'll go, but I'm *not* dancing with anyone. I'll just sit and listen to the music."

"DANCE WITH ME?"

Dorothy glanced up at the lanky young man standing in front of her. She steeled herself.

"Thank you, but I'm not dancing. I'm just listening to the music."

"You got a sprained ankle or somethin'?"

She narrowed her eyes and pursed her lips. "No, I'm just not dancing; that's all."

"Oh, I see. Not dancing with *me*, is that it? I'm not good enough for you to dance with?"

"No, not at all. That's not it at all."

"Well, then, can I sit down and join you? We can listen together. How 'bout that?"

"You are persistent, aren't you?"

"When I see a girl as pretty as you, I get real persistent."

Dorothy reconsidered her stance. In spite of herself, she began to enjoy the attention and determination of this flaxen-haired young man. "Well then, sit down. What's your name?"

"Tommie—well, it's really Michael Thomas, but everyone around here calls me Tommie."

"My name is Dorothy, but most people call me Dottie."

"I thought maybe they called you Peaches cuz of your cute little peachy cheeks."

"No, no one calls me that. And I would prefer that you not start, if you don't mind."

"That's fine. I didn't mean to upset you."

"You didn't. I just don't like to be called Peaches."

"Dottie it is then."

"Are you from around here?"

"Yup. I went to school right here in Stamford. I live with my ma and pa out east about ten miles. We got a farm out there."

Dorothy grimaced. "A farmer, of course."

"So what's wrong with bein' a farmer?"

"Nothing. My pa is a farmer too." She forced herself to smile. "Let's dance. How about that? We can dance and not talk so much."

Tommie jumped from his seat, smitten by the opportunity to hold her in his arms. "Glad ya changed yer mind."

The band began playing "Tennessee Waltz." The playful look left Dorothy's eyes.

"Now what's wrong?" Tommie asked, bewildered by her sudden mood change.

Dorothy took Tommie's hand. "Nothing, nothing at all. I thought you wanted to dance. Let's go."

Tommie slid his arm around her waist. She smelled like a garden of roses. He stifled the desire to pull her close to him and relaxed into the one-two-three rhythm of the music, confident that his waltz moves were some of his best.

Dorothy attempted to follow Tommie's clumsy, awkward

movements. Something wasn't right—or was she comparing his moves to those of somebody else?

"So, do you work?"

Startled out of her trance, Dorothy looked up to discover Tommie, not Smitty holding her close. "What?"

"I said, do you work?"

"I work in the Triple-A office. I measure farmers' property so we can determine how much the government needs to pay them not to plant a crop. But you probably know all about that since you're a farmer." She became transfixed by his deep blue eyes, which seemed engrossed in every word she spoke. She blinked several times, trying to regain her composure.

"Doesn't your pa get payments from the Triple-A?"

For a moment, neither of them spoke, lost in the rhythm of the waltz, and enjoying the closeness of their bodies.

"So does he?" she asked.

"Does he what?"

"Get payments from the Triple-A?"

"I don't know. I guess so. If he does, I'll be the one pickin' up his checks from now on if it means I can see you."

Dorothy blushed. "That would be nice."

The waltz ended, and the band began to play "In The Mood." Dorothy relaxed. She liked this good-looking, charming young man. "Do you jitterbug?" she asked.

"I try." Tommie began swinging her under his arm and then pulling her back.

Smitty wouldn't have even tried this, she thought with some satisfaction. *I like this guy's gumption, even if he isn't that good at it.* Her energy and mood rose with each move of the dance.

The song ended, and Tommie headed for a nearby chair. "I'm bushed. Let's sit down for a minute. You just plain wear a guy out. Can I get you some punch? Hey, do you have a ride home? Where do you live anyway?"

Dorothy cocked her head to the side, pleased at his barrage of questions. "One thing at a time, Tommie, please. Yes, I would like some punch. I live in Beaver City, and, no, I don't need a ride home. Maybe next time."

DOROTHY REVIEWED THE previous year: a whirlwind of dances, movies, and parties. Tommie adored her; that much was obvious. With him, she felt desirable again, and, maybe best of all, he made her forget, at least some of the time, about Smitty.

Comfortable with their relationship, she didn't hesitate to tell him about her experience with Smitty. "It's OK," he said. "I'll wait for you forever. As long as it takes for you to forget about him, I'll wait."

And now, here he was, sitting beside her under an elm tree, parked on a dirt road, waiting for her response to his marriage proposal.

She pondered her answer. "Tommie, I..."

"I love you, Dottie. I know this is fast, but I *have* to know now."

"I don't know, Tommie. Can't you let me think about it just a little?"

"No! I wanna marry you, and I need to know *now*."

"Why now? What's so special about now?"

"I signed up for the army, and I'm leavin' in a couple of

months. But I do love you."

"You joined the army?"

"I had to. The farm is goin' broke. There's no way to make a livin' there. I had to figure out a future for us. The only way I could figure doin' it was by joinin' the army. They pay good—well, better than farmin', anyway. I can save up, and it's only for a year. Then I'll be back, and we can be together. I couldn't tell you cuz I was afraid you'd talk me out of it, and I just gotta do this. It's for us, honey—you and me. Will you wait for me?"

Dorothy looked out the window at the setting sun. *Wait for you? Why am I always the one left waiting?*

"I wanna marry you. I know it's fast, but will you at least think about it, please? I got it all figured out. We can get married as soon as I get out of the army. Then we'll buy a trailer, one of them Airstream trailers, and we'll take off, go to Colorado, and never come back here again."

Dorothy's eyes glazed over. She could see every detail of the Airstream trailer.

"You mean California, right? We can stop in Colorado and maybe even go up to Yellowstone."

"No, Colorado's the place for us. Have you ever been there?"

"No, but we have to go to California if we want to see the ocean."

"Honey, once you see the Rocky Mountains, you won't give a hoot about the ocean. I promise you."

"OK, I guess, but it's sort of always been my dream."

"You'll get over it. I'm tellin' ya, you're gonna love Colorado. Anyway, honey, are you goin' to answer me?"

Dorothy put her hand on the back of his neck and pulled him to her. "Yes, I'll answer you. Yes, I will marry you. Yes. Yes. Yes," she repeated between each kiss. They fell into each other's arms, half-laughing, half-crying. They held each other closer than they had allowed themselves in the past. She didn't bother stopping him this time when he ran his hand down her back, along her side, and over her breast. It all seemed so perfect. He loved her. He would come back for her. He had a plan, and yet despite herself, she began drifting off to a familiar place.

SMITTY STOOD BEFORE her. "I should never have left. I love you so much." They held hands as they walked along the beach. The ocean waves splashed against their bare feet. With her thumb, Dorothy touched the wedding band on her left hand, assuring herself that she was, indeed, a married woman. They continued walking, meandering their way back to the beachside motel.

Smitty picked her up and carried her into their room. They fell across the bed into each other's arms. He moved his hand from her breast down her side to her thigh.

"NO!" SHE SHOUTED, and she sat straight up in the seat.

"No? No, you won't marry me; no, you don't love me?"

"Just no, Tommie, no more. I choose you. I love you, and I want to marry you. That's all."

Tommie put his arms around her. He kissed her ear. Dorothy shivered in response to the sensual pleasure and then pushed him away. "Please stop, Tommie. I need to go home. Please take me home."

"Sure, honey, anything you say. You love me and we're getting married; that's all that matters."

She took in the darkened landscape beyond the car window, holding back tears, willing herself to forget Smitty's arms holding her, of his lips pressed against hers.

"That's right," she whispered. "That's all that matters."

11

Spring 1941
Fort Knox, Kentucky

The irksome sound of a trumpet blasting reveille over a loudspeaker came too fast for Tommie's taste. He sprang out of bed and prepared for Friday morning inspection.

He took extra care to ensure a smooth shave with no nicks. The pungent smell of match-heated shoe polish soon filled the air. When the dim light in the barracks tent reflected back at him from the toes of his shoes, he knew they were ready, but he gave them an added buff for good measure. Stepping in front of the mirror, he saluted the meticulous image: hair shaved to within a quarter-inch of his scalp, military hat sitting at the correct angle atop his head, shirt pressed and tucked into pants with a perfect crease down the center. He studied his image one last time to determine any oversights as his father's words echoed in his mind: *Give to the world the best you have, and the best will come back to you.*

One last detail remained: making his bed with military precision. "I don't get military corners," he complained out loud.

"I'll make the bed if you'll help me with this damned tie. *That's* what *I* don't get." Grant, Tommie's buddy since the day they arrived at Fort Knox six weeks earlier, was struggling to make a Windsor knot.

"It's a deal. Here, let me do your tie first. Jesus, Grant, did you even iron your shirt?"

"I tried, but I always sorta look like this, no matter what I do." His large frame waged a constant battle with his clothes: shirt half-tucked, pants two inches too short and wrinkled in spite of ironing, and shoes with eternal scuff marks across the toes.

Tommie finished tying the Windsor. "It's just gonna have to do."

Just then, their sergeant made his entrance. Tommie stood at attention. "Chin up, chest out, shoulders back, and stomach in," he repeated to himself in an attempt to remember proper form. The sergeant began his rounds, scrutinizing each man with an eye on pointing out shortcomings rather than praising correctness. He spent extra time on Grant.

Tommie stood next in line. The sergeant dissected every aspect of his uniform, shoes, and stance. Tommie strained to maintain his military bearing and expressionless face, focusing on the wall in front of him. The sergeant gave a nod of approval and moved on. *Two hours work for a ten-second* glance at me, Tommie mused. *It's not worth it.*

With inspection completed, Tommie and Grant walked to class. They arrived right on time and corralled chairs closest to the door. Tommie chewed on his pencil, bounced his knee, yawned—anything to stay awake while the instructor droned on about the finer points of repairing a radio. *Hell, I'd just as soon milk a damned cow as sit here and do this—at least that's real work.* He squirmed in his chair, and his stomach growled. *Noon ain't gonna come any too soon for my liking.*

TOMMIE VAULTED FROM his chair and made it halfway to the door before the instructor finished saying, "Class dismissed." He pulled a Camel cigarette out of his pocket, lit it, and took a deep drag, enjoying the calming sensation of the nicotine as it entered his bloodstream. His stomach growled again at the sight of the mess hall. *I hope there ain't much of a crowd today. I hate the noise and everybody bumpin' into ya, reachin' over ya to get more food. I'd rather wait and eat later than eat with a bunch like that.* He took another deep drag on his cigarette, crushed it against his heel, and tossed it into the butt-can at the entrance of the mess hall.

"Over there." Grant pointed across the room. Tommie cringed at the cacophony of silverware clanking, dishes clattering, and a hundred young men talking, yelling, and laughing. *Sounds like a bunch of mad cattle milling around in here.* He worked his way across the room, clenching his jaw as soldiers bumped his shoulder or shoved in front of him. He sat down beside Grant, who was already half finished with his lunch.

The soldier sitting on the other side of Tommie reached in front of him for the salt. "Ever heard the phrase 'pass the salt,' asshole?" Tommie snapped.

The soldier jumped to his feet. "Who you callin' an asshole, jerk?"

Tommie snatched the apple off his tray, mashed his sandwich into his napkin, and steamed toward the door. "I can't eat in here, Grant. I'll see you later."

SATURDAY BROUGHT A new kind of tension. Tommie opened his eyes and with a heavy sigh sat up on the edge of his cot. Another sigh emanated from deep inside his lungs, and he flopped himself back on his cot. He checked the time: three in the afternoon. He pulled out his wallet. *Nothin' in here but mothballs and memories.* Two long empty days stretched before him. *I'll write to Dorothy. That'll fill up some time.* He removed the ink bottle and pen from his footlocker and arranged the paper in preparation.

"Dearest Dorothy..." *What do I write? What do I say that's interesting?* He commenced a tedious recounting of his week as a private in the Headquarters Company, Nineteenth Ordinance Battalion.

When he finished, he read through his letter. *That'll do. Must be gettin' late by now.* He glanced at his watch. *Three thirty? Maybe one more page.* He pulled out another sheet of paper. Several minutes passed. The paper that lay on his makeshift desk taunted him.

I wish my year was over. It's kinda fun to lay around and build air castles and then let them burst. I still have hopes of not having to go over the pond and blow Hitler off the map. But maby I can be lucky. Who knows? We are sure going to have fun when I get out, ain't we? I've got it all figured out; where, when and how.

He paused. *We'll take the Airstream trailer and hitch it to my Ford. I hope Dad's taking good care of that Ford. We'll start early in the morning and take Highway 34 to Denver...*

TOMMIE OPENED THE door to the Airstream trailer and stepped out into the warm Colorado sun. The sky matched the color of a robin's egg.

He found Dorothy lying under an aspen tree, staring at the sky. Her green sweater clung to her just enough to hint at the enticing body underneath. "Whatcha up to, honey?" he asked.

"Good morning, sleepyhead. It's about time you got yourself up. I'm just looking at the clouds. Don't you just love clouds? Look at that one. It looks like a rabbit. Can you see its ears?"

"Well, I'm more interested in breakfast, honey."

"Don't worry. Breakfast is all ready. I made eggs and bacon, nice and crispy, just the way you like it. Want some coffee?"

"Sure, honey." He sat down under the tree. The crisp mountain air filled his lungs. The roaring sound of the Big Thompson River made hearing anything else impossible.

Dorothy arrived with his coffee. He took a sip. "Honey, you make the best coffee. Nice and strong, just the way I like it."

"Thanks, sweetie." She took in the magnificent canyon walls and the raging river next to their campsite. "Ya know, we could settle here. Big Thompson Canyon is a gorgeous place, don't you think?"

"I thought you wanted to go to California."

"No, I want whatever you want, Tommie."

"Whatever I want, huh? Well then, get over here."

GRANT KICKED TOMMIE'S cot. Dorothy, the Airstream trailer, and the Rocky Mountains dimmed and disappeared like the fade-out at the end of a movie. "Hey, dreamer. Wake up! There's a football game with the Twenty-Eighth. What position do you wanna play today?"

Tommie checked his watch: 4:10 p.m. He forced himself to stand. "I'll play center. Anything's better than sittin' around an empty barracks."

"HUT, HUT." THE quarterback barked out the signals. Tommie shoved the ball back into the quarterback's hands, ran forward to block the nearest defensive man, and found himself staring into the eyes of the guy in the mess hall with crude manners. The lineman hooked Tommie's left leg, hurling him to the ground. "Asshole, huh? We'll see who's the asshole."

A loud whoosh emanated from Tommie's lungs. The field swirled around him, and he gasped for air. He sprang to his feet, determined to hide the excruciating pain now running down his left leg. He focused on the running back crossing the goal line. Raising his middle finger toward the lineman, Tommie yelled, "Touchdown!" and sauntered to the sideline, making sure he showed no signs of limping.

The final whistle blew with the score 35 to 28 in favor of Tommie's team.

I do love beating those bastards, he thought, savoring the final score. He limped his way back to the barracks. His watch read six o'clock as the endless day continued. He sat on his bunk and struggled to finish his letter.

DOROTHY WALKED TOWARD the post office. Her steps quickened as she neared the front door. "There *will* be a letter. There *will* be a letter," she chanted in rhythm with her steps.

The contents of the post office box dictated her daily mood. A letter postmarked "Fort Knox, Kentucky" promised a bright and cheerful day. If no letter appeared, a sense of gloom would envelop her. She expected a letter every day, as promised, but yesterday marked three days without a letter. Her mind raced: *Maybe he doesn't want to hear from me. Maybe it was just a winter fling. Maybe he'll be just like Smitty and leave me high and dry. Why did I tell him I would write him anyway? He said he loved me, but so did Smitty. He even proposed to me. So what? I'm twenty-three years old and single. I'm an old maid!*

She pulled the door of the post office open with such vigor it slammed against the building, attracting the attention of everybody waiting for mail. "Sorry, guess I don't know my own strength," she said to no one in particular.

She opened the box and peeked inside. A small squeal echoed against the marble walls of the post office, once again making her the focus of everyone's attention. Not one, but three letters sat in the box, all with the return address of "Fort Knox, Kentucky."

She studied the postmarks: "May 17," "May 19," and "May 21." She opened the letter postmarked May 17, making sure she preserved the stamp for her scrapbook, and began to read the latest installment in Tommie's training camp odyssey:

Dearest Dorothy,

Thursday, I spent the day washing dishes and peeling Spuds, etc. Had to work for the 28th Co. and did they ever take advantage of us. We washed their dishes and even shined their darn silverware. Their dishes were greasy from not washing them clean before. The Battalion commander came in for inspection.

He sure gave us a compliment. He told the cooks
we had the dishes washed cleaner than they
had been for some time. The 28th and us are
just like two ball teams. Each trying to out due
the other one.

Tiring of reading the finer points of Tommie's day, Dorothy began to skim through the letter until her eyes fell upon the word "married":

The way my brother wrote in his last letter
he figures on getting married this summer if
they don't call him to the army too soon. If
they do he plans to get married before he goes.
I think he's foolish. I would much rather do
it our way, go to army first & get married
afterwards.

Dorothy's brow furrowed. "Did we say that?" she wondered out loud. She read on:

Then, if we get in war & get blowed to
bits wont leave a widow. Don't you think that's
best?

She stomped her foot. "Oh, Tommie, don't talk like that!" Surprised by her own voice, she perused the area, making sure no one saw her talking to herself. *Why are men like that? Don't they know we don't want to think about things like that?*

She favored an earlier comment by far:

We are sure going to have fun when I get out, ain't we? I've got it all figured out; where, when, and how.

She stopped reading. She knew exactly where, when, and how.

DOROTHY AWOKE TO the smell of coffee wafting through the window. She heard bacon sizzling outside on the campfire and yawned. "Nothing like the smell of coffee and bacon."

She dragged herself out of bed, taking in every detail of the Airstream trailer. She ran her hands across the table in passing and rearranged the red and white checkered tablecloth, a wedding gift from her sister. She peeked into the icebox, helped herself to an apple, opened the door, and stepped out into the crisp, clear morning. She could hear the ocean waves crashing into the cove behind their campsite.

He turned from the campfire and smiled up at her, exposing the slight gap between his two front teeth. "Good mornin', darlin'."

"Smitty?"

"SMITTY?" CAROL SAID. "Did you just call me Smitty?"

"No. Why would I call you Smitty? I hate that name."

Carol finished applying her red raspberry lipstick as they began the short walk to the office. "Sure you do, honey."

Dorothy held up the letters. "It's not about Smitty anymore; it's about Tommie. Three letters today. Three! He's talking about getting married and buying an Airstream trailer. We're going to California first, but we're never settling down. He's the sweetest thing. I love him, Carol; I really do."

Carol opened the door to the Triple-A. "You love *him*, or is it the Airstream trailer you love?"

A rush of turbulence rose within Dorothy, like a pot about to boil over. "How can you ask me that? I love *him*. You can't love an Airstream trailer. You are such a pest."

"You can't love an Airstream trailer—that's true—but maybe you're just in love with the idea of getting out of here. You've always said you wanted to travel and never settle down, and here he is, offering that to you. You need to think about that."

"No, you need to mind your own business. We're going to get married, and, yes, we're going to leave Nebraska, and we're going to travel all over, and then we're going to settle down in California right by the ocean.

"Now he's saying he doesn't want to get married until he gets out of the army, but I don't want to wait. I've done all the waiting I'm going to do. I want a Christmas wedding. What do you have to say about that, Miss Nosy Pants?"

Carol nodded over Dorothy's left shoulder. "I think we have a lot of work to do today. Good morning, Mr. Anderson.

How are you this morning?" Carol's smile had a way of dissipating many problematic situations. She used it then.

"Good morning, ladies. Glad to see you're getting an early start."

Dorothy slid into her chair and pulled herself up to her desk. Not as charming or quick-witted as Carol, she blushed. "Yes, sir, we surely are."

Mr. Anderson retreated to his office and closed the door. Dorothy attempted to calm the turmoil that churned within her. She slammed her day's work file on the desk. *Why does Carol do that to me? She gets me all balled up inside. But I know what I want—I want a Christmas wedding. I'm sure of that!*

Mr. Anderson's door remained closed. She retrieved the stash of stationery she kept hidden under her ledger and began to write:

Dearest Tommie,

It sounds like you are really busy. We are busy too. I'm really enjoying my job more all the time, and I'm getting really good at it. Mr. Anderson told me so. I never thought of myself doing anything but getting married and having babies, but this is sure fun while it lasts.

I made pa a baked chicken last night. I've never done that before, but it turned out really good. It's not as good as Mom's, of course. She made the best baked chicken I have ever tasted. Don't worry. I will keep working on it, and by the time we get married, it will taste as good as hers did.

Speaking of getting married, I have something for you to think about. I know you said you want to wait, but I don't. I want to get married when you come home on leave. I don't care about the army or war or anything but you. I want us to be married. Didn't you say you thought you would be home for Christmas? What if we got married then? What do you think, honey?

I am sending a surprise for you in a different mailing, so keep your eyes open. I miss you.

Love,

Dorothy

TOMMIE SCANNED DOROTHY'S letter for the fourth time. "She wants to get married at Christmas. I told her it wasn't a good idea to get married until I get out. What am I gonna do?"

Grant slapped Tommie on the back. "Ignore it. *That's* what you're gonna do, buddy."

"I've *been* ignoring it. I haven't written her since I got this letter two weeks ago. She's gonna start thinkin' I'm mad or I don't love her. I gotta tell her somethin'."

"If she's made up her mind, you're pretty well stuck, but if you don't mention it, maybe she'll forget it. Women are funny about stuff like that. They just get an idea in their heads, and then that's all they think about. I would..."

"You don't understand. I *love* her. Her letters are the only things that keep me sane around here. Maybe we *should* get married at Christmas."

"You love *her*, or do you just love her kisses?"

"No, well, yeah, I love her kisses, but I love her too. She's wonderful, and when she smiles, her cheeks look like peaches, and her eyes light up."

"Oh, boy, you might as well just give in and marry her at Christmas. She's got you wrapped around her little finger. You're kinda makin' me sick. Think I'll just go buy myself a soda pop."

Tommie began to read the letter for a fifth time. "Hey, wait a minute. She said she's sending me a surprise. It's gotta be at the post office by now. I just forgot to check."

Grant rubbed his hands together in anticipation. "On second thought, maybe I'll just go with you to check on that surprise. Maybe it's some more of those homemade cookies of hers."

TOMMIE TORE THE paper off the package in one tug. He yanked open the box, pulling the last bits of wrapping out of the way. Grant smacked his lips. "What is it? Is it cookies, like you thought? I could sure use some homemade goodies."

"Nah. It's ten times—hell, a hundred times—better than cookies. It's her!" Tommie made a sweeping gesture at the smartly framed photo. "Grant, I would like you to meet my lovely fiancée, Dorothy. Dottie, this is Grant—another grunt, just like me."

"Ah, I see why you wanna keep writing her. Pretty girl, man, mighty pretty girl, even with glasses."

"I know. That's a new hairdo. One of them new "'dos," all rolled back in the front. I like it. Her hair is real soft, and it's the prettiest brown color you ever saw—sort of like Nebraska topsoil right after you plow it. And her eyes, every bit as brown as her hair. See, look at her cheeks. I told ya. Don't ya think they look like little peaches?"

"They sort of do look like peaches, yeah. I see what you're saying. Tommie, my man, you are one lucky son of a gun."

"I know. I know. Maybe we *should* get married at Christmas. Ya know, she's thousands of miles away, and I bet every guy in Furnas County is wantin' to court her. But it just don't seem right." He threw the photo onto his bed. "I'm so damned mixed up. My insides are all flutterin' around like a bunch of miller moths around a street light in June. I gotta get off this base for a while. Between this place and bein' all confused about Dottie, I'm about to go bonkers."

"You got it bad, man," Grant agreed. "How 'bout we just go for a walk, maybe see if there's a dance or a movie that we can go to?"

"Anywhere's fine with me, as long as it's off this stinkin' base."

TOMMIE SLOUCHED DOWN on a bench outside the bus station on the Dixie Highway.

"You're a barrel of fun, ain't ya? Come on, Tommie, there's gotta be something more exciting than this," Grant groaned.

Tommie pulled his wallet out of his pocket, opened it, and turned it upside down. "Do you see anything green fallin' out? I'm broke—not a dime to my name. Where am I gonna go? Besides, the only dances they have are on the weekend. Good luck finding anybody to dance with. There's ten GIs to every girl. You go on if you want to—I'm just gonna sit here for a while and watch the cars go by. It kinda settles my mind."

"Well, I ain't got any more money than you do, so guess I'll join ya."

Car after car rushed by, melding into a blur of color and sound.

TOMMIE TURNED UP the volume on the radio. "Scoot over here, baby. I wanna have you as close to me as you can get."

Dorothy put her hand on Tommie's leg and closed the six-inch gap between them. "Is this better, soldier boy?"

He pushed the accelerator to the floor. "Oh, yeah. If you were any closer, I'd hafta pull over."

Dorothy adjusted her silk scarf and tightened it under her chin. "I love your new car. You know, red is one of my favorite colors."

"Sorry, honey, forgot about your hair. Do you want me to put the top up?"

"No, I love the wind in my face. Where are we going today, honey?"

"Just cruisin' down the Dixie Highway. Hey, look at those soldiers sittin' in front of the bus station with nothin' to do. Poor bastards. Are you hungry? There's a real nice

restaurant up ahead. Let's stop, and I'll buy you anything you want to eat."

She massaged his leg. "No thanks. I'm not that hungry. Besides, I like just sitting here close to you."

A SPEEDING TRUCK flew by the bus station and blew its horn at the car in front of it. Tommie winced. "Think I'll go back to the barracks. See ya later."

He ambled toward the barracks, hands in his pockets, deep in thought, kicking stones off the road on the way. He stopped. "Wait a minute. Her picture! It's waitin' for me."

Sprinting the last hundred yards, he opened the door to the barracks, dashed to his cot, and picked up the photo. "Hey, baby. What did you think of my new car?"

DOROTHY UNLOCKED THE mailbox door and peeked inside with one eye shut. She shuddered and reached for the lone letter in the box, ripped the envelope open, almost ruining the precious stamp, and began to read, taking her time as she meandered her way to work:

> Dearest Dorothy,
>
> Thanks for the photo. You sure look beautiful. I'll keep it with me always. Honey, just seeing you makes me feel better.
>
> My old side kick and I was down by the bus depot this afternoon and just sat in the shade and watched the people go by. It is on

the Dixie Highway and lots of traffic. Rather gave me a homesick feeling to see them riding around in cars and having a good time. I knew that if I was only home I probably would be doing the same thing.

I have sure come to one definite conclusion though. One can never appreciate the outside as much until they have been here a spell.

Had no idea that I was as lucky on the outside as I was. If only one could read his future.

Words can never explain the value of your letters. I sure do enjoy them and surely look forward to them.

I want to say you mean more to me every day. It is far greater than words on paper can explain.

Good nite now. Gosh I wish I could have you here to hold in my arms and kiss you good nite instead of thinking how much like heaven that would be. I'm glad you are enjoying your job, but I'll be happier when you can quit, because no wife of mine is going to have a job. That's what's really important.

I'll write again in a day or so.

Loads of Love,

Tommie

PS Yes I am pretty sure I'll be home Christmas & I'll be there if we aren't across the pond *which I don't think we will be. I am really planning on a good time & no foolin. Be just back from 4 months in the rough and rearin to go.*

Dorothy crumpled the letter. *A good time? We're going to have a good time? What about, 'We're going to have a wedding'? And what if I don't want to quit my job after we get married?* She tore it into pieces, threw it into the garbage, and set off toward the Triple-A office, determined to hold back tears. *To hell with men. No more waiting for someone to come back. No more praying for letters every day. Who needs it? I am going to make a mark for myself right here in Beaver City. I don't need a man to take care of me. I can take care of myself. I can do my job with my eyes closed. The Triple-A is where I belong—not in some kitchen waiting on a man day and night.*

With the possible exception of Carol, no one did the aerial survey analysis with Dorothy's level of precision. Being a farmer's daughter spurred her to take extra time toiling over the photographs, ensuring the accuracy of her work. She inherited that attention to detail from her pa, a trait not lost on Mr. Anderson, who prided himself on only distributing compliments to those who did exemplary work. His latest assessment echoed in her mind: *You're the best operator we have.*

"Here, let me get that for you, missy." Mr. Lundquist, her least favorite farmer, stepped in front of her and opened the door to the office. She disliked him on many levels, including his shoddy, unkempt appearance. His overalls, always missing a fastener, appeared to have never seen the inside of a washtub. The stench of a feedlot preceded him into the room, and his boots never failed to leave a track of dried mud behind him.

"How are you today, Miss Ayers?" he asked in his shrill, harsh voice, another trait Dorothy detested. He made it even worse by winking.

"I'm fine, Mr. Lundquist. Just fine."

"Got that check for me?"

"Yes, sir. It's right here." She reached into the safe and pulled out his check.

"Now, is it accurate? Did you make sure I got paid for every damned acre I'm leavin' fallow?"

"Of course, sir. That's my job, and I take pride in doing it well. Now, let me record that check for you so you can be on your way."

"Oh, no hurry. No hurry. Let me see that left hand of yours, missy. Still no ring? Now what's the matter with that boy? You better be careful. I'm beginning to wonder about his intentions. You know he has a reputation, don't ya? Sorta like that Smith boy you were so wild about."

"Mr. Lundquist! Please! My private life is none of your concern. Now, here is your check. Good day, sir."

"I'll be on my way, missy, but you know I'm right. You're as red as one of them beets my wife's cannin'." He cackled as he waved the check at her.

Dorothy snatched the check out of his hand. "Oh, I'm so sorry, Mr. Lundquist. You are a day early. I can't give you this check until tomorrow."

She walked briskly into the back office before he could

protest. Mr. Lundquist began to speak, changed his mind, turned on his heel, and slammed the door as he left.

Carol opened the door to the back office. "Hey, kid, you OK?"

Dorothy leaned against a desk, arms crossed. "I'm fine." She balked at her own answer. "Actually, I'm not fine at all. That old coot! He teased me, *again*, about not having an engagement ring. The funny thing was, I got more upset when he accused me of not doing my job. The other thing is I got a letter from Tommie, and it sounds like he just wants to have a good time at Christmas; no mention of getting married at all, *and* he doesn't want me to work after we get married, but what if I *want* to work? He doesn't seem to understand that I'm not just filling time until I can be his wife. I like working!" She crossed her arms and shook her head. "I'm starting to think I don't want to get married at Christmas either. We *should* wait. We need to think this through."

TOMMIE'S HANDS BEGAN to sweat as he read Dorothy's letter:

> Dear Tommie,
>   I got your letter. I don't mind telling you I'm not quite sure what we should do, but I think you may be right. We should wait until you get out to get married.
>   You need to know that I'm pretty proud of my work, too. I don't mean to sound conceited, but I'm really good at what I do. My job makes me feel free, like I can take care of

myself. I make good money. I've even thought about finding my own place. Can you imagine what Pa would say? Ha.

Writing this letter has really helped me clear my mind. You're right, let's wait. It sounds like you're more interested in a good time than settling down anytime soon. So, what's the rush, right?

See you at Christmas time.

Love,

Dorothy

Tommie crushed the letter into a ball and threw it at Grant. It hit him on the forehead. "I should never have listened to you, asshole."

"Hey, take it easy, buddy. What are you talkin' about? What did she say?" Grant picked up the crumpled letter and smoothed it out on his lap.

Tommie snatched the letter away from his friend. "She wants to wait!"

"Congratulations, man, I thought that's what you wanted."

"So did I, but something isn't right."

He stormed out of the barracks and rambled around the base. His confusion baffled him. She agreed with him. They should wait, but all that talk about her job left him uneasy. She sounded so sure of herself, so independent.

An hour passed. Tommie opened the door to the day-room. "Take the A Train" was playing on the jukebox. He found a seat and began to hum along.

"Wish I was on a train," he mumbled. He stopped

humming. "That's it!" he yelled.

He swung the door open and ran the five hundred yards to the HQ, charging up to the first clerk he came to inside the building. "What do I gotta do to get a leave?"

"Well, private, when does your training end?"

"It won't be done for another four weeks, and we don't go on maneuvers until two weeks after that, but I gotta go before that. I gotta."

"Yeah, you and half the company. You won't be going anywhere until you're done with class, so just get *that* idea out of your head right now. Girl problems, right? She cheatin' on you, private? What did you expect? You're a helluva long ways from home, and there she is, alone and wantin' a little lovin'."

"Just give me the damned papers, will ya, and shut yer trap."

"You want the papers, private? You shut *your* trap, or you get nothing from me."

"Yes, sir. I'm sorry, sir. Just a little anxious; that's all." He seized the papers from the corporal's hand and moved to a side counter, where he could fill out the leave request undisturbed.

DOROTHY SCANNED THE letter. "He's coming home!"

"Tommie? When?"

"August fourth. He'll be here on August fourth. That's only twenty-one days. He wants to talk about our wedding!"

Carol pulled her unruly curl into place and squinted her eyes. "Um, I thought you said you wanted to wait."

"I did. I did say that, but he's coming home. It's been a long time. Maybe I just need to see him."

TOMMIE ARRIVED IN class fifteen minutes early. He tapped his pencil on the desk. "Ten days and I'll be home. Oh, man, just ten more days."

"Yeah, Tommie, I know, and yesterday it was eleven days, and tomorrow it'll be nine days. Little hard to miss since you start every damned class the same way," Grant grumbled.

"Gimme a break, man. I'm just excited; that's all."

"No, you're just a lovesick puppy; that's what you are."

Tommie started to protest, but the instructor entered the classroom, and they all stood, saluted him, and waited for him to be seated. "Gentlemen, there have been some changes in the schedule. We have moved maneuvers back a month. The extra month gives us time to dig a little deeper into radio maintenance. Class will end twenty-eight August, and maneuvers begin one September. Any questions?"

Tommie's hand flew up. "But we still get to go on leave, right?"

"Were you listening, private?" He raised his voice even louder and accentuated each word.

"Class has been extended until three days before maneuvers. You will get three days off at the end of class. Any other leaves are canceled as of right now."

"No! Sir, that can't be right. My leave is signed and everything. *You* don't understand."

"No, private. You don't understand. All leaves are canceled. Now let's get to work."

Beaver City

Dorothy opened Tommie's latest letter with great anticipation and began to read:

Dearest Dorothy,

I wrote you a while back we were to get out of school August 1. I put in for a furlough starting August 4 for 10 days, just like I told you. Then yesterday they said we wouldn't get out before manaevers, or just in time to go. Manaevers were put off until September 1.

Had the leave all signed and everything. I got right down on my knees & begged the captain to let me go, but no dice. Gosh darn

I was disgusted. The devils built us all up for an awful let down. There was a bunch of us in the same batch, but that's the way of this army. So now it looks like it'll be Christmas if something else doesn't happen. Right now I wouldn't be surprised at anything. I feel like I could just bawl if it would do any good. Was so set in seeing you again that now I feel like I lost all I ever lived for.

Carol put her arm around Dorothy. "Hey, kiddo. What's up? You looked so happy this morning. Besides, it's Friday, and isn't Tommie coming in on Monday?"

"*Was* coming, you mean? He says he can't come now. I don't know what to think. All this confusion. First he wants to wait until he's out of the army to get married, then he wants to get married at Christmas, and he's coming home so we can make plans, and I get all excited and think maybe we *should* get married; then he writes and says he's not coming, and I'm thinking maybe I don't want to get married at all!"

Carol patted Dorothy's back. "Well, maybe this is for the best. It'll give you time to get your head on straight about everything."

MR. ANDERSON CALLED Carol into his office. He cleared his throat several times. "Carol, there is a position opening at the main office in Lincoln. I would hate to lose you, and, to be honest, I thought about not even mentioning it, but I couldn't do it. The job would be perfect for you. Here's the information. I want you to give some serious thought to taking the position."

Carol had waited for this moment for a long time. She knew her work was exemplary; she knew she could do the job in Lincoln without even reading the job description. She also knew her father was dying slowly, painfully, and that her mother had no way of managing without her help. Without hesitation, she walked to Dorothy's desk and placed the letter on top of a pile of photos where Dorothy would see it when she came in.

DOROTHY READ THE letter, and then looked around, wondering how it found its way to her desk. She spotted Carol, and in one colossal moment of perfect clarity, she knew what had happened.

She marched to Carol's desk with the letter in hand. "You *have* to do this, she proclaimed. "I can look in on your parents every day. I can even help your ma cook and clean."

"You have enough on your plate with your pa and Walter, and what happens when you leave here like you always say you're going to do? No, I can't. I belong here, but you could take the job. I put that on your desk for you, kiddo. It fits you to a T."

A shift began within Dorothy, a lightness she hadn't experienced since before her mother died. She couldn't quite put her finger on it. What was it?

No attachments, no strings, just me being me. I can be Dorothy or Dottie, not Frank's daughter or Jessie's niece. I could even change my name if I wanted to.

"So, what do you think?" Carol asked, pulling Dorothy out of her trance.

"I can't believe I'm saying this, but I think I'm interested."

"And what about Tommie? What will he think?"

Dorothy stopped, dumbfounded. Not once had Tommie entered her mind

Sooner or later, the truth always emerges. Once the façade begins to crumble, there is no turning back, no pretending it didn't happen, that it isn't true. Tommie had filled an emptiness, a vacant spot, but filling a void isn't the same as filling a heart. The truth nearly knocked her over.

Dorothy spent that evening writing Tommie a letter, trying to explain her uncertainty. Crumpled sheets of paper covered her bedroom floor. How do you tell someone that you don't love him, or at least that you're pretty sure you don't love him, maybe even that you wanted it to be true so desperately that you convinced yourself he was "the one"? But, maybe he isn't.

Two Weeks Later

Tommie sprang off the still-moving Pullman coach. He spotted his old Ford at the edge of the train depot, right where he had asked his father to leave it. He jumped in, revved up the engine, and drove down Main Street, heading straightaway for the Triple-A office.

It's now or never, Tommie, old boy, he thought, watching Dorothy through the office window.

Opening the door to the office, he motioned for Carol to be still. He cleared his throat in a loud harrumph. "Can a guy get a little service around here?"

Dorothy dropped photos on the floor. "Tommie! You said

you couldn't get a leave. What's going on?"

"I explained it all in my letter. Didn't you get it? It shoulda come last week."

Dorothy hesitated. *Should I tell him I threw the letter away unopened?* "Well, I didn't get it, Tommie, so answer my question; what's going on?"

"Things just worked out. The army's like that; they just change things whenever they want. One minute you're goin' on leave; the next minute you ain't. Then they change everything again. Anyway, honey, I'm here. I only have five days, but I came anyway. I missed you so much. You have no idea."

Every woman in the office sat motionless, pretending not to eavesdrop on the conversation. "I can't talk to you here. Meet me at the five-and-dime after work. I'll be there at four thirty sharp. Now leave—we'll talk later."

Tommie tried to touch Dorothy's hand. She pulled it away.

He backed out the door and walked the block to the five-and-dime. He sat in a booth, walked around the store, sat back down in the booth, ordered a Coke, drank two sips, left the store, and walked around the block. Returning to the five-and-dime, he ordered a cherry Coke and put money in the jukebox.

DOROTHY THREW HER purse on the booth table. "So, Tommie, what's going on?"

"I had to come. All that talk about your job, and then all of a sudden you don't mind waiting to get married. I started reading between the lines, and I thought I was losing you. But I'm here now, and we can make plans. There's only one girl for me, and if you look in the mirror, you'll see her. She's the girl I wanna marry. Come here, honey. Sit down; just sit down for a minute."

"You're the one who didn't want to get married until after you got out of the army. I agree with you, and suddenly you decide you don't want to wait? You want to get married now?"

"Yes! I think I've changed my mind. If I do get leave at Christmas, let's get married, Dottie. What do ya think, honey?"

Dorothy couldn't move. He was asking her to marry him at Christmas, just like she had wanted only a few months ago. Now, her thoughts were focused on the new job, not marriage. She debated telling him about the job, but his words haunted her: *No wife of mine is going to have a job.*

"Dorothy, look at me. I want to marry you. We can get married right now if you want to. I don't care, as long as you are my wife. Then you won't need that silly job. I'll take care of you, and everything will be perfect. We'll get our Airstream trailer and take off for Colorado."

Dorothy frowned. "Silly job? That job is turning into the best thing that ever happened to me. It's not a silly job. Furthermore, we're going to California, to the ocean, *not* to Colorado! I'm so mixed up." She stood and started towards the door.

"But you still love me, right?" Tommie asked.

Dorothy didn't answer. "I need some time to think about everything. Just give me some time."

Tommie followed her out the door. "Dorothy. Wait a minute." She kept walking. "Dorothy, there's a dance tonight. If you want to get married, just show up at the dance, and

I'll know you still love me, and we're going to get married at Christmas. If you don't show up, I'll know you don't love me anymore," he shouted down the street to her back.

DOROTHY BENT OVER her mother's grave, pulled up the dried weeds around the base of the gravestone, and replaced them with a bouquet of freshly picked daisies. She sat, leaned against the tombstone, and gazed at an afternoon thunderstorm gathering itself on the horizon.

"I'm making a name for myself at work," she said out loud, as if her mother were sitting next to her. "You would be real proud of me, but I don't know, Ma. All my friends are married except for Carol, and she *likes* being single. I thought I wanted to get married, but lately I've been thinking more about work. It isn't just a job. I'm good at it, almost like an expert. Then Tommie shows up out of the blue. He says he wants to get married at Christmas, but he wants me to quit my job and he wants to go to Colorado. He doesn't get it. I don't know what to think anymore."

As was her custom, she sat in silence, then, waiting.

TOMMIE SAT DOWN in a corner booth that provided a clear view of the entrance and the people walking down the sidewalk outside. He drummed the table with his fingers and sipped his beer. *She'll show up. I know she will. She has to.*

The band returned from its break, and before long the dance floor was filled with people dancing to "Chattanooga Choo Choo."

"Hey, Tommie, where's your girl?" a friend yelled from the dance floor.

"She's just runnin' late. She'll be here."

Forty-five minutes passed. "Moonlight Serenade" began to play. "Last dance, ladies and gentlemen," the emcee barked over the loudspeaker.

Tommie left the booth and strolled to the bar, ready for another beer. He felt a hand on his shoulder. *I knew she'd come!*

"Hey, good lookin'. When did you get back in town? We're having a party tonight. Wanna come? You can be my date. We always had a lot of fun, didn't we?"

"Ellen! I—we—I'm sort of waiting for someone."

"I saw you sitting in that booth all night. Waiting for that little Ayers girl, weren't you? Well, where is she? I don't see her, and it's the last dance. Come on, at least dance with me for old times' sake. Maybe I can change your mind."

Ellen knew Tommie well. Her long blonde hair, not by accident, was parted so that it fell over her right eye in a seductive, come-hither style. She had the kind of body that made men want to hold her close.

Tommie followed her onto the dance floor. She positioned his arm around her waist, leaned into him, and brushed her tongue across his earlobe. "Close your eyes, baby. Just dance, and pretty soon you won't remember who Dottie is." She stood on her tiptoes and kissed his neck.

"Ellen, stop. I..."

She kissed him again and pressed her hips against him. "Just dance, Tommie. Relax. She's not coming. You know it. I know it. I'm the one in your arms, not her. We're good together, remember?"

Tommie closed his eyes. He could smell her, taste her, feel her soft skin against his. He backed away. "Ellen, I'm sorry. I can't." He walked to the entrance and flung the front door open, almost knocking Dorothy off her feet.

Dorothy stepped back, tripping over the curb. Tommie took her hand and led her to his car.

"No, I can't go anywhere with you," she said. "I just came to tell you that I need time to figure this out. That is the only thing that's clear to me right now."

"Shh, just be quiet for a minute," Tommie urged. "Look. You came to the dance, so you love me, right?"

Dorothy remained silent.

"Dottie? Right?"

"I need time. Please, Tommie, we need to slow down."

Tommie pressed her against the car and kissed her, holding the kiss until her resistance waned. She made a faltering attempt to push him away, but the longer his lips pressed against hers, the less she cared to stop him. His touch coaxed her, pulled at her, and then she knew. She pulled him even closer, desperate for him to continue the embrace. She was sure that, as long as he held her close, her bewilderment would be kept at bay.

A long minute passed. "Don't argue with me," he whispered. "We're getting married at Christmas. If you want to keep that job, keep it until we leave this place. What does it matter as long as we're together." He kissed her again and again and began singing, "We wish you a Merry Christmas, we wish you a Merry Christmas, we wish you a Merry Christmas, and a Happy Wedding. Well, Mrs. Thomas, how does that sound?"

Dorothy tried to clear her head. "I don't know what got into me. It's perfect, just perfect."

"It doesn't matter now. Everything is OK again. That's what matters. You're always talking about going to California, right?"

"Yeah, it'll be our first stop in our little trailer. What do you think, honey—Los Angeles or San Francisco?"

"How about Santa Monica?"

"Where?"

"It's where I'm gonna end up after Fort Knox. We're goin' there on maneuvers the first of September, so I'll be finishing out my year of service there. You could come see me."

Dorothy tilted her head to the side and raised her eyebrows. "Maybe we can have our honeymoon there."

"Maybe." He kissed her forehead.

She pouted. "What about a ring?"

13

Two Weeks Later

Dorothy frowned, her eyes focused on the word "disappointment."

> Dearest Dorothy,
>
> Well, honey it begins to look like I now have disappointment 99, & 100. 99 is we aren't going to California to make our new home, I'm quite sure. 100. You won't get to come to California. Company A of this battalion are slated for the Phillipine Islands. They leave here the end of this month for San Francisco Calif & go from there to the Philippines. They are asking for volunteers out of the other

companys to go with them. Shall I volunteer
or do you want me to stay in United States
as long as I can? Some of the kids are sure
hoping they get to go. I hope they can. I don't
believe I'll volunteer unless you want me to.

"Carol, where are the Philippine Islands? I mean, are they a long ways from California? Tommie is talking about volunteering to go there. He wants to know what I think. How do I know? I don't even know where they are. Can he get home for Christmas; that's all that matters to me."

"I'm not sure where they are, but I think they might be close to California."

Dorothy folded the letter and put it in her purse. "Think I'll pay a visit to the library on the way home."

THE PHILIPPINE ISLANDS cover 115,831 square miles and are located in the western Pacific Ocean. The islands have a hot and dry season between March and May, a rainy season between June and November, and a cool, dry season from December to March.

Dorothy put the book down and crossed the library to the world globe on a table in the corner of the reading room. She spun the globe, slapped her hand on the Pacific Ocean, and began to search. "There they are. They're so tiny, and look at all that ocean around them. Why is the army going there?"

"Shh, please, Miss Ayres, we insist upon total silence so that people can read in peace."

Dorothy looked at the empty reading area, started to protest, and thought better of it. "Sorry, Miss Lambert, I was talking to myself," she whispered. "I didn't know I was doing it out loud."

Miss Lambert's stern features softened. Library patrons rarely looked at the world globe. "That's fine, dear. What are you looking for?"

"Oh, my boyfriend—or rather, my fiancé—might be going to the Philippines. I just wanted to find it, and I want to read about it too. I found one book about the islands. Do you have others?"

Miss Lambert tapped her index finger on her nose. "We have two or three books about that region of the world. Would you like more pictures or information?"

"Oh, pictures would be nice. It sounds tropical and exotic."

"That's true. It has one of the most diverse populations of birds and sea creatures in the world."

"Then I want the picture books, please. Do you know where I can get a world map?"

Miss Lambert removed her reading glasses. "I will order one for you, dear." She smiled at Dorothy. "I think it's charming that you are taking such an interest in where your fiancé is going."

"That's because he's going to take me there someday."

Miss Lambert started to say something, stopped, and said, "That's nice, dear."

"No, Miss Lambert, he's going to take me there, honest. We're going to travel all over the United States and then all over the world. We're never going to settle down. It's so exciting."

"Yes, dear, it's nice to have our dreams."

"It's not a dream. It's really—never mind. Where are those books?"

Fort Knox

"At ease, men. As the commander explained earlier, we need thirteen volunteers from Headquarters Company to become attached to Company A on their mission to the Philippines. Out of the twenty who volunteered, only ten were qualified for the mission. That leaves us three short."

The First Sergeant stepped forward, clipboard in hand. "The following men are to report for transport to San Francisco at 0800 hours on thirty-one August: Private Small, Alan; Private Little, Henry; and Private Thomas, Michael."

Grant wiped his brow. "Whew. Guess we made it again."

"No, that's me. They said my name."

"Are you sure?"

"Michael Thomas. That's my name, ain't it? They said my damned name; that's all I know."

TOMMIE COLLAPSED ONTO his cot. "I can't go; I just can't. I thought maybe they would let me go home so we could get married before we leave, but there's no leaves, no nothin'. We leave on the 31st and we'll be gone 'til next spring when my year is up. What am I gonna do?"

"Not much you *can* do, buddy. But it won't be so bad. The Philippines, man. It's a tropical paradise. At least it's not fightin' Nazis."

"There is *one* thing I can do. Fuck this man's army. I'm outta here." Tommie flung open his duffel bag and began to pack.

"What the hell are you doing? You can't leave. You can't go AWOL. You'll end up in jail, and then you sure as hell won't be home for any wedding."

"I'm goin'. I don't care. I'll hitchhike if I have to, but I'm not stayin' here. I almost lost her once—I can't take another chance."

"Tommie, if you're gonna do it, then do it right. You should wait until after class. You can't be absent for no reason and think no one will notice," Grant advised.

"Right after class is perfect; lots of commotion goin' on." he said, throwing his duffel bag down. "And I ain't takin' a duffel bag. I don't need it. I can get clothes and stuff when I get home. My big problem is money. I don't have even half what I need for a ticket, and we don't get paid until after we're supposed to leave for San Francisco. Guess I could hitchhike, right?"

"You're such a dumb hick. You can't hitchhike. They'll pick you up in a New York minute. I'll loan you the money."

"I ain't takin' your money, and I ain't no dumb hick. I'll walk all the way there if I have to."

"You'll take my money and you'll by god pay me back once you get settled in, and that's all there is to it. Otherwise there ain't a snowball's chance in hell you can pull this off."

"Okay, okay. You're right, I am a dumb hick, but you don't have any more money than I do. How the hell can you afford to loan me anything?"

"Well, some of us believe in savin' for a rainy day. It just so happens your rainy day came before mine."

Grant rummaged through his footlocker and unearthed a metal box. He fished the key from his pocket, opened the box, and handed Tommie a wad of cash. Stunned, Tommie took the cash and stuffed it into his pocket. "I don't know how to thank. . ."

Grant cut him off. "Nuff said, buddy. I'll just expect my money back with interest," he joked.

They started toward class when Tommie abruptly swung around. "I'll catch up with you," he said as he ran into the barracks.

Out of breath, he reached for Dorothy's photo, pulled it out of the frame and tucked it under his shirt. "This is all I need to get me home," he whispered.

GRANT PUNCHED TOMMIE in the arm as he sat down beside him. "Jesus, man, quit shakin' your leg like that. Yer makin' me nervous."

"I can't help it. It's the only way I have to get rid of these nerves, and where the hell you been? That didn't help my nerves at all; walkin' into class and you ain't nowhere in sight."

The captain entered the room and they all stood. "At ease, men. Before we begin class Sergeant Wilson would like a minute of your time. He has some important information that you all need to be aware of, so listen up."

The First Sergeant paused to survey the class, looking every soldier in the eye. "It has come to our attention that many of you are considering going AWOL. Some of your fellow soldiers actually took that step. I want to make it clear to you what is going to happen if you go AWOL and we apprehend you—and, be perfectly clear about this, we *will* apprehend you. You will go straight to the brig, and you will be court-martialed. It will be considered a wartime crime. Article 85 of the Articles of War clearly states that we can hang you for such a crime. If you think you can accidentally miss the train to San Francisco or the boat to wherever else we might be going, you will be apprehended, and you will then pay for your own way. Be very clear about this, gentlemen. Leaving now is an act of cowardice. Your country needs you. Be brave, be stalwart, and may the good Lord watch over each and every one of you. That is all."

Tommie tried to remain standing, but his legs wouldn't hold him. Sweat ran down his forehead. Grant pretended not to notice, and Tommie pretended not to know the truth about why Grant had been late to class.

Beaver City

Dorothy waited for Mr. Anderson to close his office door. She pulled Tommie's letter out from under her ledger and began to read:

> Dearest Dorothy,
>
> Honey as I told you I've been an unlucky whelp since I registered for the draft. A year in the army isn't bad enough I guess. As I wrote you Company "A." was going to California the 31st of this month and under sealed orders from there and everyone seems to think they

are going from there to the Philippine Islands. Well I'm one of them tonight.

I sure hate to think of us being so far apart but nothing can be done about it. I thought of going over the hill, but you can see & I know that its foolish not to take it & make the best of it rather than do the wrong thing & be either in jail, dead, or a man without a country. Remember, what's 8 months of a lifetime if we can be happy the rest of the time.

Honey I'm awfully sorry we won't be able to get married at Christmas like we planned...

Dorothy stopped reading. She pushed her chair back with such force it fell over.

Mr. Anderson came to the door of his office. "What's going on?"

Carol flaunted her hallmark smile. "Oh, don't worry about it, Mr. Anderson. Dorothy was so anxious to finish plotting the Larson farm before lunch, she knocked over her chair. Come on, honey, I think you need some lunch. You can finish that afterwards." She led Dorothy out the front door.

"Dottie, are you all right? You look like you're about to cry."

"I'm fine, Carol. It's Tommie. He's going to the Philippines for sure. He won't be back until next spring, so we can't get married at Christmas."

"Well, no wonder you're so upset. I'm so sorry, honey."

"The thing is," Dorothy began, "I'm not crying because he

isn't coming home. I'm crying because I was actually relieved he isn't coming home. I am just as mixed-up as I was before he came home on leave. What's the matter with me?"

Carol bit her lip. "Dottie, I know you don't like it when I bring things up, but you're right, you are extremely mixed up, so I'm just gonna say it. You said you decided you did love him after he came home on leave. Did you, or did you just *want* to be in love so badly you convinced yourself this was it?"

Dorothy started to protest but stopped herself. "I don't know; how's that for honesty? Tommie says, 'What's eight months of a lifetime if we can be happy the rest of the time?' He should be discharged in May next year. That gives me eight months to figure it out, right? Maybe that's all I need— just time to figure it out."

DOROTHY ROLLED OVER in bed and finished reading the letter she had started reading earlier at work.

> If you still want that diamond ring, which I hope you do, you are sure going to get it but it may have to come from the Philippine Islands.
>
> So you hope & pray & I will & maby we can be together before too long. I know its hell but honey if you only knew what I've been through within the last few days & what I have ahead of me I think you can understand. It's a lot to ask but I do hope you won't make

a decision for someone else for a while. You are all I have to live for & I'm coming back if I have to swim.

Well honey I know you are disappointed and so am I, but I guess the thing is to make the best of it. If you love me like I love you we won't have to worry about getting together. Will write again tomorrow and am expecting one from you.

Bye now
Loads & loads of Love
Tommie
S.W.A.(big)K.

He's talking about buying me a ring, she thought. *I can't let him do that— not yet. Maybe when he comes home, but not now.* She yawned.

"WITH THIS RING I thee wed." Tommie *slipped the magnificent ring onto Dorothy's finger. She readjusted it so that the diamond became the central focus on her hand.*

"Dorothy, did you hear me?"

"Oh, sorry, Reverend Nelson."

"Well, dear, do you have Tommie's ring?"

"Of course." She reached for the ring bearer's pillow, tipping it in the process and knocking the ring to the ground. It began to

roll down the aisle.

"No. Stop! Someone stop it!"

FRANK POUNDED ON Dorothy's bedroom door. "Stop what? Dorothy, what's going on in there?"

"I'm fine, Pa; just a bad dream."

"Well, there's someone here to see you. Didn't you hear the doorbell?"

"Who is it?"

"Just get up and make yourself decent and come on down," he yelled as he stomped down the stairs.

Dorothy threw on her robe and ran her hand through her hair. *I wonder if it's Tommie. It can't be Tommie, but what if it is?* As she turned the corner from the stairs to face the front door, she stopped cold, almost tripping over her own steps.

"Hi, Peaches, how ya doin'?" Smitty asked, sauntering through the front door and brandishing his patented grin.

"Smitty, what are you doing here?"

"I got my draft notice and figured I'd come home and get deployed from here."

"No, I mean, what are you doing here, in my house?"

"I just wanted to see you and tell you that you were right. I did regret leaving. Dottie, I'm sorry..."

"Stop! You're too late, Jack Smith. I waited for you to write me. I waited." She remembered the waiting, the conversation with Annie, the anguish she had endured. The uncertainty about her future with Tommie, Smitty's fortuitous arrival, and her desire to, once and for all, leave the confines of her restrictive hometown coalesced in one crystal moment. Her future lay before her as clear as a Nebraska spring morning with not a cloud in the sky.

"No," she said with a new-found resolve. "You're too late. I'm leaving."

Jack took a step back. "What do you mean you're leavin'? Where're you goin'?"

"I'm taking a job in Lincoln with the Tripe-A. And, what about you, Jack? Annie said you had a girl. Lucky? Isn't that her name?"

"Yea, she's a nice enough gal, but not like you. Please, Dottie..."

"Don't! You're too late, and now you need to go."

Jack walked out to his pickup. He sat behind the wheel for a long time, Dorothy's words reverberating through his mind. *Story of my life. A day late and a dollar short.*

Dorothy sat on the edge of her bed. Her breath came in short erratic bursts. Seeing him for the first time in three years replayed in her mind like a vinyl record stuck in a groove. Muddled feelings of happiness mixed with despair and anger darted through her bewildered mind.

He's too late. I'm leaving. I'm starting a new life. He's too late.

Fort Knox

Tommie opened his footlocker and started to fill it. He checked his area for a final time; his eyes stopped on the photo of Dorothy. He began wrapping the photo in one of his T-shirts and laid it in his footlocker as if it were a newborn. He wrapped his arms around himself. *God, but I do love you, Dottie, and I can't store you in my footlocker for four weeks. I gotta have you with me.*

He pulled Dorothy's photo out and studied it. If he could only run his fingers through her hair or touch her cheek. She looked straight at him, so tranquil, never wavering. He found some cardboard and sandwiched the photo between two pieces, placing it with care into his duffel bag. "You're the last thing in, and you'll be the first thing out, baby."

THE ENTIRE HEADQUARTERS Company stood at attention while the band played "The Star-Spangled Banner." The last notes faded, and the general rose. "Boys, you leave today on a great mission. As you journey across this great land, remember you are soldiers of the United States Army. You will be our representatives on the Philippine Islands. What they think of you, they will think of us. We thank you for your service. Now, climb aboard, and let's get this mission under way."

Everyone cheered. Some soldiers boarded the train, while others held back, giving a last hug to family members or a lingering kiss to a sweetheart. Tommie's breathing became shallow. He shook Grant's hand while Grant cleared his throat several times. Tommie spoke first: "See ya later." Grant said nothing. Tommie pulled his hand out of Grant's grip and walked away. He boarded the train and chose an aisle seat, thus avoiding the scene outside the window.

The train left the station, and silence filled the air, each man immersed in his own thoughts about his own future.

LETTERS FROM TOMMIE lay strewn across Dorothy's bureau. She picked up the latest one.

> Dearest Dorothy,
>
> The gang was all there that could be. They were working yesterday afternoon but took off anyhow and was there until we left. I sure hated to bid them all goodbye and they sure hated to see us go. There were tears on

several of us back just a little ways and they were showing on the ones we left behind. We are on a special train. All of our own. Have 26 flat cars that have our trucks on them, one baggage car, one kitchen car and 5 pull man coaches. It's quite nice and we aren't crowded. Only 2Ø-3Ø to a car and room for 5Ø, so it's not so bad. I wish you were right here beside me now and we were on a pleasure trip. Gosh darn I betcha' we'd have a jolly time. I expect will see some pretty country in the western part of the U.S.A. I'll keep you posted on our progress.

Your poor Poppy is going to be a wreck by the time he has to set on his fanny for 26 more days. I'm afraid I might settle. Then I would be cute if it all went to waist.

But we got miles & miles to go, so I'll fold this up & write the next chapter tomorrow.

By now.

Miles & miles of Love,

Tommie

She folded the letter and opened her hope chest. Her keepsake box sat in one corner, crammed with packets of letters from Smitty. She plucked the packets from their resting place and headed for the trash can. For a long moment she stood, staring at the letters. In the end, she put them back in her hope chest in a corner under a blanket her mother had quilted for her. She picked up all of Tommie's letters from her bureau, wrapped them in a blue ribbon, and placed them inside the keepsake box.

"There." She nodded her head, as though the act of changing the location of the letters could change her as well.

MR. ANDERSON CAME to his office door. "I thought I heard you, Miss Ayers. I'd like to talk to you in private."

"Maybe it's about the job in Lincoln," Dorothy whispered to Carol.

Mr. Anderson shut the door behind her as she sat down, steno pad in hand. "As you probably know, Carol has turned down the job opportunity in Lincoln. She seems to think you could do the job just as well as her, and I'm inclined to agree. Are you interested?"

"I am, sir. When would it start?"

"Well, this is an entirely new program that they've developed, so it won't start until January. How would that work for you?"

"That's just fine. I need to talk to my pa and make arrangements for him and Walter. Neither one of them knows a darn thing about cooking or cleaning, so we'll have to figure that out."

Mr. Anderson stood up, opened the door to his office, and escorted her to her desk as she continued going through all the necessary arrangements. He shook his head and inserted an occasional "uh huh" to emphasize his feigned interest. Dorothy's banter continued as he walked back to his office and closed the door.

Carol slipped Dorothy a note: "Congratulations! Let's celebrate tonight. There's a dance at the Legion. Go with me."

Dorothy wrote back, "I can't. I have to help Pa with his books."

"You've been helping your pa an awful lot lately," Carol responded in a hushed voice.

"Maybe we could go to church together on Sunday."

Carol gave Dorothy an incredulous look. "Some celebration," she mouthed.

Dorothy shrugged her shoulders. "Church is the only safe place in town. I *know* I won't run into *him* there."

"Him? You mean Smitty? I thought that was a thing of the past."

Dorothy stared at Carol, refusing to answer her.

Carol shrugged her shoulders. "Suit yourself. If you change your mind, I'll be there!"

15

September 1941

Aboard the Train to San Francisco

"Breakfast! Get yo' breakfast here!"

Tommie awoke with a start. He held out his mess kit, and the porter gave him scrambled eggs and a slice of toast. Tommie took a bite of the toast. The swamps and oil wells of Mississippi rolled by outside the window.

A field full of unfamiliar plants appeared. *It ain't wheat. I know that. And it ain't corn.* "Wonder what they're growin' in that field?" he asked to no one in particular.

"Where you from, boy? Ain't you never seen a cotton field?"

Tommie stared over the seat at the soldier from Texas sitting behind him. "We don't grow cotton in Nebraska, so, no, I never seen such a thing. Besides, I don't see cotton on those plants—just green plants. Where's the cotton?"

With that the Texan let out an extended belly laugh. "It's too early. You are dumb, now, ain't ya?"

Tommie spilled his breakfast on the floor as he lunged over the seat toward the Texan, who dodged to the left and fell into the aisle. "What's up, boy?" he sneered at Tommie. "Don't like hearin' the truth?"

Another soldier pushed himself between Tommie and the Texan. "Let's just cool down here. We got a long trip ahead of us. No sense starting something now."

"Mind your own damned business!" Tommie retorted.

"Yeah!" yelled the Texan. "Ain't no business of yours, you little runt, if this dummy from the hills and I wanna have a little argument."

The soldier pointed to his corporal's stripes, all the while maintaining eye contact with the Texan. "Gentlemen, we are not going to do this. We are all going to sit down and enjoy the rest of this trip. We've barely started, so just calm down and have some more eggs."

The Texan glared at the corporal, who stood unmoving, hands on hips, his ice-blue eyes matching the Texan's glare.

Tommie sat down first, his father's words filling his thoughts: *Give to the world the best you have, and the best will come back to you.*

The Texan retreated to his bench, and the corporal sat down beside Tommie. "Here, you can have the rest of my eggs, since you spilled yours. My name's Bob." He extended his hand to Tommie.

"Everybody calls me Tommie." He shook the corporal's

hand. "I guess I should thank you, but you need to mind your own business."

Bob, once again, pointed to his stripes. "It is my business. I'm a corporal. They asked me to keep an eye on you guys."

"Sorry, sir. Am I supposed to call you 'sir,' or what?"

"Nah, I'm still a corporal, not a sergeant. So where you from, private?"

"I'm from Nebraska. Lived there my whole life. I joined the army last spring. Now, I'm sittin' here tryin' like hell to remember why I did that."

"Yeah, I wonder that myself sometimes. I'm from Iowa, right next door. Bet you're a farmer."

"Yup. Sure am. But, that's not what I'm gonna do when I get out. I have this girl back home. Her name's Dorothy, but we mostly call her Dottie. She and I, we're gonna see the world. I got it all planned out. We'll buy one of them Airstream trailers and hook it up to my Ford."

Bob sat up. "Where you gonna go first?"

"We're goin' to Colorado, first thing when I get out. I'm gonna pick her up, and we're gonna get married and drive out to the Rocky Mountains. I've been dreamin' about doin' that as long as I can remember."

"Ever been to California?"

"Nope. How about you?"

"I've been there plenty of times. My sister used to live in Frisco, and we used to go out every summer to see her. I'll show you around."

"Thanks. Sorry about the fracas, Bob. I'm not usually a hothead, ya know? He just got to me. I don't like loud assholes like that."

"Who does? Trick is to keep your cool, and it drives types like that crazy. Just do your best to keep your cool, and they'll melt right before your eyes."

Tommie thought for a moment. "Makes sense."

Cotton fields soon gave way to more oil fields, followed by rows and rows of shacks built on stilts. Black people sat on porches and waved to the train. Tommie waved back. "Houses on stilts. Who ever heard of houses on stilts?"

Bob shrugged his shoulders and rearranged his cap over his brown hair. "Sure not in Iowa. Guess if you live in a swamp, you gotta do something, now, don't you?"

The train came to a complete stop outside Jackson, Mississippi. Immense towers from an adjacent oil refinery filled the window.

DOROTHY CHECKED THE time: seven on a Friday night. She meandered down the stairs to the living room, where Frank sat reading his newspaper. "Going out tonight, dear?" he asked.

"I don't know. I might just stay at home."

"You haven't been going out so much lately. Is everything all right?"

"Pa, did you ever love anybody besides Ma?"

"What kind of question is that?"

"I was just wondering."

"Is everything OK with Tommie?"

"Oh, yeah, everything is hunky-dory. I just got a letter from him. He's on his way to San Francisco. They're going by way of Jackson, Mississippi."

"That's nice, dear."

Dorothy stared at the back of her father's head. She contemplated another night at home shuffling through magazines, doing cross-stitch, or completing housework.

"Maybe I will go out after all. I'll probably be home late."

Frank put down his paper and picked up his pipe, pointing it at Dorothy. "Where are you going––exactly?"

"Pa, I'm twenty-three years old. Do you need to know where I'm going? I'm going to a movie."

"As long as you live in my house, you will tell me where you are going. To a movie? You aren't going to that dance, are you?"

"I said a movie. That's where I'm going. I'm going to see if Carol wants to go."

Frank shuffled his newspaper. "Be home by ten."

"Of course. Aren't I *always* home by ten?" She resisted the temptation to slam the door behind her. *Why do I always end up lying to him?*

DOROTHY OPENED THE front door of the Legion Hall, conducting a thorough search of the dance floor before entering. She spotted Carol.

"Decided to come out of hiding, huh? I haven't seen him, so you're safe," Carol said before disappearing onto the dance floor with her date.

"Tennessee Waltz" began to play. Dorothy stood. *That's an omen. This was a bad idea.* She headed towards the exit.

"Wanna dance, darlin'? They're playin' our song." Smitty moved so close to her she could smell his aftershave. His mischievous grin lit up his face. "So, Peaches, you said you're leavin', and yet here you are. Change yer mind?"

Dorothy debated whether to answer or walk away. "Not at all. I'm still leaving but not until January. Don't doubt me. I'm going, and I'm going to make a name for myself."

Smitty backed away, taking her in from head to toe, relishing the fact that she was standing right in front of him instead of in a dream.

"Don't yell at me, darlin'. I know you, and I know you're just stubborn enough to take off. Ain't that what we used to talk about all the time? Gettin' outta here and seein' the world?"

"So, you don't think I'm silly?"

"Silly? Hell, no! Lincoln is your start, Peaches. It's the start of your adventure. Just wish I was goin' with you."

"You know I'm engaged, right?"

"Engaged? Well, I heard you're pretty serious with some guy from Stamford. So, what does he think about you traipsing off to the big city?"

"Right now he's in the army and headed for the Philippines, so he doesn't know yet, but I'm sure he'll be happy for me."

"Lucky bastard. Hope *I* get a cushy assignment hangin' out in a tropical paradise. Look, Peaches, he's not here. I am. What can one little dance hurt, anyway? Besides, I'm leavin' town in a couple of days."

"Of course, that's what you do, right? Leave town."

"Hey! Since the army ain't takin' me right away, I'm goin' up north for awhile and shuck corn for Mr. Franklin, that's all. Anyway, I told you I was sorry. I was just all mixed up.

Maybe I should have explained everything a little better."

"Maybe? You know when things got tough for Tommie, he didn't just up and leave town. He had a plan that included me."

Smitty stood silent in his thoughts. She didn't seem to care anymore, so why should he? But, he did.

"Peaches, darlin', one last dance, that's all I'm askin'." He nudged her toward the dance floor.

Their bodies touched. His cocky grin disappeared, and she saw the anguish on his face. Her resolve softened. She pressed her lips together in an attempt to remain calm, baffled by her emotions.

They began dancing. "You gotta believe me," Smitty said in a low voice. "I hated every day in Washington. The only thing that got me through it was a pint of whiskey every night. You don't know how many letters I tried to write, but I ain't much good at talkin' about this stuff."

He tried to explain the agony he endured with the failed crop, just one more disappointment in a long line of failed dreams. Dorothy found it more and more difficult to disregard his words. While it was true that Tommie had a plan for the two of them, wasn't it also true that Tommie had never faced the same adversity as Smitty? The abject poverty? The failed attempts?

"Smitty, it wasn't right that you just left like that, but—I don't know what to say."

"Don't say anything; just forgive me. At least do that. Let's just start over."

"No! You don't understand; we can't start over. I'm leaving, and there's Tommie. You can't just come home and say you're sorry and think that makes everything OK again."

"I don't. I don't. Just say you forgive me; let me at least have that."

They stood on the dance floor in each other's arms long after the song had ended. Despite her newfound determination, tears welled up. Her heart slammed against her chest, and the words she thought she would never say slipped from her mouth with ease and grace.

"I forgive you."

16

New Orleans, Louisiana

Tommie sat on the edge of his seat. He moved from side to side, trying every conceivable position to rest his backside. His reflection stared back at him through the darkened windows.

The train moved through New Orleans to the ferry, where six cars at a time crossed the Mississippi. Tommie took the opportunity to stretch his legs on deck and have a cigarette.

The expanse of the Mississippi overwhelmed him. He couldn't imagine a river so wide the other side was barely visible. A somber, melancholy mood engulfed him. *Wish Dottie was here*, he thought, taking a deep drag on his cigarette before returning to his seat.

The crossing completed, the train chugged forward into

the darkness, rocking back and forth in a gentle motion that Tommie never tired of feeling. He peered out the window into the shadows. *Yes, indeed, my dear, darling Dorothy, I wish you were here.*

"DOTTIE, YOU ARE beautiful." Tommie moved over to make room on the bed for his bride. A breeze fluttered the curtains and filled the room with pine-scented air. Thunder rolled across the mountains outside. "Come here."

Dorothy moved across the room, taking her time, breathing in the mountain air, and removing her sheer white negligee along the way. She crawled into the bed on her hands and knees, never taking her eyes off Tommie. Throwing her leg over his hips, she sat down so she could feel the power building in his groin. She slid forward, her breasts skimming his chest. Leaning into him, she moaned and whispered in his ear.

"WHAT DID YOU say, darlin'?"

The porter serving breakfast burst into laughter. "You better wake up now, sir. Yo' darlin' is long gone."

Dorothy's image dissolved into the smell of bacon.

Dearest Dorothy,

I sure had a swell dream about you last night. But, doggone just a dream. We sure had a time on our honeymoon. Just went through Gladewater, Texas. Crops in these parts are almost ripe. Corn is brown and everything else is green. Saw them picking cotton in one field but I never got to get a picture. I guess the next place we get to get off is in Sweetwater, Texas. I think it's a fair sized burg.

Dorothy attempted to stay focused on Tommie's letter. "He had a dream about us on our honeymoon."

Carol raised her eyebrows. "Your honeymoon? So you still haven't told him that things have changed a little?"

"I can't. He won't get any mail from me until he gets to Frisco, remember? Besides, I'm still not completely sure what to do. He's out there seeing the world; he's getting to do the things we talked about doing together. I'm still giving myself the eight months to decide for sure. Who knows? Maybe I can even talk him into seeing the benefits of having a working wife."

Dorothy picked up her planimeter and began to plot the dimensions of the Olsen farm. The photograph blurred into Tommie lying on a bed with a white satin sheet covering him from the waist down.

SHE GAZED OUT the window of their honeymoon suite, watching wave after wave crash against the shore. Tommie lay in bed. "Come here, honey. Come lie beside me."

Dorothy walked across the room, untying her pink satin robe, breathing in the salt-scented air. Underneath the robe she wore a matching pink satin gown. The snug lace bodice emphasized her breasts. She crawled under the sheets, and they embraced. He whispered in her ear.

"WHAT DID YOU say, darling?"

"I said, here are the Olsen farm photos. You dropped them on the floor."

Dorothy's eyes popped open. She took the photos from her boss's hands. "Thank you, Mr. Anderson. Can I help you with anything else?"

"No, but you might want to pay a little closer attention to your work, Miss Ayers." He pointed to the letter sitting on her desk.

"Yes, sir. I will, sir. I promise. It's just that..."

"No need to explain, dear. I understand. Just try to stay focused on work while you are at work."

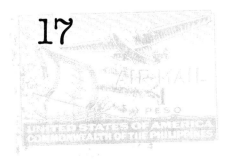

17

New Mexico

Mile after mile of sagebrush provided the only scenery visible through the window. Tommie picked up a magazine and leafed through it. *Man, I've read every magazine on this stinkin' train three or four times.* He threw the magazine down. *Will we ever reach Frisco?*

Outside, the desert scenery transitioned from sand to green grass to foothills. "Those mountains are huge," drawled the Texan from the seat behind Tommie.

"You call those mountains huge?" Tommie responded, mimicking the brash Texas accent. "Son, that's just foothills. You want to see real mountains? Go to Colorado. The Rockies, now that's real mountains. I seen 'em on a postcard once when I was a kid," he said with a certain amount of pride and satisfaction. He winked at Bob.

"Tommie, Tommie, Tommie. You're gettin' there; maybe next time just keep it to yourself."

"Hell, can't a guy have some revenge?"

"Sure, but you can also get a black eye. Everybody is just a little tense right now. It's been a long five days. Now's the time to try your best to keep your cool, Tommie. Just keep your cool."

The foothills in New Mexico gave way to tree-covered mountains in Arizona. Tommie wiggled his butt back and forth on the seat. Each mile closer to San Francisco meant a mile farther from Dorothy. *I shoulda run when I could.*

Beaver City

> Dearest Dorothy,
>
> Gosh darn Honey I wish I wasn't going to the Philippines, but someone has to go. As long as I know I'm helping someone else though I don't mind.
>
> Darling I sure hate to leave the states. The last couple of days I've had a terrible feeling and I, for some unforeseen reason, hate to even think of it. Maybe it's just my imagination. I hope. Time will tell I reckon.
>
> Bye now. I love you and I always will.
>
> Tommie

Dorothy opened the hope chest and put Tommie's latest letter into her keepsake box.

A pressed flower sat in the corner of the box. It came from the bouquet Smitty had given her while staying home that one summer. She picked it up and shuffled through the contents of the box, looking for something she might have saved from the year she and Tommie had been together. Nothing. She was sure there must be something—perhaps something from their first date or a movie ticket stub.

Instead, she found a wine label. The sight of it conjured up every exhilarating detail of that night. She flipped the label over and read the writing:

May 27, 1936.
Our first kiss.

The sensation of Smitty's lips touching hers was as intense as it had been five years earlier. She struggled to summon up Tommie's touch, his lips, his arms.

Doesn't matter. Smitty was just my first real kiss; that's why I remember it so well, but that's all. This means nothing to me now.

She crumpled the label in her hand and threw it toward the trashcan, attempting to ignore the sensual memory of that night so long ago.

18

San Francisco

Tommie gripped the handle of the trolley door. "Ain't nothin' like this back home," he shouted over the screeching of the cable car rambling down Powell Street. He sat, wide-eyed, absorbing the exotic sights and sounds of a place like none he had ever experienced.

Bob motioned toward the exit. "This is the place to get off if we want to see Chinatown."

Tommie hopped off the cable car onto Grant Street. The smell of fried fish filled the air. An old woman in baggy black pants and a black silk blouse crossed the street in front of him. A young man pushed him out of the way, yelling something at him that he didn't understand. Two more men followed the first, all carrying large boxes on their shoulders, all dressed in brightly colored flowered shirts. Lampposts shaped like Chinese lanterns adorned every corner, and red roofs covered every building. It seemed like Christmas to Tommie, with strings of white lights around windows and rooftops. A neon sign advertised silk kimonos.

He walked to the storefront. "Well, I'll be damned. Now ain't those just the prettiest things you ever saw?"

Bob peered over Tommie's shoulder. "Yeah, they're pretty nice, all right. Bet that girlfriend of yours would like one of those."

"Yup, she sure would. She'd go crazy over this, for sure."

"Well, what are you waiting for? Let's go in and get her one," Bob said, pushing Tommie towards the store entrance.

"Oh, no, I couldn't," Tommie protested. "We don't have any Chinese people back home, so I don't know the language. I don't know how to talk to them."

"Tommie, Tommie, Tommie. This is America. They speak English, at least a little. Come on. Give it a try."

"No, Bob, not tonight. Maybe later."

"Ah, come on. Let's just go in so you can see them up close."

Tommie opened the door to the shop. "Yeah, I can do that. I'll just keep my cool and act like I know what I'm doin', but I ain't talkin' to nobody."

Tommie walked straight to the rack of kimonos. He pulled one out, and it slipped off its hanger onto the floor. He glanced at the people nearby, wondering if anyone had seen.

Bob picked up the kimono and handed it to Tommie. "Droppin' the merchandise on the floor? Is that your way of not being noticed? Here, let me help you."

"Wow, it's even better when you touch it. It's softer 'n a sow's ear."

A clerk approached Tommie. "Gotta go now, Bob. Come on; time to go." He rushed out the door and into the street. Bob followed.

"Have you ever had Chinese food?"

"Now, what do you think? I already told you; ain't no Chinese people back home. Mom never even cooked rice. We're a meat-'n'-potatoes bunch. They have Chinese food in Iowa?"

"Remember, my sister used to live here. I've had Chinese food lots of times. Come on; you gotta try some. You'll love it."

BOB AND TOMMIE sat down at a nearby restaurant. "I'll order for you," Bob offered. "Just leave it to me." The waitress arrived. "We will both have the *Moo goo gai pan*, please."

"Moo goo what?" Tommie cackled.

"It's just chicken marinated in soy sauce and served with some bamboo shoots and water chestnuts."

"The only food I know out of that whole sentence is 'chicken.' How 'bout some nice fried chicken? Do they make that?"

"Tommie, we're in Chinatown in San Francisco for cryin' out loud. Just sit back and relax. You're gonna love it."

Their food arrived. "Uh, where's the silverware?" Tommie asked.

"Oh, didn't I tell you? You have to use chopsticks."

"You are an ass, ya know it? You got me eatin' some sort of weird food, and now you tell me I have to eat it with sticks? I ain't gonna do it."

Bob doubled over in a fit of laughter. "Take it easy, buddy. I'll get you a proper fork."

Utensil in hand, Tommie took a large bite of his dinner. He stopped chewing and swallowed it all at once, shaking his head. "Pretty good."

"We're gonna make you a man of the world yet, farm boy."

"Like I said, you're an ass. I told you—I ain't no farmer. That's where I grew up. That's all. I'm gonna see the world and taste all kinds of food with Dottie by my side. Just you wait and see. I got big plans."

"That's fine, Mr. World Traveler, but right now you gotta finish your meal. We're due at the wharf to catch the boat back to Angel Island. So get a move on!"

"Uh, I think I'm done for now. I mean, it tastes just fine, but I think I'm..."

"No need to explain. At least you tried it."

Bob paid their tab, and they flew out the door, chasing down the nearest trolley. Tommie pulled his photo of Dorothy out of his billfold after finding a window seat. A little over a month had passed since he had been with her. The gathering fog outside the window seeped into his thoughts. He dreamed of her soft touch, the sound of her reassuring voice whispering in his ear, and the smell of her rose perfume, but most of all her comforting presence.

Bob tapped Tommie's shoulder several times. "Hey, buddy. Wake up! This is our stop, and we're late!"

"Damn, man, you pert near scared me ta death. I was enjoyin' myself. Can't ya just leave a guy alone?"

"No. We gotta sprint to the pier if we wanna get back to

the barracks. I'll bet you were doin' a little hoochie-coochie with that girlfriend of yours, weren't ya?"

Ignoring Bob's ribbing, Tommie pushed past him down the steps of the trolley and sprinted down the hill toward the pier. "What's the matter, Bob, can't keep up?"

"Hey, wait for me! Whoa!" Bob tripped over a rise in the sidewalk, fell forward, scraping the palms of his hands and tearing a hole in his uniform pant leg. "Dammit, Tommie, wait up! Come help me, man!"

Bob lay sprawled across the sidewalk. Tommie continued to run toward the pier as he shouted back to Bob, "Get up! Move! Now! I'll tell 'em to wait for you, but hurry up, will ya? We gotta go!"

DOROTHY GRIMACED AS she read the last line of Tommie's latest letter. "Oh no, I've got to write him before it's too late."

"Why? What's up?" Carol asked.

"He's in San Francisco. They went into the city, and he got to see Chinatown and the Golden Gate Bridge. He almost missed the boat back to Angel Island. Sounds like they had a gas, but here's what disturbs me. He says, 'P.S. A surprise package is coming your way. Hope you like it. Would have sent it sooner, but I didn't get the chance.'"

Carol tugged at her hair. "Ah oh. That sounds like engagement ring talk."

"He said he was waiting until he got to the Philippines. I was sort of counting on that."

DOROTHY'S EYES WIDENED as she opened the mailbox to see the promised package. She pulled at the wrapping paper until the last piece fell to the post office floor. "This is it," she said, opening the box and moving the last piece of tissue paper out of the way.

She stared at the object that lay before her—a deep blue kimono with an exotic flower embroidered on the front. A sense of relief surged through her, and yet, she had to admit, a tiny bit of disappointment tiptoed its way into the recesses of her mind.

She ran her hand across the sensual material. As she removed it from the box, a photo of Tommie fell to the floor.

"Are you all right, honey?" Mrs. Nelson put her arm on Dorothy's shoulder. "Oh, no wonder you're crying. What a pretty robe. Must be from someone special, someone who thinks a lot of you."

"Yea, it is," she sobbed, looking from his photo to the kimono and back again.

"And look, such a handsome young man. Those must be tears of joy."

19

San Francisco Harbor

Tommie sauntered up the ramp and onto the SS *President Coolidge*, taking in the full scene, trying to make sense of it all. Hundreds of people lined the dock, waving good-bye to loved ones, getting in one last kiss before their sweethearts departed—laughing, crying, yelling across the dock to men already on board. On the ship, soldiers moved about the deck, getting their bearings, searching for their room assignments.

"Let's find our room, Bob. No use standing around up here in this herd of people. Kinda makes me think of the mess hall." They ran down the stairs.

"AFTER YOU, SIR." Bob took a sweeping bow and opened the cabin door.

Tommie perused the room and removed his shoes. His feet sank into plush green carpeting.

"Wow! Ain't never felt anything like this before."

Bob followed Tommie's lead and removed his own shoes. "They call this a luxury liner." He wiggled his toes, digging his feet deeper into the carpet. "Now I know why."

Flowered green sheers covered the two portholes. A mahogany dresser with scrolls engraved on each drawer sat in one corner of the room. In another corner stood a small desk with a Victorian chair upholstered in green brocade. Bunk beds to sleep eight took up the rest of the room.

"Now *this* is livin'!" Bob glanced at Tommie, and they secured bottom bunks before anyone else came along and snatched them.

Tommie opened his duffel bag. He put Dorothy's photo on a shelf beside his bed. "Hello, Dottie. Ready to go on a cruise with me?"

Bob emptied his duffel bag, covering every inch of his bunk. "I'm starving. Let's go get some chow. No one will take this bed; that's for sure. Come on, Tommie. Let's go."

The two took off in search of the ship's dining room. Walking up and down the length of the vessel, they soon understood the significance of belonging to the headquarters company. Cots stacked one on top of another lined every inch of the ship's ballroom. Canvas stretched between two pipes became beds for other soldiers.

Tommie walked down the hall, investigating every room along the way. "Our bunk beds and mattresses are lookin' better and better, don't ya think?" Entering the dining room, they both took a step back.

Tommie whistled, "This is like some sort of palace." Corinthian columns painted in glistening white decorated the room while soft-yellow walls completed the picture. Tables lined up end-to-end sat prepared to feed the thousands of men aboard. "I've never seen anything like it, not in all my years. Dottie would faint if she saw it." Spareribs, sauerkraut, sausage, potatoes, beans, peas, ice cream, and cake covered the serving tables. An orchestra started to play. Tommie shook his head. "Man, they thought of everything, didn't they?"

After dinner, they went on deck, where baggage, supplies, and vehicles were being loaded into the hull of the ship. At 9:00 p.m. sharp, they heard the ship's horn blow. They grasped the railing as the ship maneuvered out of the docking slip and into the harbor. Alcatraz slipped by in the darkness, as did the shadow of Angel Island.

Forty-five minutes passed. Tommie caught a momentary glimpse of the colossal orange expanse of the Golden Gate Bridge before it disappeared into the gathering fog. "This is it. No turnin' back now."

"Hey, man, whatcha starin' at?" Bob slapped Tommie on the back. "Come on. We got places to go and people to meet. Let the party begin!"

With that they ran back down the stairs to their compartment. The six men with whom they would bunk for the next two weeks gave them a raucous welcome. "Where you guys from?" one asked.

"Iowa," said Bob, and a two-hour conversation

commenced, everyone talking at once, or so it seemed to Tommie.

A lull crept into the banter. Tommie took the opportunity to reread the one letter he had received from Dorothy since his arrival in San Francisco.

Dear Tommie,

I have some really exciting news. I have been offered a job in Lincoln! Mr. Anderson recommended me for the position. I will be training people for the entire state of Nebraska. Can you believe it?

So, we are both going on quite an adventure. You to the Philippines and me to Lincoln. I hope you enjoy your adventure! I know I'm going to enjoy mine!

Love,

Dorothy

This was his fourth reading of the letter since its arrival. What did it mean?

She signed it "Love," so I guess everything is OK. Why did she have to go and take a damned job in Lincoln? Why does she even need a job? I'll take care of her just fine.

He took out his pen and paper, adjusted Dorothy's photo, and began to write:

Dearest Dorothy,

We eat in the 1st class diner. It sure is a honey. Spent a couple hours on deck after chow until it got chilly and too dark to see. We've been batting the bull here since. Are all about ready to go to bed now.

Say, how are you standing the boat ride? You are still looking good. I got you up on a shelf right by my head. All I got to do is roll over and there you are.

Honey, if you love me like I love you we won't have to worry about getting together.

Love and Kisses,

Tommie

He stuffed the letter into a large manila envelope where he would keep all his shipboard letters until their landing in Hawaii. *Hope she still loves me by the time this finally gets to her.*

SEVERAL DAYS HAD passed since their arrival on the ship. Tommie lit a cigarette, leaned on the deck railing, and inhaled, letting the nicotine do its work. He exhaled in one extended breath, waving his arms at Bob. "Hey, did you see that one? It nearly flew six feet out of the water. I didn't know fish could do that."

Bob continued to swab the deck. "How the hell can I look at flying fish while I'm scrubbing this deck? And aren't you supposed to be doing this with me?"

"Yeah, guess I'd better get busy, huh. But ya know? I never in a million years thought I'd be somewhere that you couldn't see land."

"Get your head out of the clouds, private, and grab that mop, or the only thing you'll see is the inside of the brig." Bob tossed the mop in Tommie's direction.

Tommie began moving the mop in a haphazard manner. "What's the name of that card game, again? I like it best of all the card games we've played so far. Can we play it again after supper?"

"Spades. It's called Spades. You know you do have to *move* the mop?"

"Yeah, Spades, that's the one. I love that game. I could play it all night."

Thirty minutes later, Tommie threw the mop down. "There Bob, are you satisfied? The deck is clean as a hound's tooth. Let's go play Spades."

Bob inspected Tommie's work. "Excellent work, private. Now shine my shoes, and you'll be done for today."

"You know what you can do with those shoes, don't ya?" He slugged Bob's arm and ran down the stairs to the cabin with Bob in close pursuit. Tommie opened the door to the cabin and headed straight to the shelf where he kept his cherished photo of Dorothy.

"What the hell? Where is she? Did one of you assholes take her?"

Bob put his hand on Tommie's shoulder. "Keep your cool, buddy. Let's just do a little recon around the room before you jump to conclusions."

Tommie searched the room and found nothing. He scoured his bed and still came up empty-handed. Just as he was about to give up, something bumped against his foot. "Found her!" He picked up the photo. His pulse slowed.

"Hey, baby, where ya been?"

"Jeez, Tommie. You have got it bad. It's just a picture, man."

"Just a picture? I know this might sound crazy, but as long as I can see her face, I know everything's gonna be just fine." He gazed at the photo, and his mood soon mirrored the contentment in Dorothy's eyes. "I love her, man. I just love her."

"Yeah, yeah, yeah, we all know you love her, but some of us prefer just to have a good time. Let's play Spades."

"No, think I'll drop Dottie a line first."

Bob put his cards down. He didn't understand the morose mood that had engulfed him for just a moment. "Don't forget to tell her 'hi' from me."

Hawaii

The ship maneuvered its way into Honolulu Harbor while everyone on board stood shoulder-to-shoulder on the deck. Tommie bent over the railing, attempting to get a closer look at a pineapple-shaped water tower adorning the top of a building in the distance.

Young native boys swam out to meet the boat. Bob tossed coins overboard, and the swimmers dove after them. One lucky diver came to the surface with a coin held high in his hand and a broad smile on his face, and he and his companions motioned to Bob to throw another one.

Motorboats overflowing with young Hawaiian women raced around the ship. The girls, their heads thrown back so they could see the soldiers, waved and giggled. Tommie squinted against the sun, trying to get a better view of the girls. "Do they have on grass skirts?"

"Nope, but see those big yellow flowers they have behind their ears? You know what that means, don't ya, Tommie, my man? They are available with a capital 'A.'"

"Hadn't noticed, I guess."

"Sorry. I forgot for a second that some of us are lovesick puppies. Well, the rest of us are about to *become* lovesick somethings. My God, they *are* beautiful women, ya gotta admit that, Tommie."

Tommie shrugged. "Hope we get to go into the city, at least a little while before we leave. Can't see much from here."

Bob scowled. "Can't see much? Are you blind? Tommie, open your eyes! We are getting off the ship; that's for sure. We gotta be back by four on the dot, so let's make the best of it."

Once on shore, the two walked down Kapiolani Boulevard. Tommie sprinted down the sidewalk. "Have you ever seen anything so green in your life? Look at that bush covered with flowers, and they're all different colors. I can't believe what I'm seeing. And look at the leaves on that plant!"

Two Hawaiian girls walked by. Bob tripped over a crack in the sidewalk. "You're right, my friend. There's lots of beautiful things on this island. Hey, let's buy one of those flower necklaces. They say if you throw it out on the ocean and it comes back to you, it means you'll be comin' back here again."

Tommie shuddered. "Nah, not for me."

"Hell, Tommie, why not? Maybe you can bring that cute little Dottie of yours back here."

"I don't wanna do it. I don't know why, but I think I won't be back here again."

"What are you talking about? We'll be back, you know that, and maybe we'll get to stay longer."

"Nah, not for me, man. I just gotta bad feelin' about it."

"WE'VE BEEN WALKIN'" for pert near three miles," Tommie groaned. "I gotta stop." A large white building with enormous columns rising in front of three arched doorways sat a block ahead. "Let's stop there for a while."

Bob looked skeptical. "It's a library, Tommie. Gotta a hankerin' to read a couple of books, do ya?"

"Hell, no. I'm not talkin' about the building. Don't ya see where I'm pointin', man? The lawn. I'm pointin' at my bed for the next hour." Tommie sprawled across the soft green grass under a nearby tree and covered his eyes with his hat.

"Tommie, Tommie, Tommie." Bob hesitated for a moment and then took off in the direction the two girls had gone. "See ya later."

Tommie lifted his hat. "Suit yourself. I'm takin' a nap."

The heat of the tropical sun beat down on Tommie's chest, but he couldn't shake the ominous chill that filled his gut. He closed his eyes.

TOMMIE STOOD KNEE-DEEP in the turquoise water, hands on hips, watching a large wave forming nearby. He yelled to Dottie, who was sitting on the beach sunbathing, and pointed at the wave as it continued to build. Facing the crest of the wave, he extended both arms and dove in, rolling inside the wave, waiting to glide into shore on top of it, but he couldn't break through. The riptide pulled at him, forcing him farther out to sea. The water pressed against him. He couldn't move. With every attempt he fell deeper and deeper into the wave. He began to gasp for air.

"Dottie! Help me!"

"DOTTIE!" TOMMIE JUMPED up from his napping spot in one enormous leap. His legs gave out, and he hit the ground, gasping for air. "It was just a dream, just a dream," he repeated, attempting to calm his shattered nerves.

Bob walked up behind him. "Hey, man, time to go. We have exactly thirty minutes to get back to the ship. I think we better opt for a cab. I met the most beautiful woman, Tommie—you won't believe it. She was...Tommie? You're sorta pale."

"I'm fine." Tommie pulled himself up and walked toward the harbor. "Let's just get the hell out of here."

Beaver City

Dorothy pulled a bulging envelope out of the mailbox. "Finally!" she said out loud, not caring who heard her. She counted nine letters inside, all written aboard the SS *President Coolidge* luxury liner on the way to Hawaii. She ran toward the Triple-A office, stopping halfway there to sit on a park bench, unable to go any farther without reading at least one of his letters:

> Dearest Dorothy,
>
> Another day of the long voyage almost over. We are averaging about 575 miles per day, loose 30 min every 24 hours, and have lost 6 hours since we left Fort Knox.

Gosh Honey I was afraid you had gone overboard after supper; came in and you weren't on the shelf, but I found you laying under the bed, maybe you were tired. At first I thought you had left me.

The sun shone most all day today, first day since we've been out. Could see a lot of flying fish this afternoon. We are supposed to get to Hawaii Sunday sometime, will be there a day or so.

We have a blackout tonight. All lights must be out by 10 o'clock and no light of any kind on deck, not even light a match. Getting us in practice I guess, expect we will travel that way from Hawaii.

Remember I love you always. I'll write more tomorrow.

Loads of Love,

Tommie

PS Bob says to say hello

Dorothy pondered the letter, especially the part about her picture falling off the shelf. Maybe it was a sign.

TOMMIE FOUGHT TO keep his eyes open as he lay in a deck chair tanning himself. He lifted his head long enough to appraise his tan and then rolled over onto his back. "Don't wanna end up fried like I did last week. Jesus, do you think we'll ever get there? How many days does this make?"

Bob yawned. "I don't know. I think it's day nine, maybe

ten? This is so boring, and I think we still have a good seven hundred miles to go."

"Well, we can go watch the swim race or the boxing match."

"Nah, let's play another round of cards. What's your pleasure, sir?"

Tommie lit a cigarette. "I don't know if I can play one more hand of Spades. How about poker?"

"Fine, let's go. If it gets any hotter up here, I'm gonna melt."

Tommie pulled himself off the deck chair, took one more drag from his cigarette, and walked to the railing. He flicked the cigarette into the air and followed its arc into the water. He blinked. "Bob, do you see what I see? Is that land?"

Bob raced to the railing, searching the horizon. "Nah, you're just hallucinating. There's nothin' there."

Tommie hung his head. "Nothin' but water—no trees, no mountains, no nothin'—just water and stinking fish. Think I'll drop a line to Dorothy. Then I'll catch up with you and the poker game."

> Dearest Dorothy,
>
> Have to write in the daytime now. We are traveling at complete blackout. No lights after the sun goes down.
>
> Well we've been traveling on water 10 days now & 6 on land & still have some to go. So far have traveled over 6000 miles. Every minute we are getting closer to our destination and farther from U.S.A. I'll sure

be a happy child when I make the return trip. Gosh Honey it seems like ages since we left. Hope the time doesn't all pass this slow. Had a talk by the ship doctor today on what we were getting into. He has spent 17 yrs in the army before & has been there several times. He says not to eat any green vegetables, unless you know they come from U.S. I'm afraid I ain't going to fancy that so much. He talked on people & sun. He said it was warm over there. But if its any worse than here I am afraid I'll just melt away & no one will know where I went. It was only 88 on the ship today, but I believe they left off the first figure. I've worked in 120 degrees & it wasn't as bad as this. All you got to do is drink some water & in 10 min its all boiled away. Just sweat all the time. We are about 700 miles from P.I. now. Will sure be glad to get to land again. Well that's about it for today. Bob still insists on saying Hello.

> Bye for now.
> Be back tomorrow.
> Oceans of Love
> Tommie

He folded the letter and began placing it with the others, but stopped and reopened it to add a final line, the same line he had added to the last three letters. It had now become a ritual of sorts. Surely, if he asked enough, she would answer, and the answer would be "yes."

"P.S. Do you still love me?"

22

September 26, 1941

The Philippines

Tommie climbed onto the first of the twenty transport trucks on the dock. "How far to Fort Stotsenburg?"

Bob followed him. "They say it's sixty miles. Don't worry about that now. Look around you. It's somethin'; it's downright beautiful."

Mile after mile of bamboo trees filled the space between rows of grass huts balanced on stilts. Behind the grass huts, natives worked alongside oxen in rice paddies. Swampy ground thick with green undergrowth dotted the landscape between the rice paddies and huts. Along the muddy dirt and sand road, ponies pulled two-wheeled carts through the heavy traffic.

"Yup, it's some place all right." Anxiety crept into Tommie's thoughts. "Sure is a long way from good ole Nebraska, though. A long, long way."

TOMMIE WIPED HIS forehead with his shirtsleeve. He took a drag from his cigarette and continued the work of placing the turret back on a tank. "Sure glad we got trees to work under. This could be a real bitch otherwise."

Bob sat on the other side of the tank, securing the turret. "Yeah, we're supposed to get a shop pretty soon."

"'Bout the same time they get our barracks built. Hell'll freeze over before that happens. It's been a month since we landed in this godforsaken place. I'm gettin' damned sick of living in a tent with no electricity and a stinking dirt floor."

"Tommie's got the blues, huh?"

"Don't make fun of me. I mean it. I hate this place." He took one final drag on his cigarette and flicked it onto the ground. "I just wanna go home. I never thought a person could get sick of the ocean, but I sure would like to see a big ole field of wheat, just swayin' in the breeze, instead of these swampy rice paddies—or a big ole Nebraska rainstorm with flashes of lightning 'bout make you jump outta yer skin. I even miss Beaver Creek, just the sound of the water tricklin' down the stream."

"I get it—you're homesick—but what about all that traveling you wanted to do with Dorothy?"

"If Dottie was here, it'd be a different story, but right now all I can think about is home with Dottie by my side and a big ole piece of Mom's fried chicken."

"Just keep your cool. We'll be out of here soon enough, and then you and Dottie can start your life together. In the meantime, enjoy the moment. Hey, did you hear about the tour? A couple of lieutenants from the 194th put together this entire trip. Go with me. We can see the island together, and maybe you'll change your mind a little bit."

ONE HUNDRED SOLDIERS filed into four army buses and headed for Manila, arriving just in time for dinner. Everyone gulped down his food, anxious to explore the city. Tommie patted his full belly, belched, and looked around at Bob and their other two companions. "Now what?" he asked.

All four soldiers at the table rose at once and ran to the front door, where a row of taxis waited outside. Bob opened a taxi door. "We wanna see the sights. Take us around the city and show us everything."

The taxi driver started the meter. "I'll take you all around the city; all night long if you want. But, first we go to the cemetery. It is All Saints' Day, and we must go to pay respects to the dead."

The soldiers shrugged their shoulders. "Whatever you say," said one of them. "Just show us the sights."

The taxi took off, swaying and swerving its way through the city. "Ride 'em cowboy!" one of the soldiers yelled. "Yee-haw!"

Tommie covered his ears. "Jeeze, could you guys quiet it down a little?"

They topped a hill, and the cab slowed to a crawl. Candles and lanterns glowed at each grave across the five-acre expanse of the cemetery. The soldiers fell silent. The driver parked in front of a mammoth tomb with elaborate figures carved into it and motioned the soldiers out of the cab. "Is it all right for us to be here?" Tommie asked, uneasy about what they were observing.

"Yes. Stand over there. Give me a minute, and then we can go." The driver walked over to the tomb and hugged an old woman sitting next to it. She offered him a shot glass filled with whiskey. He raised it high in the air, turned toward the grave, and said something in Tagalog. He downed the whiskey in one swallow, talked to the tombstone again, and then headed back toward the soldiers.

Tommie couldn't take his eyes off the woman with the whiskey bottle. "We sure don't do anything like this in Nebraska. Wish we did."

The driver motioned the soldiers back to the cab. "Next stop—the largest nightclub in the world."

Bob opened the cab door. "Now, *that's* much more my style than a cemetery. Sorta creepy here for my liking."

Tommie shrugged. "I don't know. I kinda liked it. Don't you like to see how other people do things?"

"Sure, like how they dance, how they drink, how they gamble."

Five miles later, the cab pulled up in front of a nightclub, which covered an entire city block. The music spilled out into the streets, along with a large percentage of the clientele, who were dancing and singing at the top of their lungs. Tommie's eyes narrowed. "Not my kind of place. You guys, I don't know about..."

Bob cut him off. "Stay cool, private. This place is swingin'.

Let's at least go in and check it out." He opened the door of the cab before it came to a complete stop. "Come on, Tommie!"

"Guess it won't hurt to try it, but I'm not stayin' if it's like the mess hall at Fort Knox. You know I don't like people reachin' over me, crowdin' me like a bunch of cattle."

Tommie and Bob walked through the swarm of people and into the front of the club. "How much to get in?" Bob asked the clerk behind the counter.

"Five dollars to get in. Then you have to buy dinner, or you can just go to the gambling hall, but you have to bet a minimum of one hundred dollars in there."

A man in a red silk shirt shoved in front of Tommie. "I don't have that kind of money, and I can already tell you I'm not gonna like it here." He walked toward the door, Bob following close behind.

"Tommie, wait up, will ya? Maybe the cab driver knows a quieter place."

The other two soldiers motioned from the door of the club. "Hey, man, we're staying here."

Tommie and Bob climbed into the cab. The driver woke with a start, surprised at their quick return. "You don't like the club?"

"Too noisy and crowded," Tommie replied. "Know any other places?"

"Sure, sure. Sit back and relax, and I will find you a quiet place."

The cab lurched into the street and headed south. Tommie slumped in the seat. "Sorry, Bob. I just can't handle it."

"Doesn't matter. I couldn't afford the place anyway. Don't worry. We'll find somewhere else to hang out."

Tommie sat up. "Pull over here! It's a roller skating rink. Can you believe it? A skating rink in Manila!"

"Let me see if I get this straight," said Bob. "You would rather go to a skating rink than a nightclub? How old are you, Tommie?"

"Oh, come on. Have you ever been skating? It's fun. I could even teach you how if you don't know. You'll like it; I promise. Just give it a chance."

"You know, if I had the money, I'd just leave you right here and go back to that club, but you're such a farm boy; I don't know if you can handle it by yourself."

"I'm sure the place is full of girls. Girls love to skate, and they love to skate with boys, and they're nice girls, real nice girls."

"Just shut up and let's go. You're serious about the girls, though, right?"

THE RHYTHMIC SOUND of skaters gliding across the polished floor greeted Tommie as he opened the door to the rink. "Chattanooga Choo Choo" blared over the loudspeaker. "What'd I tell ya, Bob? Let's have ourselves a ball."

Brown-skinned girls lined the side of the rink, waiting for someone to ask them to skate. Bob rushed to the counter. "Size ten, and make it snappy."

Tommie was amazed with Bob's ease and style as he took a lap around the rink and then did a second lap skating backwards. He approached the row of girls, doing a graceful spin in front of them. "May I escort you onto the floor?" he asked the first girl in line.

The girl smiled. "*Hindi ko naiintindihan ang sinasabi mo.*" (I do not understand what you say.)

Undeterred, Bob put his hand in hers and motioned to the floor. She giggled, winked at her friends, and followed him. He passed Tommie, who was still putting on his skates.

"Hurry up, private, or I'll have 'em all!" He pulled his partner closer. "Come on, doll, I'll teach you some English. Me Bob." He pounded his chest.

"And I am Mayala, *not* your doll. I'll forgive you this time, because I played a trick on you, but you better behave yourself. We all understand English, you know?"

Bob blushed. "Sorry—uh—wanna Coke?"

"In The Mood" played over the loudspeaker. Tommie considered the row of girls. *Why not?* He skated in their direction and took the hand of the first girl in line, pulling her onto the rink. He put his right arm around her waist, holding her left hand in his. "I love this song. Reminds me of my girl back home."

"You have a girl in America? She won't mind that you are skating with me?"

"We're just skatin'. She won't mind. Let's not talk. Let's just skate."

They glided around the rink. The blare of big band music and the rhythmic swish of skates rolling across the wooden floor filled Tommie's emptiness.

"HOLD ON, HONEY, here we go!" Tommie gripped Dorothy's hands and swung her around before bringing her back into his arms.

"This is so much fun!" Dorothy squealed. *"Do it again!"*

Tommie started skating backward, pulling Dorothy along, pleased with his skating expertise.

"I could do this all night! Especially with you."

THE SONG ENDED, and Dorothy disappeared into the eyes of the brown-skinned girl skating beside him. He looked at her for a long moment. "Wanna go 'round again?"

Midnight came, and the skating rink closed. Tommie hailed a cab just as Bob appeared from around the corner, shouting,

"Hey, wait for me! Just had to tell Mayala good-bye. How about you, buddy? How did you do?"

"Just fine. Skated a lot, and drank a lot of Coke, just like back home."

"Private, just enjoy the moment. We have a whole tour to go on in the morning, so don't get all homesick on me, please."

"I'm just sayin' I liked it." He didn't mention the vivid picture he carried in his mind of Dorothy swinging around the rink in his arms. "We'll have a good time tomorrow, just like you said."

BOB STRETCHED HIS arms and scratched his chest as he walked out of the hotel. "Last night sure was fun, wasn't it?"

He yawned, only then noticing Tommie had run ahead.

"Come on, Bob!" Tommie shouted from the steps of the last waiting bus. "We gotta hurry if we want window seats!"

Their bus headed out of Manila. One of the lieutenants walked to the front. "OK, listen up. We're headed to a place called Pagsanjan Falls. It's 390 feet high, and to get there, we will be paddling upstream in canoes.

"I'm going to tell you a legend I heard about the falls that goes way back. It's said that a long time ago there wasn't a waterfall here, just two rivers. Two brothers lived nearby. Then one day a bad drought came. Everything dried up— everything was barren. The two brothers prayed every day and every night for rain to come, but none came. Finally, the weaker brother died of thirst. After he buried his brother, the remaining brother climbed to the upper region of the riverbed in search of water. A hard climb up craggy cliffs exhausted him. To add to his misery, he found no water. He became distraught and raised his fist, beseeching the gods, 'Where is the water?' He got so angry he threw his big cane down among the rocks. Suddenly, a spring bubbled up exactly where the cane had landed. He fell to the ground and took huge drinks of the water until his energy returned. The water grew and grew and fell down the canyon walls, turning into the Pagsanjan Falls.

"That's your little bit of Filipino history for today. Anybody with a phobia about water shouldn't go up the river on the canoes. It's pretty steep, and you have to do something called 'shooting the rapids' to get back down. It's slow going up, but they say it's a fast and crazy return trip. It'll take a good hour to get there, so sit back and enjoy the scenery."

Tommie thought about the legend of the Pagsanjan Falls. "I wonder what it's like to die from no water on an island surrounded by water?"

Bob rubbed his hands together. "Who cares about that? I'm more interested in the ride down the river. Are you with me, private?"

"Oh, yeah, I wanna do it all!"

The scenery changed abruptly as the road entered the mountains. Tommie eyed the lush countryside. "It's mountains, but it's not like the Rockies, where you can see rock."

The road switchbacked up the hill. With each turn, the forest color shifted from deep olive to emerald to Kelly green. Lush forests gave way to acacia trees with purple blossoms drooping almost to the ground. Bougainvillea plants sporting bright yellow and pink flowers grew between the trees.

Tommie sat motionless, spellbound by the landscape. "This country's greener 'n green! I think I can see the whole damned island from here! How high up do you think we are?"

"Settle down, private."

"Damn you, Bob, first ya want me to stop bein' so blue, and then, when I'm feelin' happier 'n a rooster in a henhouse, ya tell me to calm down. I'm havin' a great time! Just let it be!"

In the town of Pagsanjan, the soldiers filed off the bus and moved toward primitive canoes. Each held two or three soldiers, along with two boatmen. Tommie and Bob ran to the nearest canoe, and the boatmen handed them each a paddle. One-hundred-foot walls bordered the river. Tommie clutched the oar. "Guess there's nowhere to go but up to them falls! Let's go!"

He shoved the oar into the river, determined to make it to the top. Thirty minutes into the trip, his lungs ached. His muscles burned. "Damn, my arms are gonna give out if we don't get there pretty soon!"

The guides stopped rowing and motioned them out of the canoe. "Are we there?" Tommie and Bob yelled over the roar of the rapids.

The guides eyed each other in a private chuckle. "Pick up the canoe," said one of them. "We have a long way still to go. We have to go around the rapids; then we paddle some more." Bob and Tommie shrugged in resignation and picked up the canoe.

A mile later, the guides motioned for them to get back into the river. "I am so damned tired, I don't know if I can make it," Tommie moaned.

"Gut it up, private. Just keep pluggin' along, pluggin' along, and before you know it, we'll be there." Bob shoved an oar into Tommie's hands. Tommie thrust the paddle forward into the water.

Ten more times they left the water to hike around rapids before reaching their destination. Adrenalin rushed through Tommie's blood as he absorbed the magnificence of the Pagsanjan Falls.

"Helloooo!" he yelled. A faint "Helloooo" returned. "Hey, I think I see the big cane the brother threw on the rocks!" he yelled, heady from the combination of exhaustion and excitement pulsing through his body.

The guides signaled them to return to the boats. "We go straight down now, soldier," said one, "so hold on and listen to my orders!"

Tommie gripped the oar, and they plunged into the water. Massive waves spilled into the canoe, drenching everyone. He panicked.

"Pull the oar. Good! Now push back!" the guide commanded.

Tommie's world shrank to that precise moment, and he heard nothing but the guide's voice. He wrenched the oar forward, pulled it out of the water, and with every muscle and every fiber of his body he jammed the oar into the water. With nothing left but pure exhilaration, he drove the oar back.

The river calmed. The rapids dissolved. Tommie collapsed over his oar.

"Rest now, because more rapids are coming!" yelled the guide.

Tommie raised his oar into the air. "My God, the canyon walls, they're beautiful! And could the sky get any bluer? Bob, how you doin' back there?"

Bob, his arms too limp to lift his oar, yelled, "I'm fine, just fine. I may puke, but I'm having the time of my life!"

The two-hour trek up the canyon took only thirty minutes going down. Tommie and Bob jumped out of the boat and onto the dock, whooping and slapping each other on the back. Bob raised his fists in the air. "We did it! By God, we did it!"

"I have never in all my born days ever done anything that excitin'! Let's do it again!" Tommie slapped Bob on the back. "Just kiddin', man. I'm ready for the town."

A magnificent cathedral sat in the town square of Pagsanjan. Its expansive open doors welcomed the two soldiers as they walked in. Tommie glanced to his left, where the floor shimmered in the sunlight. Gold inlay surrounded steps that led up to the statue of a female figure on an altar. Spikes of gold behind her head created a halo, which surrounded the entire back and top of the figure. Both men removed their hats.

"Who is she?" Tommie whispered.

"Virgin Mary. Read the plaque."

"It says this church was built in 1670. People were comin' in here and prayin' to her and livin' their lives a long time before Nebraska even existed. Think how many people have stood right here. Makes me feel kinda funny, ya know?"

Bob scrunched his nose at Tommie. "There you go again. Feeling stuff. Come on, man, let's go check out the rest of the town."

Tommie didn't move. "You can make fun of me if you want to, but she's been here forever, and I feel safe when I look at her—kinda like lookin' at Dottie's picture."

"Whatever you say, but I'm leaving. I wanna check out the town."

TOMMIE SAT, STARING out the window at the surrounding rainforest during the convoy ride back to Fort Stotsenburg. He thought for a moment about the cemetery, the waterfall, the Virgin Mary statue. "I can't believe I'm here, thousands of miles from home, seein' all this stuff! I gotta tell Dottie about this. I gotta bring her back here so she can see it."

"Now you're talking, man." Bob slapped Tommie's head. "That's the world traveler I've been waiting for."

"Yeah, I *am* a world traveler, ain't I? It's excitin', sorta like goin' into Beaver City on a Saturday night, but better. This is the life. We're gonna see everything there is to see in this big ole world!"

"DOTTIE! I FOUND a starfish. Ain't it beautiful?" Tommie picked up the starfish and ran the distance up the beach to where Dorothy sat sunning herself as a warm tropical breeze swept over her. She untied the top of her bathing suit and held up a bottle of oil to Tommie.

"Rub some of this oil on me, would ya, honey?"

Tommie took the lid off the bottle, and the fragrance of coconut filled the air. He poured some on Dottie's back and massaged it into her skin, taking his time, enjoying the sensation of touching her silky-soft body. He moved to her sides and down her back to her waist, sliding his hands down the inside of her suit.

"What are you trying to do?" she giggled. He continued to tug at her suit. She turned over.

"You bad boy. Now rub some of that oil on this side, wherever you want."

"GENTLEMEN, MAKE SURE you remove all your personal gear from the bus, and please exit in an orderly manner. No need to rush."

The sound of the lieutenant's voice permeated Tommie's dream, but the aroma of coconut oil lingered for just a moment. Out the window, he could see row upon row of tents that served as their battalion barracks. "Home again, home again," he sighed.

23

November 1941
Beaver City

> Dearest Dorothy,
>
> We crossed a mountain that from the top
> you could see for miles around. Out to the place
> at the falls we got canoes with natives to go
> up the rapids to the falls, about 20 miles up.
> That also was just like pictures.

Dorothy's eyes brightened. "It's Pagsanjan Falls!"

"It's what?" Carol asked.

"Pagsanjan Falls. I've been reading about it in the books Miss Lambert gave me. It's this huge waterfall in the Philippines. Maybe we can go there someday."

"You and me?"

"No, silly. Me and Tommie."

"Oh."

Dorothy knew the meaning of that response only too well. "Oh" meant Carol had an opinion about something Dorothy didn't want to think about. Nonetheless, she had to ask.

"OK, what are you thinking? You might as well tell me now."

"Dottie, you know I love you, but it's been how long now since you last saw Tommie? Three months? You don't seem to be any closer to making up your mind how you feel about him than you were three months ago, and yet here you are thinking about going to the Philippines with him. Honey, somebody has to say it, and it might as well be me. You seem to be more in love with traveling than with Tommie. Now, I'll shut up." Carol snagged the photos from her desk and headed directly into the filing room, allowing no time for any sort of rebuttal.

Dorothy sat for a moment, attempting to absorb Carol's missive. *What am I in love with anyway?* She knew the answer, but facing it and doing what had to be done seemed overwhelming. *He's so far away. Maybe I should wait until he comes back.*

She stopped at the post office on the way home and pulled a letter from Tommie out of the box. Funny, the difference six months made. She used to run to the post office and pray for a letter. Now, she prayed there would be no letter, for no letter meant another opportunity to avoid doing the right thing and delay the inevitable yet again. She opened the letter and began reading it as she ambled toward home.

Dearest Dorothy,

Don't believe it's going to seem much like Christmas over here. This year will be the first I've missed at home in my life and the hard part about it is I won't have the daughter-in-law to present to the family as was previously planned.

But honey if anything should come up that you don't want to wait I can't blame you. I can understand how it is to be waiting and giving up good years of your life for someone who isn't too sure of ever getting back. Personally I think I'll be back before another year rolls around. No matter what happens I do and always will think you are the nicest and sweetest girl I ever went with and hope someday to make you my wife and make you a good husband and also make you happy. The way the situation is now I guess every true American has lots that they are giving up to get this thing over. The sooner the better I think.

Lot of Love,

Tommie

She reached her house and sat down in the kitchen, her favorite place to gather her thoughts. Through the window, she watched the branches of the big elm tree in the front yard bend in response to a harsh November gale. Her mother's voice echoed through her mind. *Do the right thing, Dorothy.*

He's giving you the opportunity, so take it. She picked up her pen and began the letter she had so dreaded writing.

> Dear Tommie,
>> Please know that I never meant to hurt you, but I have to tell you the truth...

She finished the letter, put it in an envelope, and flew toward the front door.

Frank looked up from reading his newspaper. "Where ya goin' in such a toot? Ya know it's almost supper time!"

"I'll be right back, Pa. There's something I *have* to do, and I have to do it right now." She ran the six blocks to the post office and put the letter in the mailbox.

A gusty breeze caught the last of the leaves from under a cottonwood tree, gathered dirt from the road, and created a swirling mass of debris. She didn't attempt to outrun it but instead let it consume her.

"I'm so sorry," she whispered.

"PA, I HAVE something I need to tell you."

"What is it, Dorothy? Is everything OK with Tommie?"

"No, Pa. I broke up with Tommie, but that's not it. There's something else. I'm leaving Beaver City."

"You gonna go spend some time with Helen? I'm sure she'd love to see you. You sure about breaking up with Tommie? Ya know, you're not getting any younger."

"No, Pa, I'm sure about Tommie, and I'm leaving for good. I have a chance to work in Lincoln. Mr. Anderson recommended me for a pretty big promotion. I got the job, and I'm moving to Lincoln after the first of the year."

"No you're not! You are staying right here where you belong. What's gotten into you, young lady? You don't belong in a big city. You belong right here with me and Walter! And how can you be so sure about breaking up with Tommie? Is that what this is all about? Why did you break up with him anyway? He adores you."

"You're right. He adores me. He thinks I'm perfect, and that's just it. I'm not perfect. I'm just me. I want someone who is in love with me, flaws and all. But this isn't about Tommie. It's about my job, my career. Pa, I'm good at what I do, and I love doing it. What's wrong with a woman wanting to better herself, be independent, try new things?"

Frank stood dumbfounded, trying to take it all in. He had watched her change over the past year into a mature young woman who was, indeed, independent and passionate about her work. It was all she talked about at dinner. Why hadn't he noticed or understood? It still didn't make much sense to him, these modern women, but he knew he had to try.

"Dorothy, you've caught me by surprise. Leave me alone for a while. Let me think."

December 7, 1941

The radio startled Dorothy: "We interrupt this program to bring you a special news bulletin. The Japanese have attacked Pearl Harbor, Hawaii, by air, President Roosevelt has just announced. The attack also was made on all naval and military activity on the principal island of Oahu."

Frank ran into the kitchen. "Did he say Pearl Harbor?"

Dorothy couldn't speak.

"Is that where Tommie is?"

She stared at her father for a moment, trying to clear her head and assimilate the radio announcer's news. She opened her mouth to speak, and the truth rolled off her tongue.

"Smitty," she whispered.

SMITTY JUMPED UP, his newspaper flying in pages to the bunkhouse floor. His heart raced. "Jesus Christ! This is it! I'm a dead man!" He ran out the front door in search of his boss.

Mr. Franklin charged out the back door of the main house. "Did you hear the news? This is it, Smitty. We're not gonna just be sittin' on the sidelines anymore."

"I know, I know. I gotta get home, sir. I can't stay here. I gotta get back to Oxford and check in. You understand, don't ya?"

"Of course I do, son. Everything is gonna be different now—that's for sure. I know it's Sunday, but can you help me with this last batch of shuckin' before you go?"

"Sure. But I gotta leave first thing in the morning."

The two men stood speechless, unmoving.

Mr. Franklin broke the tension and headed to the barn. "All right, son, let's go get some shuckin' done."

Smitty walked into the barn in a daze and began to pull husks off the corn. His stomach made its way up to his throat, and he gagged. "Fuck" was the only word that made its way out of his mouth as he ran out of the barn and into the yard, retching all the way. "Get a hold of yourself, man!" he shouted, hoping the sound of his own voice would calm his nerves.

Early Monday morning, Smitty gathered his things and climbed into his Ford pickup to commence the sixty-mile drive back to Oxford. One flat tire later, he arrived and parked his pickup in front of the draft office. A line of men started at the front door, wrapped around the block, and disappeared. Smitty walked to the front of the line. "You guys got your draft notices?"

"We're volunteering," one man said.

"Well, I got my notice a couple months ago. Where's the line for reporting in?"

"There ain't one."

Smitty walked into the office and up to a harried-looking clerk. "I'm here to check in, or whatever I need to do. I got my draft notice, but that's all I know."

"Well, son, you'll be getting your orders soon enough. You'll be going to Fort Leavenworth by train, probably in a week or so. Best of luck to ya. Now, get out of the way so I can do my job."

Smitty walked out the door and into the frigid December afternoon. The sky seemed bluer than usual, the air a little clearer. He lit a cigarette, taking a deep drag on it as he climbed into his pickup. He headed south down Ogden Street toward Highway 46. The pickup slowed as if on its own as it neared the turnoff to his folks' farm. Smitty stepped on the accelerator and headed straight down the highway. The harder he pushed on the accelerator, the dimmer became the thought of seeing his mother and telling her he would soon be on his way to Fort Leavenworth for basic training.

The landscape blurred into shades of brown as the pickup continued down Highway 46. At its intersection with Highway 89, he turned west toward Beaver City, where he turned right down Ninth Street, then left onto O Street.

Pulling into a parking place across from the town square, he could see through the window of the Triple-A office. There she was. He watched her walk to the front counter, in deep thought about something, and then move back to her desk, picking up her planimeter and studying a map.

Smitty sat there for a moment longer, watching her every move, and then started the pickup and drove north out of town toward his folks' farm. Maybe facing his mother would be easier than facing Dorothy.

He spent the week packing his things and preparing for the 300-mile train ride to Fort Leavenworth, Kansas. One question haunted him and ran unceasingly through his mind. *Is it too late?*

He opened a fifth of cheap whiskey and took a healthy swig before twisting the cap on tightly and placing it in his bag. As he prepared to close the clasps on the suitcase, he stopped, opened it, found the bottle, and gulped down more of the golden, soothing liquid. His shoulders relaxed. *That's better. I think I'll pay one last visit to Beaver City. There's a dance tonight. Nothin' like a little dancin' to calm the nerves.*

WHISKEY-INDUCED BRAVADO SURGED through Smitty's blood. He grinned at a woman sitting closest to the front door. "How about a dance, sweetheart?"

"Sure, Smitty. I'd love to dance with *you*."

"How'd you know my name?"

"Everybody knows your name. Who can forget that grin of yours? Besides, I hear you are one of the best waltzers in Furnas County."

"Well, don't just sit there, then. Let's get ta dancin'." The band began to play "Tennessee Waltz."

"Sorry, honey, I gotta do somethin'." He winked at the young woman. "I'll catch ya next time."

The band's singer began crooning as Smitty headed

toward the exit. "Dammit!" he muttered under his breath. "To hell with this. I don't need it. I don't need any of it."

"Smitty! One dance, for old times' sake? Remember, this used to be our song."

The whiskey kicked in and began to speak for him. "Well, look who showed up. Peaches, darlin', how ya doin'?" He flashed his grin in a defensive move to conceal the fact that he couldn't breathe.

"This was our song? I thought it was me and Lucky's song. But sure, I'll dance with you, Peaches." He grasped her hand and jerked her toward him.

"Oops. Sorry about that, darlin'. I forgot—you're engaged, right? Hey, did you ever tell him you were leavin' to go to the big city? Bet you didn't. Too big a chicken, ain't ya?"

Dorothy could smell the stench of alcohol on his breath. She spoke softly, not ready to retreat from her mission. "I'm not going. Mr. Anderson said everything is on hold until they figure out how all this mess will affect the Triple-A, so I'm staying here for the time being."

Smitty wanted to hold her in his arms and assure her that her dreams would come true, maybe not right now, but soon. Instead, words laden with alcohol-induced rancor assaulted her.

"Tough break, but, hey, speakin' of tough breaks, ain't that fella of yours in Hawaii, or somewhere like that? Guess he wasn't such a lucky bastard after all."

"Smitty! He's on the Philippine Islands. You know as well as I do that they were attacked the day after Pearl Harbor. No one has any idea what's going on over there. He could be dead!" Her words brought to life the harsh, simple truth.

Overwhelmed, her intention in shambles, she walked away.

Smitty stumbled forward. The effects of half a bottle of whiskey disappeared. "Dottie, don't go! I shoulda kept my damned mouth shut. He's probably OK. He's a farm boy. He knows how to take care of himself."

"I didn't come here to talk about Tommie. I came here because you keep pushing your way into my mind, my dreams. I can't stop thinking about you, and then when I see you, you say something so stupid, so inconsiderate, I can't believe I care about you at all! But dammit! I do!"

Without a word, Smitty pulled her into his arms and began dancing. He craved the feeling of hope he absorbed whenever she held him close, and he didn't want her to see the tears that came dangerously close to betraying him. The one-two-three rhythm of the music filled the room.

One-two-three—she acquiesced to his touch.

One-two-three—with measured steps he allowed himself to enjoy her body against his.

One-two-three—they danced as one, and their embrace stopped time altogether.

The song ended, but they continued to sway back and forth, unwilling for the moment to end.

"Walk me to my pickup, would ya, for old times' sake?"

"Sure."

Smitty opened the door, and they walked out into the moonlit night. *It's now or never*, he thought, garnering his courage. "Peaches, I'm just as mixed up as you are. I'm sorry about your job and your fiancé, and I'm sorry I'm such an ass, but I do care about you. I..."

Dorothy stood on tiptoes, put her hand behind his neck,

and pulled him to her. Five years of stored emotion poured from her into that kiss. She kissed him again and again. He responded by pulling her even closer. "I should've listened to you back then. I should've never left."

"I'll write you," she said, hiding her face and walking away.

She disappeared into the darkness. He started to run after her but stopped. "I love you, Peaches," he cried.

Stored tears can be stifled for a while, but not forever. Dorothy allowed those tears to fall down her cheeks and onto her coat. She ran, putting as much distance between herself and Smitty as possible, stifling the powerful urge to run back to him. Instead, she whispered into the darkness, "I love you too, Jack Smith!"

25

Aboard the Train to

Fort Leavenworth, Kansas

Traces of clear-blue sky, the only color in the otherwise dismal landscape, struggled to show themselves between billowing steel-gray clouds that commanded center stage. Smitty took in the view. The gentle rocking motion and clickety-clack of the train speeding down the track consoled him.

DOROTHY ROLLED OVER on her back and put her hands under her head. "Oh, Smitty, don't you just love the big ole Nebraska sky? Look at that cloud! It's huge! It looks just like a train engine. See? There's the front of it, and there's the smoke coming out of the engine, and, see, there's the wheels. You can almost hear it, can't you? Hey! Did you hear anything I said? Look at the cloud, you silly boy." She began to giggle. *"Why are you looking at me that way?"*

"Why? Can't I just look at ya, Peaches? Why don't you stop lookin' at those silly clouds?" He rolled over toward her and pinched her cheek.

"Peaches."

THE CONDUCTOR TAPPED Smitty's shoulder. "Peaches? We don't have any peaches, son. I just need your ticket."

"Oh sure, sure." He searched through his pockets until the ticket appeared. "Here it is."

"Must have been some dream, son. I don't believe you were referring to the fruit, now, were ya?"

Smitty shrugged. Out the window the countryside rushed by in a blur of brown and beige. He pulled his suitcase from under his seat, opened the latch, and pulled out the bottle of whiskey. He took a long swig, and then shoved the bottle between the seat cushions. The familiar calming sensation began to take over, and he closed his eyes.

"CLOSE YOUR EYES, Jack. I'm coming out, and I want it to be a surprise." Dorothy peeked around the doorway of the bathroom

and into their honeymoon suite. *"You're peeking! Close them, or I won't come out."*

Smitty closed his eyes. "They're closed for now, darlin', but you better hurry. I don't know how much longer I can wait."

After assuring herself that his eyes were, indeed, closed, Dorothy took one last look in the bathroom mirror and entered the bedroom. "Don't look until I tell you to open your eyes."

Smitty opened his eyes. "I can't wait anymore, darlin', I gotta...Oh, my God, but you are a sight for sore eyes! You're beautiful, Peaches. Come on over here."

Dorothy tried to slow her pulse. She couldn't speak. She walked across the room, letting her robe fall to the floor on the way. She slipped into their wedding bed and into Jack's arms. He pulled down the straps of her negligee and began to kiss her neck, working his way to her breasts.

"BELLEVILLE, KANSAS, NEXT stop!" Smitty awoke with a jerk and faced the conductor. "Five more hours and we'll be in Leavenworth, son."

Smitty folded up his coat to fashion a pillow and placed it under his head, attempting to find a comfortable position on the train seat. He began to doze off. Dorothy's words from five years before echoed through his mind: *"Mark my words,*

Jack Smith. You will regret this day. You should never leave me. You'll regret it."

"NEXT STOP, FORT Leavenworth!" the conductor yelled out as he paraded down the aisle. "Fort Leavenworth, next stop, ladies and gentlemen. Get ready. We'll be there in thirty minutes."

Smitty put on his jacket and pulled the bottle of whiskey out from under the cushion folds. He took one last swig from the bottle. *I do regret it, Peaches. More than you'll ever know.*

26

February 1, 1942
The Philippines

Dearest Dorothy,

We are permitted to write but whether it reaches its destination remains yet to be seen. Hope so at least.

How is every little thing getting along in Nebraska now? Better than here I hope. We are not as bad off yet as we could be. At least still all together and looking forward to the outcome. Things are not as rough as they could be. We are still eating 2 meals per day and get coffee and bread for breakfast when they can get the bread, so are fairing pretty well that way..

Tommie dropped his pen and winced at the roar of Japanese bombers flying low overhead. He waited for the piercing sound of bombs falling. Nothing. The temperature inside the tent was eighty degrees, but every muscle in his body convulsed as an icy chill settled into his body.

Bob sat down on Tommie's cot. "Everything's fine, buddy. They're gone. Let's go have a smoke."

Tommie got up and started to move toward the door of the tent, clenching his jaw. His stomach churned. He reached with trembling hands for his last American cigarette, retrieved it, and moved outside.

"Where the hell did you get that cigarette?"

"I saved it, man. I can't stand those native pieces of shit they call cigarettes. They about blow my head off—they're so strong."

"Will you at least share it with your old pal, private? I ran out of American cigarettes last week."

Tommie handed him the butt. "Maybe this is a good thing. Maybe we should quit smoking anyway. What do ya think?"

Bob's eyes narrowed. He inhaled. "Bullshit." He handed it back and blew smoke in Tommie's direction.

Tommie took the cigarette and drew it in, trying to slow his breath. "So, when do you suppose those reinforcements are gonna get here? I heard a rumor that they ain't comin'. Do ya think that's true?"

Bob concentrated on the surrounding jungle, then on a row of foxholes, avoiding Tommie's eyes. "Sure, they'll get here eventually. I know they gotta fight two wars, but they'll get here, probably pretty soon."

The sun beat down on them. "I hope so. I mean, I'm real fond of coffee, but when it's all you get for breakfast, it gets a little old. I'm ready to head out of here, ain't you?"

"Sure am, buddy. Sure am." Bob walked away.

Tommie returned to the tent and slipped into the safe haven of his sleeping bag. The distinctive buzz of the Japanese bombers started once more. He tugged at the sleeping bag, trying to get it closer to his shivering body. He focused on the top of the tent. "Shit!" Throwing the blanket to the floor, he pulled the crumpled photo of Dorothy out of his pocket. He waited for the familiar calming sensation to take over, but it didn't come. He resolved to finish his letter to Dorothy.

> Have had hell scared out of me a few times and expect plenty more to come, but none so close but what it could have been worse. Our outfit has had no bad casualties yet. One kid got a leg broke in a motorcycle crack up and another got hurt pretty bad in an air raid but is out of the hospital and back now.
>
> Jap planes visit us all the way from 3 to a dozen or more times a day but as yet haven't bombed us. All have fox holes for those occasions that make it somewhat safer.
>
> I dread to think of the rainy season which isn't so far off. (about 1 mo) So far have only got soaked one nite. These tents aren't very much water proof, but things might be different before that time comes.

We are all looking for reinforcements but can't tell when they will get here, guess they are needed worse other places than here. They say we can hold here for quite a while yet and personally I think we can. If we could believe the roomers we hear we'd have it in the bag.

Well there is a lot more I'd like to write but would be of no use. I wanted to let you know I was still alive and thinking of you. You can tell the rest of the bunch if you will. If you want you can write me at the same address, but I wouldn't swear it would do much good.

So Long for now. Hope they aren't treating you too tough over there. It's a crazy war.

Oceans of Love

Tommie

27

April 1942

Beaver City

"Have you heard from Tommie lately?"

"No, Pa. It's been six weeks. The last letter came in March, and it didn't sound good at all."

Frank put his hand on Dorothy's shoulder. "I know this must be hard, dear, but it's not easy for anyone. You're not alone. Did I see you were writing Smitty, too?"

"We're just friends, Pa. I think I'll walk down to the post office. Maybe something will come today."

Dorothy left the house and meandered up the five blocks to the post office lost in thought. She crossed both fingers before entering the post office and murmured, "Let this be the day. Please, God, let there be something from Tommie.

Let him still be alive."

She opened the mailbox door. A letter lay inside with a red stamp across its front. "RETURN TO SENDER," covered Tommie's address.

That night, Dorothy sprawled across her bed, the last letter she had sent Tommie in hand. She pondered its contents and the significance of its return. Her eyes grew heavy as she reread the letter.

TOMMIE STRUGGLED TO stand upright in the pouring rain as his feet disappeared into quicksand. "Dottie, where are you?"

"Tommie, I'm over here!"

Tommie stood engulfed in the sand up to his knees. "Help me! I'm sinking! I can't move!"

Dorothy tried to run, but the sand pulled at her feet. "Tommie! Hold on—I'm coming!" She fought to move her legs, but they wouldn't budge. She searched for Tommie and saw only his head protruding from the sand.

DOROTHY SAT UP in bed. Three nightmares in three days had all ended with Tommie disappearing into the sand. She gathered the letter from her bed and tore it into pieces.

"I'm so sorry, Tommie. I'm so sorry."

28

April 9, 1942

The Philippines

The incessant heat of the tropical sun beat down on Tommie. He pushed himself up, attempted to crawl forward, and fell into Bob.

"Come on, Tommie. We gotta get out of this damned sun. Try again."

Tommie struggled onto his knees, gritted his teeth, and crawled into the shade. "What I wouldn't give for some of my mom's fried chicken with some of those mashed potatoes and her gravy. She makes the best gravy."

"Well, we don't have any gravy, but I just found a lizard if you want to share it."

Tommie licked his dry lips. "Thanks, man, don't mind if

I do." He pulled himself farther into the shade and took the lizard leg, his portion of the day's meal.

The sergeant walked toward them, pacing himself, saving his strength for what he had to say: "Gentlemen, I just received word from General King. We are surrendering to the Japs." He stifled his angst, cleared his throat and continued. "Get rid of everything you can. Don't leave anything on you that could anger the Japs, and, for God's sake, if you have anything that says 'Made in Japan,' throw it away now."

Tommie reached for Dorothy's photo in his left hip pocket. He tried to clear his mind. "Surrender? Would they have food? Surely the Japs have food, so maybe it isn't a bad thing, right?"

Bob grimaced. "Maybe. I don't know. I was hoping for something to treat this damned diarrhea. These cramps are killing me. It doesn't matter anyway—just keep your cool, remember? Keep your cool, and we'll make it through this. That's our deal, remember?"

TOMMIE WINCED AS Japanese soldiers yelled orders. One approached him, shoving him toward the road with the butt of his rifle, yelling something in Japanese.

"You don't have to yell! I can't understand you anyway!"

The soldier yelled louder, almost knocking Tommie over as he continued to shove him toward the road.

Bob lay on the ground doubled over in pain. "I can't move. I can't get up." A brown streak covered the back of his torn pants and ran down his leg. "Tommie, come help me."

Tommie pushed his way past the Japanese soldier and

ran to Bob. He struggled to pull him up, dragged him several feet, stumbled, and fell to the ground in a heap on top of Bob. "Get up!" Tommie motioned over his shoulder. "The Jap's right behind me, and he's not happy."

"Dammit, Tommie, ask them for a cot or a truck or something for me to ride in! I can't move! I'm not kidding!"

"Get up! Move, now! We gotta go! I'll tell 'em to wait for you, but hurry up, will ya? We're in this together. We'll just keep our cool. That's what you said. Jesus, Bob, get up!"

Tommie accosted the Japanese soldier and told him, "Look, I'm sorry. I don't mean to be disrespectful, but my buddy needs help." He pointed in Bob's direction. "He's sick as a dog. He needs your help. You can help him, right?"

The Japanese soldier came over to Bob and yelled into his ear. Bob's body began to shake. His eyes were filled with terror. More shit ran down his leg. "I can't move! I'm sick!" he cried.

The Japanese soldier raised his rifle high in the air above Bob's head, then thrust it down.

"No!" Tommie screamed. "No, no, no! Bob, get up! Just keep your cool and get up!"

The sickening, rhythmic thud of the rifle-butt pummeling Bob's skull marked Tommie's first day on the Bataan Death March.

29

Bataan Death March

The sixty-mile, five-day march to Camp O'Donnell, their final destination, began with Bob's murder. Nothing that happened after that affected Tommie; not the continued lack of food and water, not being forced to stand in the scorching heat while Japanese soldiers waited for them to collapse so that they could be executed for disobeying orders, not the constant prodding, pushing, and yelling of orders he didn't understand; nothing touched him. One atrocity after another unfolded in front of him, but all he could see was the terror in Bob's eyes as the Japanese soldier crushed his skull. He couldn't afford to care, only to survive, with a hazy image of Dorothy keeping him alive.

On the fifth day of the march, a Japanese soldier pushed him up the ramp into a boxcar. Tommie moved forward, too weak to do anything but obey. More prisoners followed behind him. He stood in a corner, waiting for them to close the door, and still more men crammed into the car, pushing against him. Built to carry fifty men, the metal boxcar was now jammed with one hundred bodies. The tropical sun beat down, creating an inferno inside.

"I can't breathe! I need air!" yelled a soldier in front of him. "I can't breathe!" he repeated, his eyes consumed with fear. He attempted one more breath and then passed out. No room remained for the soldier to fall to the ground. His head lobbed back and forth with the rhythm of the train, six inches from Tommie's face.

THE MEN JERKED forward, then backward, as the train came to a halt. The door opened, and everyone began to rush toward the door. Tommie pushed the dead soldier in front of him out of the way. He tripped over several more soldiers as they fell to the floor, one after another. He tumbled off the edge of the boxcar and collapsed on the ground, sucking in the less-fetid air. A Japanese guard screamed at him, shoving the butt of his rifle into Tommie's ribs. Tommie gritted his teeth and willed himself to stand. They began to march the final nine miles to Camp O'Donnell.

The incessant sun hammered at Tommie's back through his threadbare shirt. He tried to swallow, but his throat was stuck together, and he gagged.

At the risk of a beating, he suddenly stopped marching

and stood dead still. What was that sparkling at the edge of the road just ahead? Frantic, he rubbed his eyes. Absolute clarity surged through him and he lunged forward.

"It's the falls! It's Pagsanjan Falls!" He squeezed his eyes shut and listened. *I can hear it! They're real!* "Water!" he roared as he careened toward the falls. He knelt down, cupped his hands, and filled them with the crystal-clear liquid, gulping large handfuls, oblivious to his surroundings.

A sharp pain on the side of his face and something warm running down his cheek caused the precious water to spill from his hands. "No!" he shouted as he strained forward, desperate for another handful of water. A second blow, this time to his cheek, made him stop. He rose from the ground, choking and gagging, and the cool clear water dissolved into a brown, stagnant puddle of muck on the side of the road.

Hours later the gates to Camp O'Donnell came into view and his face lit up. *They gotta have water, and maybe even food. They just gotta.*

30

May 27, 1942

Camp O'Donnell

Bataan Peninsula, The Philippines

Tommie opened his eyes and squinted into the merciless tropical sun. His skin throbbed from layer upon layer of blisters and peeling epidermis. Blood caked the side of his face, and the putrid smell of diarrhea filled the air. A continual stream of shit ran down his leg onto the ground. Endless cramps stabbed at his belly. He raised his arm in a feeble attempt to shield his eyes from the sun; he squinted at an image in the distance. His vision cleared, and he relaxed as he took in the silhouette of a woman standing under a palm tree. "My dear, darling Dorothy," he whispered.

DOROTHY CAME CLOSER and smiled down at Tommie, who lay sprawled on the ground. "Come on, honey. Let's go for a walk along the beach."

A smile crossed his parched lips. "I must be the luckiest man alive." He filled his lungs with the fresh, salty air. As her hand touched his, a sudden surge of power filled his body. He rose and ran down the beach, his renewed strength mounting with each step.

HE AWAKENED WITH a start. Maggots swarmed over his body and what was left of his pants, now covered in excrement. Blood oozed from his rectum. The stench of death filled his nostrils.

A tear tried to form, but no fluid of any sort remained in his body.

He closed his eyes. The relentless cramping began to subside; no need to struggle; no need to breathe any longer, no need to do anything but find Dorothy on the beach.

DOROTHY CAUGHT UP with him and pulled him down onto the sand. She rolled him over and lay down on top of him. "I love you," she said. He smelled her perfume, felt her gentle touch.

"I love you too, Dottie."

Dorothy pushed him away and ran back into the surf. He rose and followed.

"Dottie, wait up, will ya?"

Part 2

31

May 1942
Camp Blanding, Florida

Lewis twisted the throttle, and the motorcycle responded with a deep rumble. "Hey, buddy, wanna take it for a spin?" Lewis was the only Texan in a barracks full of Texans whom Smitty cared to talk to.

"Oh, big-shot corporal with your motorcycle. What if the sergeant catches you usin' it for somethin' other than official business? You'll get your Texas ass kicked."

"Don't worry about the sarge. He doesn't care." Lewis's six-foot-four-inch frame and massive physique predisposed the sergeant toward an attitude of leniency. "Y'all wanna try it, or not?"

"Hell, yes, I wanna try it. Are you serious? I'm gonna get me one, one of these days."

"Well, 'one of these days' is now. Give this one a whirl."

Smitty jumped on, opened the throttle, and took off. The unadulterated pleasure of such a magnificent machine under his absolute control mesmerized him. "God, but I do love it!"

He shifted and opened the throttle. The speedometer read 50. "This is what I wanna do for the rest of my life!"

The road became a black line; the landscape blurred. He threw his head back and yelled at the top of his lungs. The cool breeze coming off Kingsley Lake slapped at his face as it rushed by. He goosed the throttle again, and the speedometer climbed to 55.

He beheld the open road, and it led straight to California. The machine he controlled transformed from an army-issue olive drab motorcycle into a cherry-red Indian Scout. The speedometer leapt past 60.

The startling clamor of the cycle's chain breaking and wrapping itself around the rear tire shattered his reverie. The rear tire fantailed wildly first one way and then another.

"What the fuck!" His mind raced; his thoughts concentrated on what he had to do in that second and the next and the next in order to survive. Smitty held on, resolute in his effort to regain control of the bike and unwavering in his decision that his life would not end on that day, on that road.

He willed the cycle to a stop but continued gripping the handlebars until he awoke to the severe cramping in his fingers. He scrambled to dismount, clutching his thighs in a struggle to control his wobbling legs. A Gene Krupa drum solo pounded in his chest as he fought the urge to puke. He fumbled for a cigarette, lighting it with trembling hands and sucking the smoke deep into his lungs. The nicotine surged through his blood, and he began the arduous task of manhandling the motorcycle back to the base.

Walking along the road, reliving his fleeting adventure again and again, a sense of giddiness began working its way up through his body. A snicker soon turned into a chuckle, which quickly morphed into laughter that left him gasping for breath. He dropped the cycle.

"I'm alive!" he yelled, hands raised to the sky. "What a ride! What an amazing goddamned ride!"

STEAM FROM THE heat of the day permeated the tent barracks and fused with the sweat of fifteen GIs sitting around with nothing to do. An unrelenting drizzle seeped through the roof. Smitty took a long drag on his cigarette in an attempt to calm his still-trembling hand.

"Hey, man, you look a little green. Motorcycle too much for ya?"

"Lewis! Man, am I glad to see you. I'm sorry about the motorcycle. I guess I just got a little carried away. I think I fixed it, though. Did you get in trouble?"

"Nah, you fixed it better 'n new. Yer somethin' else when it comes to fixin' machines, but you do look a little green. What's up?"

"It's this damned tent! All I can see is green. Green tents, green uniforms, green cots. And the damned rain, it never stops. That on top of the heat. I've never sweated so much in my life. I'm about to go nuts! If I have to sit here another minute, just starin' at all this green and all these damned Tex—never mind. It's all just gettin' to me. Course, it probably doesn't help that I pert near killed myself on that damned cycle of yours. I'm just feelin' a little wacky, that's all."

"Well, let's go over to the service club. We can write our girls over there."

"Wish I'd thought of that an hour ago!"

"Well, buddy, it's tough to think of things when your brains get left out there with the motorcycle."

"I wish I coulda just kept goin'."

"Little hard with a broken chain. Anyway, I'm glad you came back. Not that I would of missed yer ass, but I might of had a problem explainin' to the sarge what happened to his motorcycle."

They headed out the door, holding their army-issue stationery under their rain ponchos, running double time toward the service club.

SMITTY SURVEYED THE scene. Tables and chairs surrounded a large black and white tiled dance floor. An "OPEN" sign sat atop a spotless red counter at a small café near the entrance. On the opposite wall, a jitterbug tune blared over the speakers of a jukebox.

"Now, *this* is more like it." he said. "Let's get a Coca-Cola. We can pretend it's beer. It'll help us write prettier to our girls."

The jitterbug ended, and "I Remember You" started playing:

> "I remember you,
> You're the one who made my dreams come true,
> A few kisses ago..."

They found a table and smoothed the damp stationery in front of them. Smitty began to write:

My Darling Dorothy,

My buddy Lewis and me are sitting in the service club. Lewis is from Texas. He has the darndest accent. Nice guy, for a Texan. He's a big football player in his hometown, and he makes me look like some sort of skinny kid.

You won't believe what I did today. Lewis let me ride on his motorcycle. I do love those machines. They are a real thrill.

Hey, they're playing I Remember You on the jukebox. It's making me a little homesick for you. You want to know how I feel about you, well, just listen to this song while you read my letter...

The crooner continued:

"I remember you,
You're the one who said
'I love you, too,' I do,
Didn't you know?
I remember too,
A distant bell
And stars that fell like rain
Out of the blue."

Smitty lit a cigarette and blew smoke rings as his mind drifted back to the motorcycle ride.

"HOLD ON TIGHT, darlin'; here we go!"
Smitty opened the throttle, and the motorcy-
cle reciprocated with a thundering rumble,
something Smitty never tired of hearing.

Dorothy wrapped her arms around him
and threw her head back, laughing, "This is
a gas! Let's just keep going forever!"

"That's the idea, baby. We'll keep going
until we reach California, and then we'll ride
it right onto the beach. Just you and me—
that's all that matters."

TORRENTIAL RAIN BEAT against the metal roof of the service club, like a freight train roaring overhead. Smitty began to hum along with the jukebox:

> "When my life is through
> And the angels ask me to recall
> The thrill of them all,
> Then I will tell them
> I remember you."

He took another drag on his cigarette. "When my life is through," he whispered, reliving the day's events. "When my life is through," he repeated, as his ambiguous future, something he tried hard to ignore, lurked in the shadows. He continued writing:

> You only live once and I am going to live it
> up while I can. I'm going to buy a motorcycle
> as soon as I get out of this damned army and

> go all the way to California and then on from
> there. I'll take you with me if you'll come and
> we'll have a grand time.

A sense of urgency swept over him as he wrote out the last lines of his letter.

> You know I love you, don't you? I want you
> to marry me. I know you are engaged to that
> other guy, but you loved me first, remember?
> Please say yes.
>   All My Love,
>   Smitty

He stuffed the letter into an envelope, slapped on a stamp, and wrote the address in a hand that only an experienced postman could decipher. "I remember you," he sang, knocking over his chair as he flew toward the front door of the service club.

"Hey, buddy, where ya goin'? It's rainin' cats and dogs out there. Can't it wait?" Lewis asked, perplexed at Smitty's abrupt departure.

"No, it can't wait!" Smitty bolted out the door, holding the letter inside his rain poncho and sprinting all the way to the mailbox. He shoved the letter through the slot.

I've waited too long. I can't wait anymore.

DOROTHY TRIPPED OVER a rise in the sidewalk and dropped the letter.

Carol caught Dorothy's arm. "Careful! What did he say

that got you so flustered?"

Dorothy made a frenzied attempt to pick up the pages. "I think he said that he loves me and he wants to marry me, and he'll take me to California on a motorcycle..."

"Whoa! Slow down, honey. He wants to marry you?"

Dorothy held a page of the letter up in the air. "Here, read it for yourself. Isn't that what he said?"

Carol began reading the letter and then stopped. "Oh my God! He *did* say it. What are you going to do?"

Dorothy mulled over the question for a moment. "I don't know. It's so fast. I mean I just sent a 'Dear John' letter to Tommie six months ago. I thought I was going to work in Lincoln, a free woman, not tied down to anything. Now, here I am, new job dissolved into thin air and the man that I have loved since that dance six years ago is asking me to marry him and I'm hesitating." She threw her arms into the air. "What's wrong with me?" she asked the heavens.

A PRICKLING SENSATION ran down Smitty's spine as he read Dorothy's letter.

> Dear Smitty,
>
> Your letter really caught me by surprise! I never expected a proposal from you, at least not this fast.
>
> I never told you, but I sent a "Dear John" letter to Tommie in November, but it was returned as undeliverable after Pearl Harbor.
>
> You know he came along after you left, and

he loved me and I wanted to love him back. But I knew in my heart there really was only one guy for me, and that was you.

You hurt me pretty bad, though. Now, I'm a little scared to trust you again. I want to, but it's going to take awhile.

I also don't want to rush into anything again and hurt you like I hurt Tommie or like you hurt me. I need to be absolutely sure. Just give me a little time.

I do love that you want to take me with you to California, but not on a motorcycle. I think an Airstream trailer would be a better idea, don't you? I'm sure it's just as much fun as a silly old motorcycle.

Love,

Dorothy

His thoughts came in rapid succession:

It's happening all over again. I can't hold onto anything: a crop, a job, the woman I love. Fuck this. I may be dead in a few months. I'm not gonna waste my time worrying.

He threw the letter onto his cot and lit a cigarette.

"Hey, Lewis, you goin' to the dance tonight?"

"Wouldn't miss it. How 'bout you?" Lewis drawled.

"Damned straight! Come on. There's never enough women to go around, so let's go before anybody else gets there."

SMITTY SURVEYED THE dance hall scene. "Guess we weren't the only ones who thought of coming early, huh?" Young women stood against the walls, and a line of GIs stretched around the room and out the side door. The jukebox began to play "You and I."

He scanned the line of eligible dance partners, sauntered across the floor, and took the hand of the first petite brunette he saw. "How about a dance?"

"Sure." He took her into his arms with expert skill and slipped into the crowd of dancers.

"You're almost as good a dancer as my husband."

"Your *husband?* What the hell are you doin' here?"

"He's already overseas. I come here because I get lonely, and it seems like the patriotic thing to do, ya know?"

"Sure," Smitty lied.

The music stopped and started again with a jitterbug. Smitty continued to hold her in his arms. "What's your name anyway?"

"Deborah, but everybody calls me Debbie."

"OK, Debbie, can I walk you home after the dance? It's not too safe out there, ya know?"

"How thoughtful. I would love that."

SMITTY AND DEBBIE strolled toward her house. As they neared the front door, she stopped.

"Thank you so much for walking me home. You're a great dancer. Some girl is going to be mighty lucky."

Smitty grinned and leaned forward, putting his arm around her. She pushed him away. "I'm married, remember?

I never meant for you to get the idea that..."

Smitty blinked. "Of course, of course. I get it. Sorry. Good night." He walked away clenching his jaw.

Back at the barracks, he cornered Lewis. "Wouldn't ya know I would end up with a married woman who wants to stay loyal to her old man."

"Well, I'll be. Even the infamous Smitty couldn't break through, huh?"

"Ah, shut up, ya big ape." He picked up a magazine and threw it to Lewis. "Look at this article. It's all about all the bad girls in Boston. How about you and me go check 'em out when we get to Camp Edwards?"

32

Beaver City

Dorothy propped her pillow against the headboard and began reading Smitty's latest letter, her eyes growing heavier the farther she read.

> Darling Dorothy,
>
> I understand why you don't trust me, but just remember all the dreams we had. They can still happen. You and me together, just like we planned. Remember?
>
> You just wait until you sit on a motorcycle. You'll change your mind I guarantee it. It'll be a gas. Anyway, you worry too much. No sense worrying. You know my motto, you only live once so let's do it up right.

An Airstream trailer is for fuddy duddys or people with kids. We won't be old or having kids any time soon. We will be having too much fun cycling around the country, without a worry to our names...

"TOMMIE! YOU'RE ALIVE! Why didn't you write me?"

"Does it matter, honey? I'm back." *Tommie intertwined his hand with her right hand. "Come on. Let's run down the beach together."*

"But, Tommie, I have something to tell you. I wrote you a letter..."

Tommie held on tightly, pulling her forward. "Come on! Let's go!"

Smitty took Dorothy's left hand and began tugging her in the opposite direction, toward his motorcycle. "Hey, Peaches, don't go with him. Come on. You and I can have some fun."

Dorothy's arms stretched like rubber bands. Her chest began to ache as her skin split.

"STOP!" THE LETTER fell to the floor, and her breaths came in shallow, rapid succession. The sheets on her bed were drenched in sweat.

"Stop!"

Frank stood in the doorway of her bedroom. "Dorothy, honey, what's going on?"

"Just a bad dream, Pa. I'm fine."

"You've had an awful lot of those lately. Maybe you should see Doc Olson tomorrow."

"No, Pa. I'm fine. Go back to bed."

"Suit yourself."

Dorothy waited for her father to close the door and then knelt at the side of her bed. She folded her hands and bowed her head. "Ma, it's me again."

SHE AWOKE IN the morning on the floor beside her bed. Ambling her way to the bureau, she sank onto the chair and began brushing her hair while scrutinizing her reflection in the mirror.

"Guess I have to figure this one out on my own, huh, Ma?"

An irresistible urge to rearrange the bedroom furniture came over her. She put on an old housedress and started surveying the room. It seemed imperative that the bureau and the chest of drawers switch places. She tugged on her bureau, jerking it forward. A crumpled wad of paper at the back of the bureau caught her eye. Curious, she picked it up and unfolded it. Like a squall that begins as a soft spring breeze wafting its way through the leaves of a cottonwood tree, the recognition of what she held in her hands left her dumbfounded. She turned the wine label over and read the words: "Our first kiss." The memory of that night—every touch, every word, every dream they had shared, vibrant and alive.

She walked to her hope chest and lifted out her box of keepsakes. Tommie's photo lay on top. She touched his cheek in the photo, lingering for a moment before she smoothed out the wine label, placed it on top of the photo, and closed the lid.

33

Boston, Massachusetts

Smitty and Lewis bolted off the train and entered Boston's South Station. "Hot damned!" Smitty exclaimed. "Where the hell did all these people come from? Look at 'em! And, look at that floor. It's marble, ain't it? Sorta like the post office back home, but we never had anything so fancy as this place."

Lewis furrowed his brow. "Hey, you hick. Keep your mouth shut! We don't want anyone to know this is our first time in a big city."

"I can't help it. Look at those big windows. Hey, there's a place to buy candy bars. Let's get some." Before Lewis could protest, Smitty was across the terminal, snagging a Butterfinger from a kiosk.

"Candy? We didn't come to Boston on our first leave to

buy goddamned candy bars! Remember, we are here for a *different* kind of sweet stuff." Lewis winked at Smitty.

"We'll get to it; don't worry. They say those bad girls are everywhere—at least that's what the magazine said. Hey, let's ride on one of them streetcars. We sure don't have anything like that back home."

Lewis ran after Smitty. "Slow down, buddy. I can't keep up with you!"

SMITTY HELD ONTO the ceiling strap of the streetcar. "Here we go!"

A young woman stepped in front of him. Her perfume smelled exotic and earthy, and it captivated Smitty. He took her in—from her brunette hair layered in curls on top of her head to her eyes made even greener by the dress she wore that flowed over her perfect body. Her eyes were filled with mischief. "New to Boston?" she asked.

"Sure am. Bet you ain't. I can tell by your accent."

"I've lived here my whole life. Want the grand tour?"

"Sure! I'd love it. What's your name?"

"Sarah. You're not Errol Flynn by any chance?"

"Could be. What's it worth to ya?"

"Hmm. Well, we'll see. Should I just call you Errol, or do you prefer Mr. Flynn?" she asked, continuing the flirtatious banter.

"No, baby. You can call me Jack, but most people call me Smitty."

"Smitty it is then. Let's get off here."

"Got any friends for my pal, here?"

Sarah narrowed her eyes. "I'm not a dating service, Smitty. Now come on. Let's go."

Smitty waved to Lewis. "Hate to ditch ya, buddy. Hope your luck's as good as mine."

SMITTY AND SARAH walked together down Washington Street. "So, when do you leave for the war?" Sarah asked.

Smitty frowned. "I don't know, and no sense worryin' about it. I'm here to have a good time and live it up." He grinned and winked. "You don't happen to be one of them bad girls I read about by any chance?"

Sarah hesitated, taking in this soldier's strength, good looks and that mischievous grin. "I guess time will tell."

"That's good enough for me. Hey, do you know how to dance? I'm pretty good. I'll take you wherever you wanna go. Oh boy! What's that building?"

"Settle down, soldier boy. That's called the Old State House. It's been around since the 1700s. See that balcony? That's where the Declaration of Independence was read to Boston citizens in 1776. Lots of other historical things happened here too. Ever heard of the Boston Massacre?"

"Sarah, I can hardly understand a word yer sayin', and I don't know much about history, so let's just *look* at the building. What else is there to see anyway?"

"Surely you know about Paul Revere, right? Everybody's heard of him."

"Hell, yes, I know about him. I'm not dumb, ya know."

"Wanna see where he warned everyone about the coming of the British troops?"

Smitty shrugged. "Sure, Sarah, I'll go wherever you take me. There's so much going on here, people everywhere. Where the hell are they all going anyway? Look at all the shops and the cars. I can't get over it."

"Just how small a town are you from?"

"Let's just say it's in the boondocks, and nobody back there could even begin to imagine this. I mean, get a load of this place!"

"Well, let's just make sure you get your money's worth, shall we?"

SARAH LOOKED AT her watch. "Getting tired of riding the streetcars yet?"

"No, unless there are more elevators we can ride."

"I hope you're kidding. We've ridden this streetcar for well over fifteen miles today. I think it's time for a different kind of entertainment."

"So, you are one of those bad girls I read about. What did you have in mind, doll?" He winked at her.

"You said you were a good dancer. Wanna see what a big city dance hall is like?"

"Hell, yes, let's go!"

They walked down Piedmont Street. Sarah stopped in front of a nightclub where people were shuffling in and out with the regularity of city traffic.

"It is *the* place to be in Boston if you wanna dance, especially on a hot Saturday night. They have a rooftop dance floor! Come on, my treat."

"Sarah, you've done enough. I can't..."

"Hey, you're about to leave to go to war. I'm not sure about giving you everything you want, but I *can* give you this. Besides, you said you were a good dancer. Prove it!"

They entered the lobby. Fake palm trees lined the walls of the first floor. Smitty gawked at the scenery. "Hey, this is like the tropics! This is somethin'."

Sarah pointed to a stairway. "Wait till you see the upstairs."

Smitty took the last step onto the rooftop. "Oh, boy! I can't believe what I'm seein'! Look at all the lights. There's more lights up here than in the entire state of Nebraska!"

Sarah snickered. "You *are* a small-town boy. Come on. Show me those dance steps you've been bragging about."

Smitty took Sarah in his arms and glided across the dance floor as the singer crooned,

> "At last, my love has come along,
>
> My lonely days are over,
>
> And life is like a song."

Smitty's chest tightened.

> "At last, the skies above are blue,
>
> My heart was wrapped up in clover,
>
> The night I looked at you."

He pulled Sarah closer. "Nice song, huh?"

"One of my favorites." She began to sing along:

> "I found a dream that I could speak to,
>
> A dream that I could call my own."

Smitty stopped dancing. "I think I need to call it a night. Thanks for everything, Sarah. You're a swell gal." He leaned over and kissed her. She began to wrap her arms around his neck.

"I gotta go," he said backing away from her.

"You do what you gotta do, Smitty, but if you're ever in Boston again, look me up. I'm usually here on Friday and Saturday nights."

Smitty wandered back to the train station, his thoughts churning along with his gut.

34

Beaver City

Dearest Smitty,

Honey, I've made up my mind. I do want to marry you, and the sooner the better. I just needed some time to sort things out, but I'm sure now!

"Here's your m-mail, sis," Walter interrupted. "Got another letter from Smitty," he grinned, holding the letter just out of Dorothy's reach.

"OK, snoopy, hand it over!" She snatched the envelope out of Walter's hand and tore it open, anxious to read its contents. She had not heard from Smitty in two weeks.

Darling Dorothy,

Say, Honey, got three letters from you all in one day. Just the way I like it. Keep the good work up. I guess the reason I got all them today was I wasn't here this weekend. They told us we weren't getting another week end off till the 15th so thought I better take it while I had a chance. Went to Boston. I saw the most interesting things.

I rode streetcars and elevators, something I never did before. Quite a thrill. Rode 15 miles Saturday night on twenty cents, cheap enough, huh?

The reason I like to go to Boston is to see those bad girls of Boston. I read about them in the last picture magazine. They're really the hot stuff. Ha Ha

I guess you know me well enough to know I'm no angel when I go to town, hardly ever sit around and twiddle my thumbs. I didn't meet any bad girls. I did meet a very nice girl up there. She showed me all over town, and took me to a dance Saturday night. I have met lots of nice girls and some bad ones too, but there still is just one that I care to marry and you know who that is. I think it's all right to have friends wherever you go as long as it don't go too far. I want you to get out and do the same, for god sake don't sit around home and worry. We can only live this life once and we will never get anywhere worrying. Honey, I hope you don't mind me going with girls as long as they're decent, now tell me the truth, do you? I don't care if you go with guys as long as you keep your place and I am quite sure that you are one girl I can trust, since I have known you so long.

Will write more later.

Loads of Love

Smitty

Dorothy threw the letter on the floor, picked up the letter she had started and tore it into tiny pieces, each tear ripping at her heart.

35

Camp Edwards, Massachusetts

Dear Smitty,

You ask me to marry you and then you tell me to date other people. Don't you get it? You are starting to act like you did five years ago. Please don't do this to me again. Make up your mind, once and for all. Is it me you want or is it bad girls in Boston?

He stopped reading and crushed the letter in his hands until it became a small ball. He threw it across the room and walked out the barracks door. *I wonder what Sarah's doin' this weekend.*

Boston

Smitty took the stairs two at a time to the roof of the nightclub. In an instant he spotted Sarah, her back turned toward him. She wore a royal blue dress that clung to her body. *I'd know that body anywhere,* he thought as he walked up behind her. "Hey, baby, how about a dance?"

"Smitty! I knew you'd come back. You missed me, now, didn't you?" The band began to play "Moonlight Serenade." She winked at him. "Just my kind of song."

She melted into his arms. He closed his eyes, leaning his cheek against her head. Her silky hair brushed against him, and the musky smell of her perfume sealed his fate.

"Can we get out of here, Sarah?"

"Sure. Follow me." She gripped his hand and led him down the stairs and out the front door. They walked in silence down the street. She stopped outside a closed storefront and motioned him to follow her. They embraced and she parted his lips with her tongue. She explored his mouth for just a moment before he stopped her.

"Where did you learn to do that?" he asked, confused about what had just happened.

"Like it?"

"Well, let's try it again and I'll let you know."

"It's called a French kiss and it's just one of the things I can teach you," she purred. She touched the tip of her tongue to his lips. "Come on, let's go to my place. It's just around the corner from here." She took off down the street, leaving him in the doorway, week-kneed and trying to catch his breath.

SMITTY LAY ON his back in Sarah's bed. He lit a cigarette, inhaled, and handed it to her. "You are one helluva woman, Sarah. One helluva woman. I was so damned confused when I came down here. But now everything seems clear."

She took a drag from his cigarette. "You certainly didn't seem confused when you lured me into bed two days ago. You seemed so sure of what you wanted and how you wanted it." She pushed him onto his back and sat on top of him. "So what exactly were you so confused about?"

"Jesus, woman, you are somethin' else! I do have to get back to the base sometime today, ya know. Ain't you had enough?"

"No, Smitty, it's '*Haven't* you had enough,' not 'Ain't you had enough.' "

"Whatever you say, baby. So, *ain't* it time for me to go?"

"Moonlight Cocktail" played on the radio. Sarah sang along, rotating her hips in time to the music. Her breasts slid over his chest as she leaned forward and began to kiss his neck. "Hey, sweetie, I asked you a question. What is so confusing? You have a girl back home?"

"Shh. We have time for one more..."

"So that's it, isn't it? A girl back home. A cute little farm girl. Does she do this for you?" She continued to rotate her hips on top of him.

"No," he groaned as he rolled over and lay on top of her. "No, she doesn't—not even close."

"I didn't think so. Now just relax and enjoy."

SARAH AWOKE TO the sounds of Smitty in the shower. She joined him. "Do you have to go back today, sweetie?"

"I do, baby, but I'll be back next weekend for sure. Give me your phone number, and I'll call you when I can." He washed her hair and rubbed soap over her voluptuous body. "Ever been on a motorcycle?"

He handed her the soap. She rubbed it over his chest. "Many times. I love the freedom. You have a motorcycle?"

"Well, sort of. I'm plannin' on ridin' one from one end of this country to the other. What do you think of that?"

"Is that an invitation, soldier?"

"Sort of, well—yeah, it is, baby, it is. Sure you wouldn't prefer an Airstream trailer? You know, they're pretty nice."

"An Airstream trailer? I think you are a lot like me. You like to live just a little on the wild side, right? So why settle for an Airstream trailer? A motorcycle fits who we are, sweetie. Where do you want to go first? My folks have a place in Florida. Ever been there?"

The lather ran down Sarah's body. Smitty put two fingers over her mouth. "Shh, baby, let me just look at you one last time before I have to leave."

She licked his fingers and backed away. "Take a good look, Smitty, and know that I don't care that you have a girl back home. I'm here, totally here, and I'm yours to do with as you please, and when you're ready to get on that motorcycle and go, just let me know."

She curled her legs around him, and they made love one last time while the shower rinsed them clean.

36

Camp Edwards

Dearest Dorothy,

Sorry I haven't written lately. I've been pretty sick. Not much to tell you about. Just the same thing day after day. I've been enjoying Boston as much as I can.

Lewis walked into the barracks. Smitty put his letter aside. "Hey, buddy, how about another weekend with that motorcycle?"

Lewis balked. "You and Sarah have been thick as thieves for goin' on three weeks now. What about that little doll back home you wanted to marry so bad?"

"What about her? I'm writin' her a letter right now. Satisfied?"

"Tellin' her all about Boston, are ya?"

"Fuck off! It's none of your goddamned business what I write or what I do, is it? Now, can I have the damned motorcycle or not?"

"All I'm sayin' is that you can't keep burnin' the candle at both ends, man. Somebody's gonna get hurt."

SARAH ANSWERED THE door naked, her bewitching green eyes a bottomless pit of seduction.

"Jesus, Sarah. What if it hadn't been me?"

"It's hard for somebody on a motorcycle to sneak up on me. Besides, I know your knock," she said with a grin, kissing his neck, his mouth, his chest and shutting the door.

He picked her up and carried her to the bed. They made love far into the night and early morning, stopping only for a cigarette now and then.

Sarah sat up and put on her robe. "Well, what do you want to do now?"

Smitty wavered. "I'm broke, baby. I can't take you dancin' or out to dinner. We better call it a day."

"OK, let's just get on your motorcycle and ride for a while."

SARAH CLIMBED ON the cycle and pressed against his back. She wrapped her arms around him and began to massage his chest, working her way downward.

Smitty threw his head back and groaned. "Don't move those hands, baby. You are in for the ride of your life!"

They worked their way to Highway 3 and then took a side road with less traffic. Smitty slowed down. Sarah yelled over the roar of the motor, "You drive this thing just like you drive me, sweetie! Nice and smooth!"

He sped up. "I know! I love it almost as much as I love you!"

"What did you say?"

"Nothin', baby! I didn't say anything worth repeating!"

"There's a bar about a mile up the road! Let's stop there for dinner!"

"Baby, I told you, I don't have any money."

"Doesn't matter whether you have any money or not, sweetie. I'm loaded."

THEY FOUND A secluded table. Smitty signaled the waitress. "Bring us some beers, honey."

Sarah put her hand up. "No, wait." She studied the menu. "No beers. We would like a bottle of Cabernet."

"Wine, huh? Ain't you the ritzy one?"

"You better get used to it. It's how I live. Wine instead of beer. Steaks instead of fried chicken, and 'aren't' instead of 'ain't.'"

"You think you're gonna change me, do ya?"

"Smitty, I heard what you said on the bike. You said you loved me. Did you mean it? Are you falling for me?"

"Hell, Sarah, I don't know. It just sorta slipped outta my mouth. I have trouble thinkin' straight when I'm around you."

"It's all right. I'm finding it harder and harder to see you leave at the end of our weekends. I don't know what it means, but let's not rush things."

"Hell, yes, let's not rush things for sure."

"So, what about that girl back home?"

"I don't wanna talk about her, Sarah. This is *our* time." He put his hand on her knee, massaging his way up to her thigh and beyond, never taking his eyes off hers. "We got a whole Labor Day weekend ahead of us. Let's just enjoy the moment."

She sighed. "That's the plan, sweetie, but if you don't stop that right now, we're going to have to go home without dinner." She caressed his thigh and continued gazing into his eyes. "By the way, my friends are throwing a big party tomorrow night. I would love to go and show you off. Are you game?"

"Game for what?" He slid his hand between her legs. She stifled a groan and moved her hand further up his thigh.

"You know you're making it hard for me to think straight," she whispered, continuing her ascent. "Maybe we'd better stop."

"No, don't stop, baby. I'll go anywhere you say, just don't stop."

SARAH MADE A grand gesture with her arm. "Everybody, this is Smitty, the guy I've been telling you about. Smitty, this is everybody."

He didn't move. "This is some swanky place you got here."

"It belongs to Brenda. She's a trust fund baby like me."

"A what?"

Sarah smiled. "She's filthy rich. Be nice to her."

A willowy blonde woman approached. "Oh, speak of the devil. Smitty, this is Brenda. He was just admiring your lovely abode."

"Well, you just look all you want, Smitty. Sarah, you didn't do him justice with your description. He's gorgeous. Now let's see if she told the truth about your dancing, dreamboat."

He faltered, still dumbstruck by the lavish surroundings. Sarah gave him a shove. "She won't bite. Go dance with her."

Brenda drew Smitty to her. "So, I hear you are quite good at a lot of things."

"That ain't necessarily so, ma'am. I'm good at ridin' motorcycles and fixin' cars, and I'm a damned good dancer, but that's about it."

" 'Ain't'? You are so quaint." Brenda winked. "Well, you're right about one thing—you can dance like a pro. Come on—hold me like you hold Sarah. You know she and I share a lot of things. We're extremely close."

Sarah tapped Brenda's shoulder. "That's all you get, Brenda. We are *not* sharing this."

"You mean we 'ain't' sharing this?" Brenda smirked as she walked away. Smitty started to protest, but Sarah intervened.

"Calm down, sweetie. She's just kidding around. That's what she does. Come on, I want you to meet the boys. They're nicer than Brenda, and they've been my friends forever. You'll love them. Smitty, meet Brian, Jeffrey, and Anthony. Boys, this is Smitty. Keep him company while I go powder my nose, and be nice."

They all watched Sarah disappear around the corner, taking in her sensual way of gliding across the room, her hips moving ever-so-slightly to and fro under her silk skirt, just enough to arouse every male in the room.

Brian raised his glass, spilling half its contents on the carpet. "Here's to the most beautiful woman in the room and to the man who has captured her fancy—this week, anyway," he laughed. "So, Smitty, Sarah tells us you're from Nebraska. I thought all they had there were hick farmers," he continued in a slurred, drunk-induced voice.

"Well, I'm a farmer, but I ain't no hick; so watch yourself."

Anthony snickered. "Oh you ain't, ain't you? Well, where did you go to school?" he asked, guzzling his drink and tipping the glass back to get the last drop.

"Hollinger, cuz it's close to the farm."

"Hollinger?" Jeffrey chimed in. "Never heard of it. Is it one of those elite liberal arts colleges that are so prevalent in Nebraska?" He gripped Anthony's shoulder to hold himself up and bent over laughing at his own joke.

Smitty considered his options. "Think I'll go find Sarah."

Better that, he thought, *than starting a brawl with a bunch of drunken, snooty bastards like these guys.*

"Ain't mad at us, are ya? Don't go tellin' yer *pa* on us," Brian yelled across the room.

Smitty clenched his fist and started back toward the group when Sarah appeared from around the corner. She kissed his cheek, oblivious to his frame of mind.

"Let's go get some hors d'oeuvres. I'm starving after all our escapades."

"Some what?"

"Hors d'oeuvres, sweetie—you know, fancy little foods you eat at a party or before dinner."

"Well, what's an escapade? Is that somethin' we're gonna eat?"

"You have so much to learn, but I'm a great teacher." She winked. "But then, you already know that, don't you?" She began to rub his chest.

"Sarah, don't, not in front of your friends. Come on."

"Are you serious? We're in Boston, Smitty, not some backwater town in Nebraska."

He pushed her away and headed for the door. "Fuck you, and fuck your swanky asshole friends too!"

"Hey, what's got you all riled up? What happened?"

Smitty walked out the front door with Sarah close behind. "Oh, sweetie, don't be mad. Come on, we don't need to stay here around all these petty jerks. Let's go to my place."

"No, Sarah, this ain't gonna work. We're too different, you and me."

"Oh, sweetie, just one more kiss, and then I'll let you go. I promise."

SARAH WALKED NAKED around the bedroom, picking up Smitty's clothes. "So, when will I see you again?"

"I don't know, baby—soon I hope, very soon."

Her breasts bounced as she leaned over to pick up his pants while Smitty watched. "Jesus, Sarah, you sure make it hard for a guy to stay mad."

She handed him his clothes and then walked to the window. "Look at that cloud. It looks like a squirrel, and he's got a nut he's holding. Don't you just love clouds? Come take a look at it."

He stopped putting on his shirt and stood motionless, staring at her. "Stop looking at the damned clouds, woman!" The angry sound of his voice confused him. He pulled on his pants, trying to regain his composure.

"What's the matter with you? I thought after last night I was forgiven for my vulgar friends and my stupid comment."

"You're forgiven, baby. I forgave you after round two—or was it three? Just stop lookin' at the damned clouds!"

"So, what do you have against clouds?"

"Sarah! Enough about clouds. Just come here and give me one last kiss before I go."

She sauntered across the room, allowing him to fully appreciate her naked body. She leaned into him and began buttoning his shirt, kissing his chest above each button. He closed his eyes, relishing the seductive pleasure of her touch. He didn't stop her when she reversed the process and began to unbutton his shirt. Nor did he protest when she unzipped his trousers and yanked them off. Unable to stand for another moment, he flopped onto the couch bringing her with him, kissing first one breast, then the other. "Oh, Dottie, I..."

Sarah sat up. "Dottie?" She shoved him away and marched to the window. "You know, I told you I didn't care if you had a girl back home, but I never expected you to call me her name while I'm kissing you and you're holding my breast in your hand. We just spent three days together, three wonderful days. You son of a bitch! You even said you loved me!"

Smitty hurriedly put on his pants and shirt. "Sarah, please. She's the girl back home, but she's nobody. I wanna stay here with you, ride my motorcycle, sleep in your bed. I didn't mean it, honey. It was just a slip of the tongue."

"Right, just a slip of the tongue. Get out of here! Now!" She threw his shoes at him and pushed him out the door, flinging the motorcycle keys at his head.

37

Beaver City

Carol massaged Dorothy's shoulders. "Still not sleeping, huh? Did you check the mailbox today? Maybe this'll be the day."

"Not a word in over a month. Nothing. He talked about touring Boston with some girl. As a matter of fact, he writes about Boston all the time. Why do I let him do this to me?"

"Well, in all fairness, he is a free man. You haven't given him a final answer yet, have you?"

"Don't start. You know you're not my mother, Carol."

"But I am your best friend. Come on, let's go check the mail."

DOROTHY CLIMBED THE stairs to the post office and handed her mailbox key to Carol. "You check. I don't think I can handle another disappointment."

Carol took the key and disappeared through the door, leaving Dorothy sitting on the steps, holding her head with both hands, waiting for the verdict. Would it be another day with no answer to her question or would this be the day of resolution?

Carol flung the door open, letter in hand. Dorothy snatched the letter out of her hand, tore it open, and read:

> Dearest Dorothy,
>
> I'm sorry I haven't written in so long. I've been sort of sick, but I'm better now. Much better. I've had a lot of time to think about us, about our future, and I have a surprise for you. I am sending you an engagement ring. I know you said you weren't sure, that you didn't trust me, and I don't blame you, but I'm sending it anyway. You asked me to choose and I choose you. Honey, I love you and nobody else. No more fooling around either. I hope you aren't. Time for that has passed. Now it's just you and me.
>
> All My Love,
> Smitty

Dorothy sobbed, wiping her tears away with a page of the letter.

Carol's eyes turned steely gray. "Oh no, honey, I was

afraid of this. He broke up with you, didn't he? That bastard! I didn't want to tell you what I thought, but he's a no good son of a..."

"Stop right there. He's sending me an engagement ring!"

"A what?"

FRANK PEEKED OVER Dorothy's shoulder. "Is that a letter from Smitty?"

"Yes, it is, and this is probably as good a time as any to tell you the news. He's sending me an engagement ring, Pa. It should be here anytime now. What do you think of that?"

"Sorta fast, isn't it? I mean, Tommie and all..."

"You're right, it is fast, but I've given it a lot of careful thought. He asked me to marry him four months ago, and, believe it or not, I didn't just answer yes right away. I do love him, I know that, but I had to learn to trust him again after what he did six years ago. I don't know why, but I do trust him. He and I, we think alike. We both want to travel, see the world. He even supported me when I thought I was going to move to Lincoln."

"He did?" Frank asked, surprised that any man would support such a bold move. "Well, I guess he *does* understand you. Okay, if he makes you happy, that's all I care about."

Now it was Dorothy's turn to be surprised. "Pa, do you mean it? You just want me to be happy?"

"Oh for heaven's sake! Don't start cryin' on me, now. What do you think any man wants for his children? I know I've been hard on you, but it was for your own good, and look how you've turned out. I get *some* credit for that, don't I?" He put his arm around her shoulder, the most affectionate gesture he knew. "So, I suppose you'll be wantin' to get married as soon as he gets back from this damned war, won't ya?"

Dorothy stopped crying. "No, Pa, I think we'll get married *before* he goes over there."

FRANK CLICKED HIS pipe against his teeth. "Say, I saw Jack's father at the seed store today, and I invited him to dinner tonight. I hope you don't mind."

"Tonight? Is Mrs. Smith coming too?"

"No, she can't make it. Just George. We want to talk to you about you and Jack and your plans."

"What do you mean, you want to talk to me? Smitty and I are getting married when he comes home on leave. What is there to talk about?"

"Dorothy, I'm *not* going to discuss this with you right now. I just wanted you to know that George will be here for dinner so you can plan accordingly. That's all."

"Well, he is welcome to come to dinner. We can talk about the weather and his crops and his family, but we are *not* going to discuss Smitty and me!"

"HELLO, DOROTHY," GEORGE said, scrutinizing her from head to toe. "You look as good as a slice of my wife's peach pie. How ya doin'?"

"Fine, Mr. Smith, just fine." Dorothy wondered how someone so short could scare her to the point of making her legs wobble like day-old Jell-O.

"No need to call me 'mister.' I'm gonna be your father-in-law soon enough, so you can just call me George. Say, speakin' of you two gettin' hitched, Frank and I wanna put our two cents in."

Dorothy put her hands on her hips. George's eyes narrowed. "Now don't get all huffy, young lady." He shook his finger at her. "Your face is about the same color as my big ole red barn. We brought the two of you into this world. We have a right to our say."

"Yes, sir."

"Now, you just sit down here, and let's talk about it. Are you sure it makes sense to get married in the middle of a war?"

Frank chimed in. "You know Jack is going to end up over there, right in the middle of it, just like Tommie, and look what happened to him."

"Dad, we don't know what happened to him. Maybe nothing happened to him."

"But that's just it. No one knows what's going to happen. It would be wise for the two of you to wait until Jack gets home."

George added his opinion. "You're young. You have all the time in the world to wait, young lady. You sure don't want to end up a widow, and you sure as *hell* don't want to end up a widow with a child, for God's sake."

Dorothy sprang from the couch. "That's enough! I won't listen to any more. He asked me to marry him, and we are going to get married when *we* want to get married. Maybe we aren't being sensible, but if something happens to him, do you think I'm going to be any less devastated if we *aren't* married? No! And what if I do have his child and something happens to him? Wouldn't it be nice to have just a little part of him still here?" She shuddered. "I can't believe we are having this conversation, as though he's already dead. This will stop now! I made a nice fried chicken dinner just for you, George. I know how much you like it. I hope you stay, but we *will not* discuss my personal life anymore. Is that understood?"

George and Frank looked at each other. After a long silence, George piped up, "Got any gravy for the mashed potatoes?" He stood and hurried into the kitchen.

Frank stayed behind, caught off guard by his daughter's emphatic demeanor.

Dorothy saw the sadness in her father's tired brown eyes. "Pa, I know you are only trying to protect me. You don't want me to experience what you did when Ma passed, but it's my life. You can't go around protecting me forever."

"I know, dear, but..."

"Stop. I'm not changing my mind."

38

Camp Edwards

S mitty grinned as he read Dorothy's latest letter.

> Dearest Smitty,
>
> The ring came today. It's beautiful! I've shown it to everyone, so I guess that gives you my answer to your proposal, doesn't it?
>
> I think we should get married sooner than later, don't you? Maybe before you are sent overseas? And we can pick out that Airstream trailer I've been telling you about. Please let me know as soon as possible.
>
> All My Love,
> Dorothy

Lewis kicked the bunk and slapped Smitty on the back.

"Hey, buddy! Guess who's lookin' for ya? Remember to ask her if she'd go out with me, OK?"

"Sarah? She's here?"

"That's what I said. Now you're in deep shit." Lewis pointed at the letter that lay crumpled in Smitty's hand. "Isn't that a letter from that cute little gal you sent a ring to back in Nebraska?"

"It's none of your goddamned business."

SMITTY SPOTTED SARAH as soon as he opened the door to the service club. She had on the same royal blue dress he tore off her the first night they had made love. She winked at him, but her eyes didn't look as mischievous as in the past. He feared his legs might fail him. His hands began to sweat. "Sarah?"

"Hi, Smitty. I hope you don't mind. I needed to see you. Actually, I had to see you."

Smitty backed up, mouth open.

"Oh, don't worry. I'm not pregnant or anything, although I sort of wish I was. Sit down, sweetie. I just want to talk."

He sat down and locked his eyes on her. "What do you want? I mean, I'm glad to see you. You look fantastic, Sarah. I..."

"Shh." She put her hands on his lips.

An electric charge surged down to his toes. "Jesus, Sarah. I'm so sorry. I didn't mean to call you her name."

"Shh." She stopped him again, this time taking his hand in hers and kissing it. "I love you, Smitty, and I decided to fight for you. You may think you love this Dottie, but I know what we have together. You don't find that everywhere. Do you honestly feel the same way when you make love to her?"

"Wouldn't know, Sarah, and it's none of your business, anyway."

She leaned back in the chair. "You're kidding, right? She's a virgin? You think you are in love with a virgin?"

"OK, Sarah, now you're starting to piss me off. It's none of your goddamned business, I said!"

"Smitty, look at me. We have something special, and it's more than sex. We click, you and me. Would she ride on a motorcycle with you, all the way to California? Come on. Give me another chance, please—just one more chance, one more weekend. We can do the town up right. I can show you some new places. It's all up to you. Please?"

He studied her eyes, searching for what he needed to end his perpetual confusion. He couldn't speak. His head began to nod as if on its own volition. She grinned and kissed his fingers. "We'll ride the streetcar all night if you want, or we can do whatever you want, any way you want, all night long."

LEWIS LOOKED OVER Smitty's shoulder. "Did you get your orders?"

"Africa, man—they're sendin' me to Africa. Never been out of the country. I get drafted, and now I'm goin' to Africa in the middle of a fuckin' war."

"Well, at least you get some leave first, right?"

"Three weeks. Then I'm a goner."

"What about Sarah? What did she want?"

"You're like all those gossipy old women back home."

"Is she pregnant or somethin'?"

"No! She's not pregnant, but she's got me all confused. Me and Sarah, we just click. She loves motorcycles and having a good time. There's this feeling I get when I'm with her—sorta free. She's just excitin', ya know? She's so damned good-looking and good in bed taboot. Damned, Lewis, you got me talkin' about my personal life like a woman. Fuck off!"

"It's worse than I thought. Two women in love with you, and you are such a dumbass you don't know which one you want."

"I love 'em both, man. One's sweet and innocent and devoted to me since she was in high school. The other is beautiful and sexy and excitin' and, man—I don't know. I just don't know."

THE TICKET LINE at the train station extended out into the main lobby and around the corner. Smitty didn't care. He let his mind drift, searching for an answer. *Boston or Nebraska? That's my choices. Which is it gonna be?* The line inched forward. *It's gotta be Sarah. She's just like Boston.* He could almost feel the motorcycle between his legs and Sarah's arms around his chest.

THE BAND PLAYED "Moonlight Serenade." Smitty held Sarah close. She responded to his every move and leaned in even closer to him as they glided around the dance floor.

The song ended, and they ran out the front door. "Come on, baby, let's take her for a spin," Smitty yelled.

Sarah climbed on the back of the motorcycle and wrapped her arms around him. "I'm ready, sweetie. Where do you want to take me tonight?"

"Let's go to California."

"OK, let's go!"

Smitty accelerated the engine until it roared. The open road expanded before them. "We're free, you and me. No worries, no one to stop us. Just you and me, baby."

SMITTY FELT A tap on his shoulder. The woman in line behind him pointed to a large gap that lay between Smitty and the person ahead of him.

"Sorry, ma'am." He moved toward the woman in front of him, who held a baby in her arms. She cooed at the baby, who responded with a smile. A soldier approached the woman. "There you are. I was afraid I wouldn't be able to find you." He kissed the woman and took the baby from her. "Hi, little bambino. How's my favorite son?" Smitty watched the family talking, laughing, sharing the moment. The soldier held the baby close to his chest and looked at his wife. The silence between them was filled with the clouded future they faced together. "It won't be long, honey. I promise I'll be back before you know it," he said with feigned confidence.

Smitty mulled over the scene as the line dragged along.

His uncertainty overwhelmed him. What did *his* future hold? When would he be home again; *would* he ever be home again?

"Where you goin', son?"

Smitty jumped. Perturbed, the ticket clerk repeated his question: "I said, where you goin'?"

Smitty stared into the eyes of the impatient clerk, who drummed his fingers on the countertop. "OK, soldier, make up your mind. There's a huge line behind you, and I ain't got all day! Hell, do you even *know* where you're going?"

Struck by penetrating clarity, Smitty slammed his money on the counter. "Yes, sir. I do know where I'm goin'. For the first time in my life, I know *exactly* where I'm goin'."

SO LONG!

Part 3

SWISH!

PASSED BY
U 41784 S
ARMY EXAMINER

WAR & NAVY
DEPARTMENTS
V-MAIL SERVICE
JUL 2
9-AM
1943
OFFICIAL BUSINESS

39

November 18, 1942

"Jack! Did you hear the question?" The judge peered at Smitty over his glasses, tapping his foot, proclaiming his impatience with Jack's hesitation. "Do you, or do you not, take..."

"Yes, sir. I heard the question, and I do, sir, I do."

The judge cleared his throat. "Don't tell me, Jack. Tell her," he said with a newfound sense of benevolence.

Smitty faced his bride. "I do, I do, I do!" he sang, swinging her in his arms, laughing and crying all at once.

"All right, son, you've made your point. Calm down and let's finish this, shall we? With the power vested in me, I pronounce you man and wife, Mr. and Mrs. Jack G. Smith. You may kiss..."

The judge shook his head at the newly married couple, already in full embrace, and walked toward the foyer to the next in an endless line of anxious couples.

40

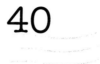

September 1943
With the United States Eighth Fleet
Bizerte Harbor, Africa

Smitty ducked as bullets ricocheted overhead.

"Jesus Christ!"

He seized his .50 caliber machine gun and gripped the handles to calm his nerves, shouting his lucky-charm phrase in rapid-fire succession.

"I'm OK. I can do this. I'm OK. I can do this."

He swung the gun and aimed it at the oncoming German fighter planes.

Don't fire. They're too far away. I'm OK. I can do this.

The sky lit up again and again as the enemy continued its unrelenting attack.

"I'm OK."

An enemy plane materialized over the right side of the deck. Bullets flew from every direction as all hands began firing at once.

"Fuck!"

Smitty swung the machine gun toward the sky. His heart beat as fast as the bullets leaving the barrel.

Seventy-five rounds later, a gloomy darkness enveloped the deck as the searchlights dimmed. Smitty continued to grip the handles of the machine gun. He began to shake, stopped himself, and howled into the night sky, "I did it!"

The thrill of the moment ebbed, and his thoughts turned to a distant place, now a faint memory.

"I gotta tell Peaches."

SMITTY TOOK A pencil and stationery from his footlocker at the end of his cot. He wrote at a feverish pace, the exhilaration of the air raid fresh in his mind.

> Talk about fireworks. The tracers lit up the sky. That was one of the biggest and the most thrilling events to me.
>
> Right now, though, I'm in the mood darling, for what? Writing letters. I have your picture sitting here but it hasn't said a word. It's taking some awful beatings riding around with me. The frame is a little beat up but the picture is ok yet. It's the most valuable piece of property I have.

Her photograph captivated him: her dark hair, pinned back in the popular Queue Curl style, never changed. Her wire rim glasses stayed perfectly balanced, and she never averted her eyes; her mouth remained forever turned into a perfect smile, and those lips, those full, luscious lips.

Those lips look like they were all in the mood for a big kiss, in fact my highest ambition right now, if possible, would be to press my lips against those lips. I hope to God it isn't too long till we can act that out together.

I'll write more tomorrow. For now, though remember that I love you and I will love you always.

All my love,

Smitty

He folded the letter and placed it in an envelope. He sat her photo on a table next to his cot. A tranquil mood overtook him as he studied her face. "I'm OK. I can do this." A smile crossed his lips as he fell into an exhausted sleep. "I *did* do this."

41

One Month Later

The entrenching tool that passed for a shovel made a shallow dip in the ground. He emptied the clay soil and dug again. He repeated the action in a rhythmic motion and continued talking to himself. *I'm safe. It's over for now. I did what they trained me to do.* He cringed at the sound of an artillery shell exploding in the distance, and his pace increased. *Gotta get this foxhole dug.*

The company clerk, his hands full of mail, jarred Smitty out of his absorption with creating a safe haven for the night. "I wish the noise would stop just for a little bit. Don't you?" Smitty asked, trying to determine why the clerk was there, disturbing his all-consuming mission.

"Hey, man, it's a war, but today's your lucky day, soldier."

He held up two boxes and a handful of letters. "This is all for you."

"For me? What is it? Is it for my truck?"

"No soldier, this is all from home. Remember home? The good ole USA?"

Smitty nodded toward his foxhole. "Better finish this first."

"The invasion is over. We're here, on Italian soil. We're doin' fine. Why don't you just take a little break and look at some mail?"

Smitty stared at the clerk, dropped his shovel, and sat down. "That's what I'll do. I'll sit down. Thanks, buddy."

The clerk handed him the packages and letters. "Take it easy, man. Enjoy yourself a little."

Smitty read the return address on one of the boxes: "Mrs. Jack G. Smith, Beaver City, Nebraska." He tried to make sense of it. *This box is from back home? How did this stuff get here in the middle of a war?* Smitty watched the clerk as he walked away. *He said we're doin' fine. The invasion is over.* He ducked as another shell exploded with a deafening blast. *Maybe I better finish my foxhole.* He began to dig—faster now, with the prizes from home waiting for him to finish.

Twenty minutes later, he slid into the dark safety of his own personal bomb shelter, grabbing his bounty on the way down. The tape holding the box shut made a loud popping sound as he tore at the wrapping paper, yanking it off in one large piece. He opened the lid with calculated movements, finding great pleasure in extending the last step before unveiling the treasures inside.

A sack of butterscotch candy caught his eye. He opened the bag, selected a piece, and popped it into his mouth. "My favorite," he said out loud to the dirt walls of his new home.

A white envelope with a lipstick kiss on the seal captured his attention. He picked up the envelope and smelled the lipstick. "Oh, darlin', you smell *so* damned good."

Photographs of Dorothy in a new fur coat, Dorothy and Annie standing in front of his parents' house, and Dorothy standing in front of his Ford pickup all spilled from the envelope and filled him with a deep sense of melancholy that seeped into his bones. He put the photos back into the envelope and popped another piece of candy into his mouth. Savoring the sweet flavor of the butterscotch, he considered the final contents of the box: V-mail stationery wrapped in a blue ribbon. Pulling a pencil out of his rucksack, he flattened the cardboard box into a makeshift desk and began writing:

> Somewhere in Italy
> My Darling Dorothy,
>
> Hello honey, how are you? How's everything by now. It's sure been a long time since I have had a chance to write. As near as I can remember it's been a month since I wrote but I've had a pretty good reason for not writing. I have been pretty busy since coming to Italy. I can't tell much about it just now. The censor would block it if I did. I can say that I've seen a lot of combat duty since I've been here. For the time being we have everything under control. I had a few scares at first but it

wasn't as bad as it could have been. Darling, please don't worry just because I'm over here, because I'm plenty safe where I'm at. I imagine you hear plenty about the whole thing on the radio and in the paper.

Honey, I sure thank you a lot for the package, the candy sure tastes delicious and I'm using some of the V-mail now. I suppose you're wishing I'd use more of it. Ha. I was digging a fox hole when one of the boys brought the package to me, what a coincidence. I also got a bunch of letters and a package from the folks too, so you see I'm doing quite well. Those pictures were good, they made me feel sort of homesick though.

Well Honey hope you're OK. Tell the rest hello for me. I don't think it will be too long till we win this war and I'll be home. I love you darling.

All my love,
Smitty

His eyelids closed. Sleep came for the first time in three days as his head rested against the dirt wall of his foxhole and his hands cradled the box full of treasures from home.

42

November 18, 1943

Smitty turned over in bed and opened his eyes, blinking several times in an attempt to focus on the figure standing over him. "Peaches, is that you? Honey, I can't stop shaking; I'm so damned cold. Can you get me some more quilts?"

The nurse refreshed Smitty's sweat-soaked blankets. "I'm not Peaches, soldier, but I'm here to take care of you. You're gonna be just fine."

The doctor entered, and the nurse began giving her report. The doctor frowned, "Admit him. How many cases does that make? Twenty or so, just in the last twenty-four hours?"

Smitty wrapped the blankets around his body, tucking them under his chin. His teeth chattered as the nurse moved him onto the gurney. "Thanks for the blankets, but I'm still freezing. Please, Honey, help me."

Several Days Later

My Darling Dorothy,

Hi Honey. How's every little thing? What's new back home?

Maybe I should tell you, I'm in the hospital. Don't get excited. It's just a slight case of malaria. I was pretty sick when I came in, but I feel better now.

The nurse arrived with lunch. Smitty put his letter down and took in her brown hair, neatly pinned under her nursing cap; her crisp, white, fitted uniform; and her long legs, made to appear even longer with white hose. "Good to see you sitting up, Jack—here's your lunch." She smiled as she set the tray down. He tried to focus on the lunch tray instead of her long legs.

"Hey, cat got your tongue?" she asked, fully aware of his focus.

Smitty coughed. "No, no, just lookin' at this delicious lunch you brought me. Thanks. Hey, any mail come in for me?"

"Sorry, not today."

"It's been ten days without mail. Seems more like ten months."

"Maybe tomorrow, Jack. Try to eat something now. You need to build up your strength."

He stared at his lunch tray, picked up the fork, and twirled it in his hand.

"I just can't get over having real silverware and china plates." He took a bite of green beans.

"Makes everything taste better."

THE CREAK OF the mail cart making its way down the hall stopped Smitty's pacing, and he headed toward the door. The orderly manning the cart saw him as he stuck his head into the hallway. "Sorry, Jack, nothing today."

"Dammit to hell!" he murmured. His thoughts came in rapid succession: *She's writing me. I know she is. She loves me. She said she would wait for me forever. The letters are just all stacking up back at my company. But why are other guys getting mail? What if that Thomas guy came back? He was MIA; maybe they found him and sent him home. No, no, that can't be it. I'll get all her letters all at once. I just have to get back to my company.*

The nurse arrived with his morning medications. "Good morning, Jack. How are you today?"

"Not so good. Still no mail. It's sorta drivin' me bonkers."

"It's probably waiting for you back at your company. Just think. When you get back, it'll all be waiting there for you. It'll be like Christmas."

"Yeah, guess yer right. Nothin' I can do but wait."

The nurse nodded toward his wedding ring. "So, how long have you been married?"

Smitty's eyes widened. He looked at his wedding band, and his heart sank.

"Jack, is everything all right? I didn't mean to upset you. I was just making conversation."

"A year. I was married a year ago on the eighteenth of this month. My anniversary came and went, and I didn't even know it."

"You've been through a lot, Jack. Cheer up. Maybe next year you'll be together."

"Yeah, maybe next year." He picked up a deck of cards and, with meticulous care, dealt out seven piles, straightening each one as he went along.

The soldier in the bed next to him chuckled. "I never seen anybody play solitaire as much as you."

"Fuck off, man, and mind your own damned business!"

Africa

Dearest Wife,

Well, Honey, they moved me back to a big hospital in Africa. I was doing okay and then came down with jaundice. Can you believe it? Still no letters. I know they are piling up for me back at my company. I know you are writing me, just like you always do. I'm afraid that if they try to send them to me now, I'll be gone by the time they arrive, then I'll have to wait another month before they catch up with me. It's all starting to drive me just a little crazy.

Smitty stopped writing and began to pace the floor. Four weeks without mail. His deck of cards in hand, he headed out the door to the solarium, tormented by his thoughts. *I wonder if they'll send me back to my company. What if they don't? I'll never get my letters. And my buddies. What about them? I don't want to start over with new guys. My buddies need me.*

"There you are, Jack. I've been looking all over for you. How's it going today?"

"Doc, am I glad to see you! I gotta get out of here—today, if possible—I mean, it *is* possible, right? You said yesterday that my numbers are better, and, look, the jaundice is almost gone."

The doctor put his hand on Smitty's shoulder. "Calm down, son. Your blood work is improving, but it's still not normal. Maybe by Christmas."

"Christmas? That's ten more days, Doc. I don't think you understand. I'm goin' a little crazy here. My buddies, they need me."

"Jack, calm down. Why don't you play that card game you're so fond of? That'll help pass some time."

Smitty stifled the urge to throw the cards in the doctor's face. "My buddies need me, Doc. Didn't you hear me? I'm the driver. I gotta drive ammo to the front lines. They need me."

"You'll be back there soon enough, son. I'll have the nurse give you a little something to calm your nerves."

December 25, 1943

> Dearest Dorothy,
> Merry Christmas, Honey. What did you do today? Sorry I couldn't get you any presents. I'm still here in the hospital.

Smitty listened to the howling wind blowing sand and dust into the air. "I bet it's snowin' back home," he mumbled, staring out the window at the stark, colorless landscape. "Some Christmas this is. No letters, no packages, no snow, no nothin'. Just stuck in this fucking hospital." He picked up his pen.

> Honey, I hope we're together next year. I can see us now with our little bambino and a big old Christmas tree in the living room, and...

A nurse poked her head through the door and looked around the empty ward until her eyes landed on Smitty. "Hey, come on down and join the fun." She motioned for him to join her. "We have a whole program planned for you guys. You can finish your letter later. Come on, Smitty. We need you down there."

"Just give me a minute. I gotta finish my letter first."

The nurse shrugged her shoulders and turned to leave. "Suit yourself, but you're going to miss out if you don't hurry."

Smitty sat motionless for a moment. He put the pen down with exaggerated care. "Wait up. I'm comin'."

January 1944

Grotsky, Smitty's best friend and assistant driver, slapped him on the back. "Where the hell you been? We thought we lost you forever, you slacker."

Smitty shook Grotsky's hand, eager to participate in the banter. "Hey, smartass. Been in the hospital with malaria and jaundice for over two months. Try it sometime, and we'll see who's a slacker, you blue-eyed Polack."

Grotsky softened. "Yeah, I know, buddy. They told us how sick you were. We saved a cot for you, though. We knew you couldn't stay away." He pointed to a cot piled with packages and layers of letters at least an inch thick.

Smitty peered around Grotsky's six-foot frame and stepped forward with trepidation. "Is this all mine, or did you just empty mail call on my cot as a joke? This can't be all mine."

"Sure as hell is. Now, stop staring at it, and let's open those packages first. I'm bettin' there's some of them amazing cookies your honey sends you in at least half those packages. Can we help you open them?"

"Sure." Smitty continued to take in the sight. "Go ahead. Dig in." He picked up a handful of letters and let them fall through his hands like water from the pump back home. He sorted each one by date and read every letter twice, looking up now and then to watch his buddies ransacking the boxes, searching for anything edible.

I'm home, he thought, and then he grinned for the first time in a long time.

43

January 24, 1944

Beaver City, Nebraska

"Pa, what's wrong? It's seven in the morning. Why are you still in bed?"

"I don't feel so good, honey. That cold is getting me down. I've never had one last so long. Walter is doing the morning chores. You better get going, or you'll be late for work again."

"Do you need anything before I leave?"

"I'm fine—just a little cold. Now scoot!"

"OK, Pa, see you around five o'clock. Love ya."

"Love you too. Don't be late."

Dorothy stifled herself. "Yes, Pa, I won't be late."

Carol waited at the foot of the porch steps, applying a new shade of red lipstick. "Good morning, Mrs. Smith."

"You say that every morning, but I never get tired of it. Mrs. Jack G. Smith," she sighed. "Did I tell you he's been sick too? He had malaria, of all things. Can you imagine? I had to go to the library and look it up. It's pretty serious stuff, but he's fine now. "

"How about we stop for a milkshake after work today?"

"Can't. Pa's not feeling well, and I told him I would be right home after work. He says he's got a cold, but this seems different. I'm going to call Dr. Olson and have him drop by."

Arriving at the office, Dorothy made a preliminary scan to ensure Mr. Anderson hadn't arrived. She removed her stationery from its hiding place under her ledger and began to write:

> Good Morning Dear Husband,
>
> How's every little thing? Glad to hear you are out of the hospital. I worried about you every day and twice on Sunday. My prayers have been answered. No sooner do I get one man well than another one gets sick. Pa has a bad cold and wasn't even out of bed when I left this morning.

Mr. Anderson tapped his finger on the letter. "That looks like interesting *work,* Mrs. Smith, but not appropriate for here, wouldn't you agree?"

"Oh, good morning, sir. I thought you weren't in yet. I mean that's not why I was writing. I just had a minute, and thought I would start this letter, but I agree it's not appropriate for here, so here it goes, under my ledger, and here goes a photo onto my desk." She made a show of placing the photo, just so, on her desk and began to measure it with her planimeter. Mr. Anderson remained standing by her desk. "Is there anything else, sir?"

He cleared his throat twice. "You do excellent work, Mrs. Smith, high quality work." He paused. "It's a good thing."

Dorothy didn't look up from her work. "Yes, sir." She moved the planimeter over the surface of the photo and made thorough notes on the side.

The door to Mr. Anderson's office closed, and Dorothy made a face and wiped her brow in an exaggerated show of relief. "That was a close one." She and Carol both giggled under their breath.

DOROTHY ARRIVED HOME at five o'clock, as promised. Dr. Olson and Walter stood in the hall outside Frank's bedroom door, deep in conversation. She clenched her jaw. "What's going on?"

"He's p-pretty sick this t-t-time, Sis."

Dr. Olson frowned. "I'm afraid your father has pneumonia. I think he'll be fine, but he's going to need some pretty close attention."

"I can take care of him. I always do." Dorothy sounded more defensive than she meant to. "What do I need to do?"

"Just feed him clear soup and plenty of water. Take his temperature every four hours and call me if it gets above 102 degrees. Do you know how to take a temperature?"

"Of course, Doctor. Is that all?"

"Sure wish we had some of that new penicillin. It could

help him a lot, but it's all for the boys fighting the war at this point. Just call me, Dorothy, if he starts to go downhill. This can be pretty serious."

"Certainly. But he'll be fine. I know he will. He has to."

Dr. Olson put his hand on Dorothy's shoulder. "Now, Dorothy, I don't mean to alarm you, but you know as well as I do that pneumonia..."

"I know!" Dorothy suppressed her anguish and lowered her voice. "I know, Dr. Olson. You don't need to remind me. I'll take care of everything."

Dr. Olsen hesitated and then let himself out while Dorothy and Walter stood in the hall, trying to avoid eye contact. Walter spoke first. "Why did he have ta b-b-bring that up? Just cuz Ma d-d-died of pneumonia, don't mean Pa will."

"I know, honey. Dr. Olson was just trying to be helpful. Can you watch Pa for a little while? I'll go say hi to him first, but then I need to go out."

"Okay, Sis, but d-d-don't be long."

"HI, PA. I just talked to Dr. Olson. Sounds like everything will be just fine. I'll take good care of you like I always do."

Frank lay motionless in the bed, gasping for every breath, sweat beaded on his forehead. He opened his eyes. "Is that you, Ethel?"

"No, it's me, Pa. It's Dorothy. Can I get you anything?"

"Well, where's your mother?"

"Pa, she's gone. She's been gone for a long time. Remember?"

"Gone? Well, go get her."

Dorothy bit her lip. Who was this fragile-looking man who lay helpless, his arms limp beside him, an ashen color replacing his eternal farmer's tan? Where was her strong, domineering father? "I'll go get her, Pa." She left the room. "Walter, I'll be right back!" She grabbed her coat and ran out the door into the bleak January twilight.

She climbed the hill to the cemetery and let herself in through the creaky front gate. She wrapped her coat around her and turned the fur collar up to protect her face. Before reaching her mother's grave, she began to yell, "You can't have him yet! I'm all alone! Pa is all I have to keep me strong until Jack gets home! Me and Walter can't make it without him! He can't come to you yet, Ma! You and God figure it out! Just don't take him yet!"

Dorothy knelt on the ground, wailing and pounding her fist on her mother's tombstone. "Please, Mama, please!"

Italy

> Dearest Jack,
>
> I don't know how to start this letter. I even thought about not telling you until you came home.

Smitty stopped reading. *Dammit!* he thought. *That Thomas guy came back. A year away is just too long.*

> Honey, in your last letter you asked me how Pa was doing. Well, the cold he had turned

into pneumonia, and he died that same day your letter came. I can't believe it. This is the first time I've written out the words – he died yesterday.

1/27/44 – I'm sorry, Honey. I had to stop writing. I cry myself to sleep almost every night. I wish...

Smitty crumpled the letter in his hand. Grotsky sat down beside him. "Hey, man, you're as white as a ghost! What's going on?"

Smitty sat silent.

"Oh, man, she didn't ask you for a divorce or something, did she?"

"Stop, Grotsky! She didn't ask for a divorce. Her pa, Frank, he..." He picked up his helmet and threw it across the tent.

"Watch it, Smitty! What did her old man do to get you this upset?"

"He died! He fucking died! I'm in fucking Italy in the middle of a fucking war. He died over a week ago, and I didn't even know it. My wife is 6,000 miles away—alone." Smitty's shoulders slumped as he put his head in his hands just as the sergeant flew into the tent.

"Off your asses and on your feet! Now, gentlemen! They need more ammunition up front. Let's go!"

Smitty scooped up his helmet and ran out the door. Three words haunted him as he jumped into his truck and headed for the front: *I wasn't there.*

Beaver City

Helen wrapped her arm around Dorothy's shoulder. "Are you sure you and Walter will be all right? You know you can come home with us for a while if you like."

"We'll be fine, Sis. You've already done enough. You've stayed the whole week since the funeral. It's time we get going on our own. I'll help you get your luggage into the car."

DOROTHY WAVED AS Helen and her family pulled out of the driveway and disappeared down the street. Only then did she allow herself to cry. *I'm an orphan. No ma, no pa, and no husband around. Just me and Walter.*

She made dinner, deep sorrow replacing the usual pleasure she enjoyed while cooking. *Pa always complimented my cooking, even if it was terrible. Guess that's not gonna happen anymore.* She set the table, reminding herself that she only needed two plates now, not the usual three.

She and Walter ate in silence. Finally, he pushed his chair back. "Gotta go milk those cows. Hey, Sis, that was p-p-pretty good chicken. Thanks."

Dorothy held back tears. "You're entirely welcome, honey. Thanks for saying so. See you later."

She cleaned up the kitchen and then meandered into the living room. The latest *Life* magazine sat untouched on the coffee table. She picked it up and began to thumb through it, relaxing into a familiar evening routine that predated her father's death.

She turned to the cartoons first. One of the captions brought a brief smile. More than anything else in the magazine, she loved the ads, especially for clothes. Alden's ads always attracted her attention. That week's ad featured a fine-looking spring coat made of wool fleece. She found solace in fantasizing about how it would look with her pink Easter dress.

She always enjoyed the photos in *Life* as well, but this issue seemed ominous. A grotesque drawing of men tied to a fence while a Japanese soldier beat them with a two-by-four made her pause. The caption read, "Death Was Part of our Life." She skimmed the page.

On the next page, a map of the Philippines left no doubt about the subject of the article. She didn't want to continue reading, but she couldn't stop. She flipped back to the beginning of the piece. An all-too-familiar sense of impending doom began to percolate inside her. She picked up the phone and asked the operator to connect her.

"Carol, it's me, Dorothy."

"Hi, honey, how's it going? You sound a little shaky."

"Have you seen the new *Life* magazine?"

Carol didn't answer.

"You saw it, didn't you?"

"I did, honey. I was hoping you would miss it. You know, those officers escaped. Maybe Tommie did too."

"I don't think so. They don't even know where he is." She sobbed into the phone.

"I'll be right over."

Dorothy draped herself in a comforter, trying to warm her shaking body. Carol didn't bother to knock. She ran into the living room and wrapped her arms around Dorothy. "It's OK, honey. Let it all out. You've been through a lot—just let it all out."

"It's just so much. Smitty's gone and for who knows how long, Pa dies, and now this. Tommie—what he must have gone through. Why did this have to happen?"

"Don't try to figure it out. You can't. It'll get better as time passes."

"No, it won't! I'm so scared. I need to get out of this town. Everywhere I look, there are memories of my ma and my pa. What if something happens to Smitty? What will I do? I'll be all alone."

Walter stood by the living room door. "N-no ya won't, Sis. You won't b-be alone. I'm here."

Dorothy rushed to his side and held him in her arms. She sensed the same vulnerability he displayed the day their mother was buried. "Oh, honey, I didn't mean it. Of course we have each other."

Holding Walter, she realized it was no longer about her. Nor was it about her and Jack. She saw the unmistakable path that lay before her. She would be the one to manage the grain and seed store and keep the books straight for the farm—not Helen, not Walter, but Dorothy. How could she not have seen it before? Her father had prepared her for this moment. She had learned to manage his books, to speak up for herself, to make up her own mind because of him.

Courage usurped panic. She patted Walter's back in a tender, comforting rhythm.

I'm OK. I can do this.

44

May 1944
Italy

Smitty positioned Dorothy's photo beside him. He looked at her, losing himself for a moment—yearning for her warmth, her touch, her voice. He cleared his head and took out his pen and paper.

> Honey, you can't believe how beautiful Italy is. We're coming back here someday after this damned war is over. I'm sitting here in the back of my truck, smoking a ten cent cigar and watching the sunset. It's almost as beautiful as it is in Nebraska.

He took a sip of his ration of 3.2 beer and frowned as the watery brew barely registered on his palate. Raising the bottle and toasting the air, he sighed, "Better than nothin'." He adjusted the letter on his leg, took a drag from his cigar, and basked in the last magnificent rays of the sunset. A bird sang its evening song in a nearby olive tree. He blinked. *Did I just hear a bird singing? Is that a cricket chirping?* He put the letter down and sat still, listening to the sounds of his nearby unit: men talking, trucks moving. They resembled the sounds on every street in every little town back home. *I'll be damned—no bombs, no shelling. I'll be goddamned.*

The golden glow of the twilight mesmerized him. His eyelids began to close, only to jerk open again in a desperate attempt to block the terrifying images that filled his mind whenever he remembered the horror four months earlier.

Rapido River Crossing

Smitty ducked at the sound of whistling shells overhead. He latched onto the steering wheel of his Deuce and a Half. "Damn. I hate that, don't you?"

Grotsky stopped playing the mandolin, his constant companion since arriving in Italy. "Yeah, who doesn't hate it? Sometimes I think we're in as much danger as the guys at the front. I mean, we're the ones carrying the ammo to them. We're probably A-number-one targets for the kraut-eaters, right?"

"Yeah, we are, but I wouldn't trade places with those poor bastards this time. The river crossing is a total fuckup. I'll just stay in my truck and bring them the ammo they need, thank you very much. Hey, play somethin' on your

mandolin—makes the time go by faster. Play 'Tennessee Waltz.' That's me and my wife's favorite."

Grotsky played while the shells continued whistling overhead. "Just a few more miles to the ammo dump."

"Yup, not long now." Smitty's stomach churned. "But I wish you hadn't mentioned that just yet. I can handle hauling ammo up to the front line just fine. I can do this all day long if I have to. I don't give a damn about the shelling. It ain't that bad. It's hauling the load goin' back the other way that I hate." He spat out the window, trying to settle his stomach. "At least I don't puke anymore. Do you?"

Grotsky clutched the crucifix he wore around his neck and kissed it. "Shut the fuck up, man!"

They drove into the ammo dump singing.

Smitty opened the door to the supply tent. "We're here, sergeant. We got a full load for you."

The sergeant, crouched over his desk, continued writing. "I've got a full load for you, too," he said. "This is a disaster up here. I'll have my guys unload for you, but I'm gonna need you and your buddy to help with the load going back."

"Yes, sir." Smitty's knees began to buckle. He held onto the counter to steady himself. "Where are they?"

"In the morgue tent, same as always."

Smitty and Grotsky walked toward the morgue. "What do you want to sing on the way back?"

"What?"

"Humor me. What do you want to sing on the way back? Let's just start practicing now. Give me a tune, Grotsky. Just give me a tune!"

Grotsky made the sign of the cross and started singing

"Pistol Packin' Mama." Smitty chimed in. They entered the tent and reported to the sergeant in charge. They opened the back of their truck and began their gruesome task. The lyrics faded into a whisper as Smitty picked up one end of a burlap-wrapped body and Grotsky grabbed the other.

As with so many trips before, they placed the body into the truck, turned back to the tent, and began the process again. Smitty tried to sing, but his lips stuck together. He tried to spit, but no saliva came. He concentrated on Dorothy, on what they would do when he got back home, on anything but the body in his hands.

They loaded another body, and another, and another. Grotsky spat and walked back into the morgue. "Are we almost done?"

New bodies arrived. One lay uncovered. A black, sticky mass of dried blood filled the cavity that used to be the chest of a young man. Ribs jutted out in all directions like the spikes of corn stubble after harvest. All that remained of his face was an eyeball hanging in a precarious spot over the left temple—or what must have been the left temple at one time. Smitty's stomach churned, and he began to gag, and yet he remained locked on the macabre scene, unable to look away.

The sergeant smirked. "What did you think they looked like under the burlap, soldier? All pretty and nice and ready for a funeral? Pull yourself together, private! Let me wrap him up—or, better yet, you wrap him up and take him with you."

Smitty began to shake. Sweat ran down his face.

They picked up the corpse, gently hoisted him onto the

burlap, and began to sing again. They sang loud, they sang fast, they sang slow, they sang every verse, and then they started again. Still, the ghoulish images lay embedded in their minds and would remain there evermore.

SMITTY SHUDDERED AND frantically shook his head, intent on stopping the loathsome images. He finished his 3.2 beer and took one last drag of his cigar. The sunset, nearly gone now, left only a sliver of orange light along the horizon. The air smelled clean and fresh. *Still quiet,* he thought, not wanting his voice to shatter the stillness. He languished there for a while and then began to drift, ever so slowly, into a cherished place, where his dreams remained safe and possible and untouched.

> *THE ROWS OF apple trees, with their branches bending under the weight of deep-red fruit, filled Smitty with a sense of pride. He plucked a Red Delicious off the nearest tree and sank his teeth into its flesh. He chewed on the succulent, tart apple, letting its juice run down his chin, confident now in their decision to move to Washington.*
>
> *A school bell rang in the distance, and he could just make out the sound of someone yelling something. He patted his stomach. "Dinner's ready!" He turned the tractor down the lane toward home.*
>
> *As he entered through the kitchen door,*

the smell of fried chicken teased his senses. He slapped Dorothy's backside. "My favorite dinner from my favorite wife."

Dorothy jumped. "You always manage to sneak up on me. How do you do that?" She placed freshly baked rolls on the table and swatted his backside.

After dinner, Smitty walked out the back door and sat down on the porch swing, pushing it back and forth with his foot and listening to the sounds coming from the kitchen: the clanking of dishes, Dorothy whistling, the baby crying. The back door opened.

"Here, you take him while I finish the dishes. Say good night; then I'll put him to bed." Smitty reached out and cradled his son close to his chest, relishing the smell of the baby's freshly washed hair. "Hey, li'l bambino, how's my baby boy?" As his lips touched the baby's cheek, a sense of abiding peace wrapped itself around him. He held the baby up in front of him. "My son," he whispered, struggling to comprehend the unconditional love that filled his heart.

Dorothy reappeared. "Our son, you mean. Don't move. I'll be right back." She slid her arms around the baby, opened the screen door with one foot, and disappeared into the gathering dusk.

Half an hour later he heard the creaking

of the screen door as Dorothy returned to the porch and snuggled into his welcoming arms. Together they watched the last purple reflections of the sun setting behind the orchard. He kissed her neck, sending goose bumps down her arm.

"Don't stop," she said, intent on watching the setting sun.

He put his hand on her chin and turned her head to face him. "Let's go inside."

A STREAK OF light filled the sky, followed by a deafening barrage of artillery. The din of mortar shells exploding in the distance dissolved the last remnants of his dream, and Dorothy slipped back into the photograph that sat beside his letter.

45

June 1944

Beaver City

Dorothy held the letter still, reading the last line for a third time.

"Carol, wait up." She ran down O Street, catching Carol as she crossed the street. "Jack wants to move to Washington. Can you imagine? I don't even know for sure where Washington is. I get it mixed up with Oregon. Which one is closest to Canada? He was working there when he was drafted. He always said he had a girl back there, but he never talked about *living* there."

"So, what do you think? Are you ready to move halfway across the US with him?"

"I'd go anywhere with him. I always thought we would be

gypsies, never settling in one place. That's the kind of guy he is, and I love it. It's exciting. Hey, do me a favor and tell Mr. Anderson I'm going to be a little late. I've got to stop by the library for a minute."

"OK, doll, see ya later."

Dorothy ran the last half block to the library. "Good morning, Miss Lambert. I'm back."

"Dorothy, I haven't seen you for a long time." Miss Lambert put down the pile of books in her arms and shook Dorothy's hand. "Say, I heard you got married. Congratulations. Is he still in the Philippines?"

Dorothy opened her mouth to explain, then stopped. "No, he's in Europe."

"Well, he gets around, doesn't he? So, what can I help you with today?"

Dorothy slipped her hand from Miss Lambert's firm grasp. "Well, I need a book about Washington. We're thinking about moving there after the war. I also need another map of the United States. And if you have anything about growing apples, I would appreciate that too."

"Oh, my, but you are an ambitious young woman!"

"Yes, I am. Do you have a map of the US that I can look at?"

"There's one on the wall right over there. I can order one for you if you like."

Dorothy walked to the map and began to look at the states west of Nebraska.

"You're getting close, dear. It's right here, up in the most northwestern corner of the country."

"Wow. It's a long ways from here, isn't it?"

"Yes, it is. Probably about eleven hundred miles or so."

"I've never been that far from home before."

"Yes, that is a long, long way. Does that scare you a little?"

"Oh, no, not at all. It just makes me so excited, I don't know if I can work today. Look at all the states we go through to get there: Colorado, Wyoming, Montana, Idaho. Do you have any books about those states?"

Three Weeks Later

"I see Walter has your father's business up for sale. Any takers?" asked Mr. Anderson.

"A few, but it probably won't sell until after this darn war is over—and, by the way, Walter isn't selling the business. I am. My pa taught me how to keep books—you should know that—and he gave me a good head for business too."

Mr. Anderson cleared his throat. "No disrespect meant, Mrs. Smith. Of course I know you're good at whatever you do. Why, you're almost as good as Carol."

"That's quite a compliment. Thank you, sir."

"I mean it. You and Carol could probably run this place when I retire."

"Well, I don't know about that, at least for me. I have a farm to run, and that keeps me plenty busy. Besides, Jack and I are moving to Washington when he gets back. We're going to raise apples. I've been reading all about it. Did you know that Red Delicious apples are the easiest apples to grow? I've been thinking a lot about it, and..."

Mr. Anderson headed toward his office. "You sure have, Mrs. Smith, but I suggest you concentrate on your work right *here* for the time being."

Dorothy was intent on continuing the conversation, but Carol raised her hand. "Not another word about apples, or I think I'm gonna croak. I know more about apples, thanks to you, than I ever cared to know! I need a little break."

"Let's talk about the Airstream trailer, then. I went over to Oxford to..."

Carol interrupted, "Next to apples, I know more about Airstream trailers than I ever thought possible—again, thanks to you!"

"Sorry. I'll stop. I promise. But I've already saved about a quarter of what we need to buy one. Bet you didn't know that!"

Mr. Lundquist entered the office looking even more wretched than usual. Dorothy attempted to disappear into the back office, but too late. Carol interceded.

"Good morning, Mr. Lundquist. I have your check right here for you."

Mr. Lundquist took the check without looking up. "Thank you, dear," he mumbled as he walked out the door.

"What happened to him?" Dorothy asked, curious about his morose behavior.

"Didn't you hear? His son was killed in Italy. You remember Willy, don't you? Hey, where're you going?"

Dorothy disappeared out the front door and ran down the sidewalk, not sure of her own intentions. "Mr. Lundquist!" she yelled.

He turned with a start. "Did I forget something?"

"No, I did. I just heard about your son, and I'm so sorry." She wrapped her arms around him—filthy overalls, reeking of manure; it didn't matter now. "My husband is over there. I know how hard this must be. How can I help?"

"Well, honey, there ain't no help'll ever bring him back." His voice trembled.

"I know, I know, but maybe we can do something together, you know, do it in your son's memory or something."

His eyes lit up. "Ya know the missus has been thinkin' about a Victory Garden, but we're gettin' too feeble to mind it. I can hardly keep up with my farmin', let alone help her. It'd sure be nice if you could help her with it. Would sorta get her mind off it for a while. Make her feel like she's makin' a difference."

Dorothy didn't hesitate. "Sure, I can help. We can plant green beans and squash and maybe some carrots. What do you think, Mr. Lundquist?"

"I think you're a mighty fine young lady, and your husband should be damned proud, honey."

46

June 1944

France

The incessant rain fell in sheets across the windshield. The thick, slippery mud made traction nearly impossible. Smitty righted the wheel preventing the Deuce and a Half from sliding into the ditch. He spat out the window. "So this is all France has to offer, huh? Could of used some of this in '36. Where's all the vineyards and French women and all that stuff?"

Grotsky humphed. "Don't hold yer breath. How many days does this make now?"

"Six. Six days of rain and gray skies. Never thought I'd get tired of rain, but this is startin' to wear thin."

They drove their Deuce and a Half down a street lined

with half-timbered houses. "Stop," Grotsky yelled. "This is the place we'll be staying. They said it'd have the number seventy-six on it, and there it is. At least we'll get to sleep on a real bed for a change."

Smitty stopped the truck. "And maybe even take a bath in a tub instead of out of our helmets. Wouldn't that be somethin'?"

They threw their duffel bags over their shoulders and walked up craggy stone steps to the front door of an unassuming, ancient home that appeared as though it would crumble in a strong wind. Before they could knock, an old woman opened the door. She wore an apron over her black dress. Her snow-white hair was pinned up in a tight bun on top of her head. She came to Smitty's shoulder, and she had to wrench her head backward as far as she could in order to look up at him.

"Welcome," she said, her ice-blue eyes and staid demeanor leaving no doubt about her expectations of the two men about to enter her home. "I know just little English. Hungry?"

"You bet. Whatcha got?" Smitty's stomach started growling.

The old woman pointed at his duffel bag. "Rations."

"Oh, I get it. We feed you, and you feed us."

She continued to point at the duffel bag. "Rations," she demanded as she began to loosen the cords that secured the top of the bag.

"Hold on. Hold on, Gramma." He produced a large white box.

The old woman became more animated, and a smile lit

up her face. "Oh! Good soldier! So big!"

"Where the hell did you get that?" Grotsky asked, amazed at the size of the box.

"They just gave it to me. There's other guys who're gonna stay here with us, so they gave me ten-in-one rations. You go cook, Gramma. We're hungry." Smitty pointed to the kitchen and rubbed his stomach.

The old woman disappeared into the kitchen, dismissing the two hungry soldiers with a wave of her hand. "I cook ze good meal for you."

Grotsky and Smitty explored the house. Smitty peeked into the first room. An ornate settee upholstered in mustard-colored velvet took up one entire wall in the small room. A battered upright piano with water stains covering the top sat against the other wall. Several mismatched chairs lined the remaining two walls. An ornate marble-topped table covered with a crocheted doily and numerous photographs sat in the center of the cramped room. He closed the door and walked toward the kitchen, the only other room on the main floor. The old woman was stirring something on the wood-burning stove. A timeworn oak table large enough to accommodate two chairs sat in the corner.

"Where are we supposed to sleep?"

She ignored him, or perhaps she didn't hear with her back turned to him.

"Up here!" Grotsky yelled. Smitty followed the sound of his voice to a narrow staircase. He climbed the steep stairs two at a time and walked down a cramped hallway to join Grotsky in a room with slanted walls and two single beds that took up the entire room. A small window looking out onto the street provided the only adornment. He threw his duffel bag on one of the beds. "Home sweet home."

Moments later, the old woman yelled up the staircase, "You come now! Ze meal is done!"

Smitty and Grotsky clambered down to the kitchen. The table was set with bowls and spoons. A chunk of homemade bread lay beside each bowl. A bottle of red wine occupied the center of the table. The smell of beef filled the air. Smitty walked over to the stove. "Where the hell did you get beef?"

"Beef?"

"Meat. You know, *moo*," Smitty bellowed.

"Ah, *bœuf*."

"Buff?"

"No. *Bœuf. It tiz zees.*" The old woman held up a can of dried beef.

"Yeah, beef. I mean buff. Wee. Buff."

She shook her head at Jack. "*Bœuf*. We eat now."

Grotsky and Smitty sat down at the table. The old woman shooed them away from the table and pointed to a bowl of water on the kitchen counter. "*Non, non, se laver les mains.*" She rubbed her hands together. "Wash."

"Oh, sure, sure, OK," Smitty replied. Like sheepish little boys caught in an act of disobedience, the two men rose and moved to the dishpan of water. "When was the last time you washed your hands before you ate?"

"Or ate at a table with a real spoon?" Grotsky added.

Returning to the table, they waited while the old woman said a prayer and filled their bowls with soup. "Or ate hot food," Smitty agreed, stuffing an entire piece of bread into his mouth.

The old woman waited. A smile began to grow on her tired face as the two ravenous soldiers gulped down her food. "Good?"

"Oh, yes, ma'am, real good. *Oui.* Good."

"Si bon."

Smitty tried. "See bone."

"Good," the old woman said, pleased with her attempts at teaching French and cooking a fine meal.

Her jovial mood shifted to one of dismay as a distant hissing sound began. She looked out of the kitchen window and motioned to the two soldiers. "Come! *Tout de suite!*"

The sound grew louder. Smitty could see her talking, but he couldn't make out her words. It didn't matter. He knew the sound all too well. "Incoming!" he yelled as he jumped up from the table with Grotsky close behind, clutching his mandolin.

The old lady moved like a woman half her age as she motioned them down narrow stairs.

"*Cave.* It is safe there."

"*Cave?*" Smitty looked around. "It's a cellar."

"*Oui. Cave.*" She motioned to a bench along the wall. The three of them sat while shelling continued through the night. Grotsky kissed his crucifix and began to strum his mandolin.

SMITTY AWOKE TO the smell of coffee. He lay sprawled across the entire bench while Grotsky lay in a corner on a pile of old blankets. Smitty rose, stretching and rubbing his stiff neck. "Hope that don't happen too often. Come on, Grotsky. Rise and shine. Time for breakfast."

In the kitchen, the old woman made scrambled eggs with the powdered mix from the box of rations. She added butter from her churn.

"I'll be damned," Smitty chuckled. "Real butter." He started shoveling food into his mouth.

Grotsky appeared in the doorway. "The radio's squawkin'. I'll go see what's up."

Smitty continued eating. Grotsky returned. "Gotta go. Now, man. They need more ammo up front. Come on! Get a move on!"

Smitty reached for one more slice of bread, started to take a bite, and then handed it to Grotsky. "Sorry, man. You can have it." He waved at the old woman. "Bye."

"Bye-bye," she said as she motioned them toward the front door.

GROTSKY SAT IN the passenger seat of the truck, tuning his mandolin. "What do ya wanna sing next?"

"I don't know. Look in that *Hit Kit* book, man. It's got all the latest songs in it. I gotta keep my eyes on the road. It's a bitch tryin' to keep up with Patton and his damned tanks, especially on these fucking roads. There's more holes than road! Play anything, man—just help me stay awake. Hey, how about 'Lili Marlene'?"

Grotsky leafed through the book. "Here it is." He began to strum his mandolin.

The sound of shells exploding came ever closer. Smitty didn't jerk the steering wheel at the sound anymore, but that old familiar clod of Nebraska dirt had reappeared, and it grew heavier with each passing day. "Maybe that's not such a good song. It's kinda sad. Let's sing somethin' else. How about 'Pistol Packin' Mama'?"

"Sorry, man, that one's ruined for life. I can't sing it anymore without thinkin' about the Rapido."

"Say no more. Just play for a while, whatever you want. I'll just hum along."

A deafening burst assaulted their ears. Grotsky didn't miss a note. "That was close."

"Yeah. I think they're gettin' closer. Let's stop and have a cigarette."

"Nah, I'll just light one for you. You keep your hands on the wheel. Can't you drive a little faster?"

"If I go any faster, we'll start flyin'. Give me the damned cigarette, Grotsky, and just keep playin'. "

Their continual chatter was interrupted as the all-too-familiar drone of a German Fw-190 filled the air, the harbinger of the death and destruction to come. Frantic, both men searched in vain for the exact location of the fighter-bomber. A piercing rumble and an explosion of dust a hundred yards in front of the truck ended the search. Smitty slammed on the brakes. "Shit!" They leaped from the truck and scrambled underneath it.

"Is this the best place for us to be right now?" Grotsky yelled.

"How the fuck should *I* know?"

"Let's move over to those bushes over there. On the count of three. One, two, three!"

Smitty's legs wobbled until adrenalin kicked in. He scrambled across the road and dove into a ditch in front of the bushes. Grotsky crossed himself, kissed his crucifix, and followed close behind.

"Ain't you glad I remembered this?" Smitty removed a flask from his pocket, flipped off the cap, and took a large swig, coughing as he swallowed. "That's better. Here, have some. It'll calm your nerves better than that damned cross you keep kissin'."

Grotsky grabbed the flask. "Maybe you're right," he said, downing the remaining whiskey.

Smitty cackled, pointing at Grotsky clutching his mandolin. "You truly love that thing, don't ya?"

"This?" Grotsky played a couple of chords. "It keeps me sane, man, and, yeah, I *do* love it. It'll stay with me till the day I die."

The shelling subsided. The two men climbed back into the truck, maneuvered their way around the shell holes in the road, and continued toward the front. They could see the tanks in the distance. Grotsky lit a cigarette for Smitty, handed it to him, and proceeded to pick yet another cheerful tune on his mandolin.

OVER TIME, A routine emerged. Every morning Grotsky and Smitty waited for orders via the truck radio, delivered ammo according to the orders received, returned to the old woman's house, ate dinner, and slept in the cellar while endless shelling took place throughout the night. This day would be different.

When two hours had passed without a single squawk emanating from the truck radio, Smitty and Grotsky looked at each other over their morning cup of coffee and smiled. "Bath," they said together.

Smitty stood. "Yup, today's the day. Now, how the hell are we going to make it happen?"

Grotsky pointed toward the barn. "Follow me. I have an idea."

GROTSKY SLAPPED HIS hand on a boiler-looking affair in the barn. "Here it is. We fill it with water, make a fire, sit it over the fire, and wait. Pretty soon we'll have nice hot water for a nice hot bath," he said, grinning from ear to ear.

"So how are we gonna get it to the tub?"

"I got it all figured out. See those two boards over there? We'll just hold them under this rim on this boiler contraption and carry it to the bathtub."

"Good plan. So, who gets to go first once we get it there?"

"Private, who do you *think* gets to go first?" Grotsky pointed to his private first class stripe.

"Oh, pullin' rank on me, huh? Hell, go ahead—you deserve it. There might even be enough clean water for the two of us. This boiler is huge."

An hour later the two men secured the boards on either side of the boiler and lifted. Smitty began to walk backward out the barn door. He stumbled over a rock. "Hold yer horses, not so fast!" He regained his balance, and they continued at a fast pace toward the house.

Having climbed the stairs to the back porch, they poured the heated water into the waiting tub. Both men stared at the tub, now filled with steaming-hot water. The old woman handed them a bar of soap and a towel and pinched her nose shut. "Wash good."

Grotsky began to unbutton his shirt, all the while staring at the old woman. "You go now, *oui?*"

The old woman left, still holding her nose as she walked back into the house. Smitty continued to stare at the bathtub.

Grotsky grew impatient. "Man, you act like you're lookin' at the most beautiful woman in the world. Come on. Give me some privacy—or did *you* wanna watch?"

"What? No, man, I'll go eat or somethin', but don't dillydally."

"I'll dally as long as I damned well please. Now, get the hell out of here."

Smitty walked into the house. A package lay on the kitchen table right where he had left it before he and Grotsky had figured out a way to take a bath. He sat down and began to rip off the wrapping paper. Pulling back the flaps on the box, he reached inside. He hesitated, sure that he could smell the lingering scent of her rose perfume. He sat for a long moment, luxuriating in the simple pleasure of looking at things from home: a pipe, a bag of marbles, cookies packed in popcorn, and a new photo of Dorothy.

He removed the pipe and held it in his hands as if he were holding a baby chick. He turned it in every direction, taking in the grain of the wood, the intricate carving on the bowl, and the smell of tobacco that still permeated the length of the pipe. He knew it had once belonged to Frank.

"Whatcha got there?" said Grotsky, who walked in wrapped in a towel. He peered over Smitty's shoulder into the box. "Ooh, cookies! OK, man, it's your turn in the tub. I even added some clean water for you."

"There'd better be cookies left when I get back." Smitty removed his shirt as he left the kitchen table. He arrived at the tub naked and shivering in the morning chill. He stuck his foot in to check the temperature of the water and then slid into the tub. In an instant, the water turned brown. He didn't care. A package from home and a tub full of hot water. What more could a farm boy from Nebraska hope for out here? He closed his eyes and lay still, relishing the luxurious sensation of the hot water before grabbing the soap and beginning the arduous task of removing thirty days of war from his skin.

47

November 18, 1944

France

The old woman met Smitty at the door with a bowl of soup. "You eat!" She shook her finger at him.

Smitty pushed the bowl away and kept walking toward the stairs. "Gotta sleep first, Gramma." He compelled his legs to move up the creaking steps, opened the door to his room, and fell across the bed in his mud-caked uniform. The constant fear of his recurrent nightmares didn't faze him as three days without sleep took their toll.

"I'LL BE RIGHT back," Dorothy whispered.
She walked past Smitty. He stood

motionless for a moment, and then followed her down the hall into the bathroom. Without a word, he slid her dress up over her head and let it fall to the floor. She unbuttoned his shirt. He pulled down her slip; she pulled down his trousers. He picked her up and carried her back to the bedroom, laying her on top of the chenille bedspread and under him. He leaned down and kissed her breast.

"SMITTY, WAKE UP!" Grotsky shoved him from side to side, almost knocking him out of his bed. "Wake up, buddy. It's your anniversary, and I wanna celebrate," he continued, slurring his words and trying to stay upright.

"I *was* celebrating, you asshole. We were right there on the bed about to celebrate, and along you came and woke me up," Smitty grumbled.

Grotsky sat down on Smitty's bed. "Sorry, buddy, but we gotta celebrate. My anniversary is next week. Yours is today. Come on." He held up an empty bottle of wine. "I got three more of these babies in my duffel bag."

"I haven't had a drink for two weeks."

"Well then, it's about damned time. What's the good of being in fucking France if we can't drink some wine and get soused?"

Smitty sat up. "I think you've got a head start on me. Don't worry; I'll catch up. Been married two years today. Two years."

"Two years next week, for me."

"Two years, and all we had were three nights together—that's three *married* nights, if you know what I mean."

"You poor bastard. At least we had a couple of weeks. Well, to hell with this. Let's go get drunk."

"Suits me just fine. I'll just finish that dream later."

Three hours passed, Grotsky and Smitty climbed the stairs to their room, arm in arm, singing "I'll Get By." Out of tune and staggering up the last few stairs, they repeated the refrain. From the bedroom across the hall, a disgruntled soldier yelled, "Hey, assholes, hold it down! Some of us are trying to sleep!"

Smitty stumbled in the dark toward the voice and began to sing again.

"I don't give a rat's ass about you getting by!" shouted the soldier. "You two ain't the only homesick soldiers in the world, so shut up and sleep it off!"

"Good idea. Uh, where's my bed?"

"Next door, man. Now, shut the fuck up!"

Smitty staggered next door and collapsed onto his bed.

DOROTHY HUMMED AS she walked around the bedroom.

> *"What's that tune, honey?"*

> *"'I'll Get By.' I like it, don't you?"*

> *Smitty grinned. "As long as you're here, darlin', I'll always get by." He sat on the edge of the bed and reached out to her as she passed him. "I love you, Peaches."*

> *Dorothy resisted. A streak of lightning*

filled the night sky, and thunder crackled
overhead. She headed toward the door.
"Dottie! Where you goin'?"

"NO! DON'T LEAVE me!" Smitty fell out of bed. His head throbbed. Streaks of light flashed passed the windows. A whistling sound followed, assaulting his ears with its deafening blast. He lurched toward the door of the bedroom.

"Smitty! Not that way. Come on. We gotta get to the cave."

The stairway moaned with loud cracks and creaks as four soldiers scrambled down two flights of stairs and into the cellar. "That sounds even closer than last night," Smitty said, trying to keep from heaving that last bottle of wine.

Grotsky shrugged his shoulders. "Nothin' to do but just sit here and wait it out." He kissed his crucifix and began to play "I'll Get By" on his mandolin.

Smitty sat in the darkness. He could still see Dorothy walking out the door. He longed to see her face for just a moment, but she disappeared into the sound of whistling shells overhead.

48

November 18, 1944

Beaver City

Carol adjusted the purple scarf around her neck. "Any letters today?"

"Nothing for three weeks—not a thing. I'm a little frantic. Why would he just stop writing me? I wonder if he's in the hospital again. Maybe his malaria came back or something."

Carol put her hand on Dorothy's shoulder. "Calm down. You know he's in the middle of a war. They can't always write on a schedule."

"I know that, but you don't understand. I just have this awful feeling that something is wrong."

"Honey, you've had a hard year. Your father died; your husband is gone. You might be overreacting just a little."

"Overreacting? Did you hear what I said? Three weeks—that's twenty-one days—and no letters, nothing. And you're right—he's in the middle of a war. How can I *not* be worried sick?"

Dorothy took out her planimeter and began to plot the Rhenberg farm. She soothed herself with platitudes. *He's fine; he's just fine. I know I'll hear from him soon. He's just busy; that's all.*

Betty, one of the bookkeepers, leaned over Dorothy's desk. Her cleavage showed more than Dorothy thought proper. Noting Dorothy's apparent displeasure at her brazen display, Betty leaned forward even more, swinging her hips back and forth as she spoke: "No letters in three weeks? Hey, wanna go with us to the dance tonight? That would get your mind off that naughty husband of yours."

"You still go to the dances? I mean, you're married. We're married women, Betty. I don't think it's such a good idea to go to the dances."

Betty snickered and tucked her long blonde hair behind her right ear. "Don't trust yourself, girly? It's just a dance. No hanky-panky or anything."

"That's not what I heard, Betty. You better be careful who you're hanging around with. It might get back to your husband."

Betty ignored the advice and finished applying her pink champagne lipstick. "Suit yourself, sugar." She sauntered back to her desk, winked at one of the women, and nodded toward Dorothy. "Prude," she said, just loud enough for Dorothy to hear. She sat down and crossed her legs, exposing just a hint of her thigh.

Dorothy swiveled her chair around and opened her mouth to protest but stifled herself at the last minute. "Are *you* going to the dance?" she whispered to Carol.

"Of course, honey. Remember, I'm not married. You know, Betty is sort of right. It wouldn't hurt you to get out of the house now and then. You *love* to dance. You should try it out. You could go with me. *I'll* make sure you behave."

An army-green sedan with a white star on the driver's door turned up the street past the Triple-A office and headed in the direction of Dorothy's house.

Dorothy rushed to the office window. "Did you see that?"

Carol looked outside. "See what?"

"It was an army car headed toward my house."

"It was headed west—not necessarily to your house. Dottie, wait!"

Dorothy was already out the door and running the four blocks toward her house. Her heart pounded. "Please don't let it be me. Please, please, please."

She reached her house and looked up and down the street. Was it lost, or making a U-turn? Then she spotted it, parked not in front of her home but that of the Larson's, four houses down. Two men in crisply pressed, immaculate uniforms got out of the vehicle and approached the front door, their faces grim and foreboding. Mrs. Larson opened the front door, saw the men, and began to scream, "No! No! Not Danny! No!" Mr. Larson held her as the soldiers attempted to do their duty.

Dorothy stood, frozen, unable to look away from the appalling scene. "It's not Jack, but it's Danny!" Relief and guilt rushed through her in equal measure. "How can I be happy?" she cried. "But I am. God help me, I am."

DOROTHY PUSHED OPEN the door to the American Legion Hall. The band played "There'll Be Some Changes Made." She straightened her shoulders and made her way through the door and into the crowd. Carol and her date followed close behind.

"There's a table, honey. Grab it before someone else does."

Dorothy headed to the table. "I'll just sit here while you dance."

"But it wouldn't hurt you to dance at least *one* dance, would it?"

"Probably wouldn't hurt, but I'm here because I couldn't stand to stay home after today's events. That's all. I just need a little diversion. Besides, it's our anniversary, and I want to celebrate, even if it is by myself."

"Suit yourself!" Carol and her date headed for the dance floor.

Dorothy hummed and tapped her foot in time to the music. The events of the day faded into the rhythm of the music. She couldn't remember the last time she had felt so lighthearted.

Hate to give Betty credit, but maybe this was a good idea after all, she pondered.

She jumped as someone's hands covered her eyes, smudging her glasses.

"Guess who? Hey, I've been lookin' for you, Dottie. Where ya been?"

"Ivan! What are you doing here? I thought you were in England."

"I was, but I'm back with a Purple Heart and a bad

shoulder. Say, I heard about Tommie missing in action. Do you know if he's still alive? Oh, Dottie, I'm sorry. I didn't mean to be so thoughtless."

"It's OK, Ivan. I don't know what happened with Tommie." She pointed at her left hand. "I'm a married woman now. I married Jack Smith. You remember him, don't you? He's Annie's brother."

"Well, I'll be darned." Ivan sat down beside Dorothy. "I didn't know. Last I heard you were going with Tommie, and I just assumed..."

"Wanna dance, Ivan?"

"Sure, let's dance. That's a good idea."

The band began to play "Blue Champagne." Ivan put his arm around Dorothy's waist, and they eased their way onto the dance floor.

"I forgot what a good dancer you are. Almost as good as my husband."

"You're pretty good yourself, Dottie."

"Thanks."

He caressed her. She started to resist, but he held her even closer, and she began to relax into the swaying motion of their bodies. *What could it hurt?* she thought. *It's just a dance.*

She could smell his Old Spice aftershave. "My husband wears that same aftershave," she said in a whisper.

The song ended. "One more for old times' sake, Dottie?"

"I don't know. You know how people talk."

Ivan winked at her. "Come on, Dottie. It's just a dance."

"Stop looking at me. It's those doggone blue eyes of yours, and you know it too." His smile, his dimples, and his eyes, the color of the Nebraska sky early in the morning before the clouds roll in, melded into an irresistible force.

"You're *always* smiling."

"Why wouldn't I smile? I'm with you, the girl of my dreams."

"The war didn't change you one bit, did it?"

"I'll Get By" began to play. Ivan coaxed her onto the dance floor. He wrapped his arm around her so their bodies touched, and he rubbed her back in a way that no one else would notice. She noticed, of course, and, try as she might, she found she didn't want to stop him. He leaned down and put his lips against her ear, "Dottie, you know how I feel about you. I haven't changed my mind one iota since our junior year. Let's leave the dance for just a little while. No one will notice. I've been away so long. The war..."

Dorothy pushed him away. "Ivan! I told you I'm a married woman." She started to go.

He took her hand. "Dottie, I'm here. He isn't. Just finish this dance with me, and I promise I'll leave you alone."

She stood there for a moment, knowing she should leave but not wanting to go. Finally, she put her hand on his shoulder and allowed herself to drift into a fantasy as Ivan waltzed her around the floor.

"JACK, YOU'RE HOME!" She ran into his arms. He picked her up and swirled her around until they both fell to the ground, dizzy, giddy, and falling into each other's arms. "I missed you so much. Happy

anniversary, baby. I told ya it wouldn't be long. Let's go home and celebrate."

In the car, Jack took a right turn instead of a left onto the highway.

"This isn't the way home, you know."

"I know, but I can't wait. We're goin' to our special place. Remember?"

He turned the car onto the dirt road by the cemetery and parked it under their favorite elm tree. She slid across the seat, and they fell into each other's arms...

"HEY, DOTTIE. THE dance is over. Come on. I'll take you home."

"What? Oh, Ivan, I'm sorry. I sort of..."

"I know, Dottie. It's so hard when your old man is off fighting a war. It's lonely; I know. You can talk to me. Come on now, and let me drive you home."

"I don't know. I don't think that would be such a good idea. I think I'll just walk home. I need the fresh air."

"I'll walk with you."

Carol moved herself between Ivan and Dorothy. "Hey, honey, I thought I'd lost ya. Are you ready to go home?"

"Yes, yes, I am," Dorothy said in a daze. "Thanks for the dance, Ivan, but I came with Carol. I need to leave with Carol. See you around."

Carol ushered Dorothy toward the door. "Looked like you were enjoying yourself with good old Ivan, but I'm not sure about him at all. What's with the tears?"

"Nothing. I'm fine, but I want to walk by myself. Thanks for inviting me, Carol. I'll see you on Monday."

The cold air swept across Dorothy's face, dissipating the heat that was now radiating through her body. She couldn't deny how much she delighted in having a man pay attention to her, caress her, whisper in her ear.

"Jack Smith!" she yelled. "Where are you?"

49

January 1945

Smitty sat on his bed, polishing his boots. Grotsky entered, frowning and holding a letter.

"Hey, man, why the scowl? Bad news?"

"My wife. She says the farm ain't doin' so good. There's nobody to do the work. She and her dad are doing everything they can to hold it together, but there's just too much work to do. The good news is she's talkin' to the draft board about how to bring me home early."

Smitty dropped his boot. "You mean you can do that? Get out early to farm?"

"She seems to think so. She's sending me papers from people back home that say I need to come home or the farm will go under. I have to get the colonel to sign off on it; then it goes to Washington, DC, for approval."

"Damned, the war will be over by the time you get all that done."

"Maybe, but it's worth a try, don't ya think?"

"Hell, yes. Maybe I can get one, too, to work on my wife's farm or somethin'. Her brother is the only one back there; if he's drafted, maybe I can take his place." He slapped Grotsky on the back. "Thanks, pal. I think I can see the light at the end of the tunnel! I'm gonna write Dottie right now and tell her."

DOROTHY TORE AT the envelope, shredding it in the process. As she walked toward the Triple-A office, she began to read:

> Darling Dorothy,
>
> How are you doing these days? The mail seems to have slowed down again. I have only got one letter since I last wrote you. Honey, I'm sure glad you are starting to hear from me. I know how you feel when you don't get letters regular. I can tell by your letters that you get pretty disgusted with me. Honestly, Honey, it really isn't all my fault. I know there are times when I neglect writing, but there is generally a reason. When a man is up here close to the front and there is shelling going on, it just seems impossible for me to sit down and write. I don't want you to think that I don't love you, because I don't write, because Honey,

you are in my thoughts every day.

Honey, if Walter gets drafted, maybe I can come home early and take his place. No fooling. Grotsky's wife is working on him coming home early. Maybe we can do the same thing. It's a long shot, but it's worth a try.

I have to go now. I'm in the middle of cleaning my boots and they're likely to call us any minute to take a load of ammo to the front.

Always remember how much I love you, Honey.

All my love,
Smitty

"Always remember how much I love you. Always remember how much I love you," Dorothy repeated, marching toward the office in step with the words. "Always remember..."

"Hi, Dottie. Got a letter from that husband of yours?"

"Oh, hi, Ivan. Yes, *finally*. I didn't know what to think. It's been four weeks since I heard anything from him. He could have been dead for all I knew. Sorry, you don't need to listen to my woes."

"You know I'd listen to you forever. I wasn't foolin' the other night at the dance. Hey, how about going with me tonight after work for a chocolate shake? Is that still your favorite?"

"How can you possibly remember my favorite *anything* from high school?"

"Oh, I remember everything about you, Dottie—the way

you walk, the perfume you wear, the way you kiss." Ivan wrapped his arm around Dorothy's shoulder.

"Ivan! Cut it out! Now I remember why we broke up. You won't take no for an answer."

"That's right. I'm a man who never gives up. Just keep that in mind, Mrs. Smith." He winked at her and crossed the street, whistling "I'll Get By."

"See you after work, Dottie!"

IVAN TAPPED HIS fingers on the counter and smiled at Dorothy. "Here I am as promised, five o'clock sharp. Ready for that chocolate shake?"

Dorothy blushed. "Ivan, you are impossible."

"Well, well, well, what do we have here, Mrs. Smith? I saw you two at the dance last Saturday," Betty taunted. "Changed your mind, Dottie? Singin' a little different tune?"

"It's none of your business, Betty. And *no*, I haven't changed my mind about anything!"

"Calm down, Dottie. Why are you getting so upset if there's nothing going on?"

Dorothy turned her back to Betty. "Ivan, I have no intention of going anywhere with you now or ever. Do I make myself clear?"

Ivan's blue eyes dimmed, and his dazzling smile disappeared. "I'm sorry, Dottie. I didn't come in here to embarrass you. I just thought we could have a shake for old times' sake."

Betty picked up her purse and walked toward the door. "Hey, Ivan, I'll have a shake with you." She looped her arm around Ivan's and whispered, "I'm not a cold fish like some people we know." Ivan, looking a little stunned and confused, nonetheless strolled out the front door arm-in-arm with Betty.

Dorothy watched in righteous indignation as the couple departed. "How can she be that way? Her husband is fighting in this crazy war, and she's back here flirting with everyone. She's going to get herself in a fix if she isn't careful. She doesn't know Ivan like I do. He doesn't take no for an answer without a fight."

Carol headed for the front door. "Well, honey, I'm not sure she's going to put up much of a fight. You know, people don't change just because they get married. Betty has always been ready for just about anything."

"Well, some people change. Jack changed."

50

March 1945

Germany

Smitty handed his repair requisition to the sergeant on duty at the motor pool. "Here you go. It's not hittin' on all cylinders. I think it needs a valve job."

The sergeant studied the orders and sniffed at Smitty. "The showers are around the corner to the left. You might wanna check them out, private."

"Sorry, sarge. I just got back from the front. We've been haulin' ammo for three days. No time to change clothes, let alone take a shower. I know it's different back here at headquarters, but..."

"That'll be all, son. I'll take care of your truck. Go take a shower and get some chow."

"Yes, sir." Smitty left the motor pool and headed for the showers.

GROTSKY STRIPPED OFF his muddy, grime-covered clothes and left them in a heap outside the showers.

"Grotsky, how did you beat me over here?" Smitty asked, adding his muddy pants to the pile.

"I didn't have to deal with the orders or the sarge. I just took off and headed straight for here. This is a little piece of paradise, ain't it?"

"Yeah, I may never get out." Smitty began to sing "Lili Marlene." Grotsky joined in.

A loud voice boomed over the splash of the showers: "Gentlemen, this is not a place for mindless chatter. There is a finite amount of hot water available and a hell of a lot of GIs that need it. Get your asses in gear!"

"Yes, sir!" Smitty and Grotsky yelled in unison.

They finished their showers, dressed, and headed pell-mell for the mess tent. "These Joes got it made, and they don't even know it," Smitty chided. "B-rations, man, someone else is gonna cook for us. I could get used to this. I bet these guys ain't even heard the sound of shelling or seen half the things we have."

Grotsky agreed. "I get what you're sayin', but I for one don't care what they have or haven't seen or heard or done. It's so quiet and peaceful back here. Let's just enjoy it. B-rations, man. This is first class."

They sat down at an open table, and Grotsky began shoveling food into his mouth. "I'm so damned hungry, I could eat a horse. When was the last time we got this much chow at one time? It even tastes pretty good."

Smitty stopped eating. "Have you heard anything about goin' home?"

"Not a damned word. I'm gettin' a little discouraged about the whole thing. It was a long shot anyway, but there's always tomorrow."

"Surely those Krauts can't hold out much longer. We're already in their damned country."

"Yeah, but they're Krauts. They'll fight to the bitter end."

Smitty piled mashed potatoes on his spoon, shoved them into his mouth, and continued talking. "Wonder what they'll do with us while the truck is gettin' repaired."

"I'm sure they'll think of somethin'. And here comes the answer now." Grotsky nodded in the direction of a sergeant who approached and loomed over them.

"Smith and Grotsky?"

"Yes, sir. That's Smith, and I'm Grotsky."

"My lucky day." The sergeant threw a packet of papers on the table. "Here are your orders, privates. Head to the transportation pool as soon as you finish chow."

"Yes, sir!" Grotsky barked.

Smitty opened his orders and began to read. "Well, I'll be damned. They're keepin' me here. I'm gonna drive a captain around all day. I think I died and went to heaven. What about you?"

"Same orders. I stay here permanently and drive a jeep all day. Hot damn, Smitty! Even if I don't get to go home early, this ain't half-bad duty."

Two Weeks Later

Smitty's eyes opened against his will. Every beat of his heart echoed in his throbbing head. He tried to push himself up into a sitting position, but his arms wouldn't cooperate. His body trembled in violent spasms as an arctic chill ran down his spine.

Grotsky stormed in, holding a letter in his hand. "You ain't gonna believe this!"

Smitty struggled onto his side. "Believe what?"

A courier ran into the room, stopping long enough to catch his breath. "Smitty! Get your ass out of bed! Now! The captain needs you! You gotta drive his ass up to the front!"

"The captain has to go to the front on a Sunday morning?" Smitty groaned. "Why? Never mind. I can't do it. It's the malaria. It's back. Ya gotta help me get to sick call."

"Didn't you hear me? The captain wants you now! Get your ass out of bed!"

Smitty sat up and attempted to focus his blurred vision. He dropped back onto the bed. "Man, look at me. I can't even sit up." He wrapped his blanket closer to his body.

Grotsky touched Smitty's forehead. "Damn, he ain't kiddin'. He's burnin' up. Tell the captain I'll drive him as soon as I help Smitty to sick call. My only day off in two weeks, and you up and get sick! Come on; let's go."

Grotsky hoisted Smitty up into a sitting position and wrapped his arm around his waist. "Let's get you to sick call so I can get back to the captain. Sounds like he's in a pretty big rush."

"Thanks, buddy. Hey, what was in that letter anyway?"

The room swirled. Smitty struggled to focus on what

Grotsky was saying, but the words fell into a blackness that absorbed him and dragged him into a deep dark hole.

SMITTY ATTEMPTED TO move his right arm, but a restraint held it in place. He followed a line of tubing from his forearm to a bottle of fluids dripping into his vein. His head no longer throbbed, and the chills seemed less severe. "Think I'll live after all."

"Oh good. You're awake," the nurse said, somewhat relieved.

"Sorry, I didn't see you. What time is it anyway?"

"It's nine o'clock at night, soldier. Your buddy dropped you off this morning. You passed out on the way. The poor guy almost had to carry you into sick bay. You're pretty sick, soldier. Your malaria has kicked up again, for sure."

"Again? Damned! Say, my buddy didn't happen to come back by, did he?"

"I don't think so. What's his name?"

"Grotsky, Daniel Grotsky. He drove for me today. Took Captain Wilson to the front, but... Hey, what's the matter? You look like you just saw a ghost or somethin'."

"You said Captain Wilson? Captain Carl Wilson?"

"Yeah, you know him? Kind of a short guy with black hair and blue eyes?"

"Yes, I know him. I'll be right back, soldier. I have to report to the doctor that you're awake. He'll want to check you out."

"Suit yourself. I'll be right here."

THE DOCTOR ENTERED the room. A grim look covered his face. "How are you feeling?"

"Not bad, Doc, but you look like shit. What's goin' on? Am I gonna die or somethin'?" All the moisture left Smitty's mouth.

"No, son, you're doing just fine. It's a bout of malaria. We're treating you for it now, and you'll be good as new in a couple of days. But if you were Captain Wilson's driver, I'm afraid I have some bad news."

"*Were* his driver? What are you talking about?"

"He died today. He was headed to the front when his jeep hit a land mine. You're one lucky guy. Your malaria actually saved your life."

Smitty tried to digest the doctor's words: *land mine, dead.* "Who is dead, Doc? The captain, just the captain? What about his driver?"

The doctor touched Smitty's arm. "No one survived, son. The driver and the captain both died in the explosion. Did you know the driver?"

"Grotsky, Daniel Grotsky. Is *that* who was driving?"

"Yes."

Smitty sat up. He took a swing at the doctor. "No, you're wrong! Grotsky brought me to sick call. He can't be dead." Pushing the doctor away, he attempted to get up.

"Settle down, son. Nurse! Bring me a sedative, stat!"

Smitty managed to take a step toward the chair that held his clothes. "I gotta go find Grotsky! You're wrong, Doc!"

"Medic! In here, now!"

"Leave me alone!" Smitty took a swing at the medic. The room spun like a top.

THE BLARING SOUND of reveille careened into Smitty's brain. He pressed his pillow over his ears. Every joint in his body ached and throbbed in time with his pulse. He could see the sun rising through the window. *Wait, wait. It was just some sort of nightmare. That's all it was.* "Nurse!" he yelled. "Nurse! Oh, good. You're here." He heaved a sigh of relief as the nurse entered the room. "I had the worst nightmare. It was my buddy. They said he blew up, him and the captain. It was just a nightmare, right?"

The nurse took his hands in hers. "Look at me, Jack. Look into my eyes and listen to me. It wasn't a nightmare. Daniel Grotsky and Captain Wilson were killed yesterday by a land mine they hit on the way to the front. Now, keep looking into my eyes. Take a deep breath. Good, now take another one and just keep looking into my eyes. It's awful. It was a shock for all of us. I am so sorry, but it *is* true."

He contorted his face, biting his lower lip and shaking his head. "No, no, it can't be. This can't be happening." An agonizing cry started deep inside and worked its way upward as he took in the truth reflected in the nurse's eyes.

"Don't try to stop it. Let it out. Let it all out. It's OK, Jack. Let it out."

Smitty's body heaved in giant waves of anguish. The nurse wrapped her arms around him.

"He was just here." Smitty looked around the room, sure that Grotsky was about to walk in and tell him it was all just a big joke.

"He has a mandolin, and we sing songs together while we're drivin' to the front. Hell, we sang our way through Africa and Italy and France."

The nurse tightened her grip on his trembling hands. "Tell me more about him. Everything you know. You said he had a wife. What was her name?"

"Doris. They got married two weeks after me and my wife did, but we didn't know each other then."

"When did you meet him?"

"We met one night when we were both soused." He laughed through his tears. "We were in the same tent in Africa. He used to grab my letters out of my hand and read them."

Smitty talked on. The nurse listened. The clod in his gut expanded, fed by an unyielding, relentless sorrow.

51

April 1945

Rest Camp in France

Birds flew in and out of a nearby birdbath. Tulips surrounded a dirt path leading to a hot spring. A breeze came up and blew white apple tree blossoms through the air. Smitty picked up his pen determined to write something:

> My Darling Dorothy,
>
> How's my beautiful little wife? Whatcha up to? You'll never guess where I am, not in a million years. I'm at a rest camp in France. I had another bout of malaria. I've been here about a week. I will probably go back to my unit next week. It's beautiful here. I'm better now.

He crumpled the letter and threw it into the birdbath. He stood up and took long deliberate steps down the path, allowing the surroundings to calm his anguish. He closed his eyes.

DOROTHY THREW HER head back and laughed. Her eyes sparkled like the Platte River under a full moon. He tasted the sweetness of her mouth against his. The rose scent of her perfume filled his nostrils. He felt dizzy, overwhelmed by her presence: warm and inviting like a front-porch swing in late May. The air seemed filled with her love and devotion to him.

"JACK, I HATE to bother you—you look so relaxed—but it's time to get going. You have a dinner engagement tonight, remember? It's your turn to have dinner with the Martin family at their house." The corporal handed Jack a box. "Here are the ten-in-one rations. Just give them to the lady of the house. She'll make a nice dinner with it. It's a thank-you gift for inviting soldiers into their home."

Smitty heard the corporal's voice, but his words made no sense.

"Jack, come on. You gotta get ready now." He took Smitty's arm and helped him stand.

"She's so beautiful, isn't she? Did you see her? My wife, I mean. She was just here."

"I think you had a pretty vivid dream, soldier. You're in France. Your wife is in the good ole US of A. Come on, let's get you dressed and ready to go. You'll have a good time."

"No, she was here. I could smell her and taste her and feel her, just like she was standin' right here."

"Whatever you say, but she's gone now, so let's get going."

Smitty pointed to his head. "No, she's still here, and she'll always be here."

"Whatever you say—just keep walking. We're almost to your room. Can you get your clothes changed on your own?"

"I'm fine. Why do I have to change my clothes?"

"Oh, brother, you are a case. Maybe you shouldn't go."

"Go where?"

"To the Martin's house for dinner. They invited you. Remember, the nice French family that hosts soldiers in their home? We talked about the whole thing this morning, and you said yes, so they are expecting you. Get it?"

"I get it. I get it. No need to be a wise guy!"

"Give them the ten-in-one rations. Do you remember what they're for?"

"I got it, man. It's a gift. She'll cook them up. We'll have dinner. I got it."

SMITTY STOOD AS Madame Martin entered the dining room, speaking French at a fast clip. Her daughter, Michelle, translated at an equally fast pace: "She says the rations were excellent, and thank you for sharing them. She has added a few of her own ingredients, and she hopes you like what she's done."

"I'm so glad you speak English, Miss. This is much more enjoyable with your help."

"Call me Michelle, please, Mr. Smith."

"Only if you call me Jack. People used to call me Smitty, but I'm Jack now. Call me Jack."

"Jack," she said with an American accent. "This is how we say it in French: 'Jauck.' That is a strong name. It fits you."

Jack fidgeted with his hat. "Thank you, Miss—er, Michelle. I'm sorry. It's just a long time since I've been around a woman, I mean, a young woman like you."

"Oh, yes. Young men are scarce these days as well."

Madame Martin served a salad made with the fruit cocktail from the ten-in-one rations.

"Is this it?" Jack whispered.

Michelle looked at him in amazement. "Oh, goodness no. It is the first course. In France we linger over our food, one course at a time. It's good to take your time, linger over things—don't you agree?" She ran her fingers through her long auburn hair and smiled softly at him.

Jack sat speechless. He took a bite of the fruit salad, and his eyes lit up. "There's apples in here. I never tasted any canned fruit from rations with apples in it. It's delicious. Where did she find apples this time of year?"

Michelle put her elbow on the table and rested her chin in her hand. "Jack, doesn't your mother put food in jars to preserve it for the winter?"

"You mean canning? Oh, sure, I just didn't know you did that in France."

"Oui, we 'can,' as you say, in France. My mother cans all sorts of things. You will probably taste more of her cans as the evening goes by."

"It meets your liking?" Madame Martin asked in English, waiting with folded hands for Jack's response.

"How do you say 'delicious' in French?"

Monsieur Martin answered, "*Délicieux*. We speak some English, but Michelle is the master."

Jack cleared his throat. "Deleasho," he muttered, turning to Michelle. "Maybe you better say it for me."

Madame Martin furrowed her brow. "That is fine. I also speak and understand a little bit of English. You tried to speak our language. It is difficult."

Michelle smirked at her mother. "What she means is, don't butcher our beautiful language with your terrible American accent."

Madame Martin shot a disapproving glance in Michelle's direction. "Michelle, that's enough! I'm sorry, Jack. Our daughter turned twenty-one, and now she thinks she is a modern woman, rude to her mother in front of guests, no less." She showed a broad smile for the first time. "A little wine will cheer us up." She disappeared into the kitchen and returned with two bottles of red wine.

"Mercy," Jack stammered.

Michelle shook her head. "It is pronounced "Mare-*see*. Try again."

Jack blushed. "Marsee."

Michelle touched his lips with her fingertips. "Hold your mouth like this, and put the emphasis on the second syllable, like this: Mare-*see*."

Jack tried to focus on Michelle's words instead of the fingertips on his lips. "Mare-*see*."

"*Trés bon*. You are a fast learner. Tell me, do you dance?"

"Do I dance? Do I *ever* dance! That's something I *can* do. I'm pretty damned—er, I mean, darn good at it too. Do *you* dance?"

"Of course. I am French. We dance from the time we are little ones. We will dance after dinner. You can show me just how good you are. Now eat. *Maman* made a special treat for you with your rations."

AFTER DINNER, MICHELLE led the way into the parlor, closed the door, and placed a record on the phonograph. Benny Goodman's band began to play "Moonglow."

"Hey, that's American music!" said Jack.

"Of course. Now, let's see how well you can dance."

Jack put his arm around Michelle's waist. She moved into Jack so that their bodies touched. He pushed her away.

"I see. Are you married, Jack?"

"Yes, I am."

"Are you a faithful husband?"

"Yes, I am."

"I am not asking you to be unfaithful, but how can we dance so far apart?" She moved her body close to him. "There, this is how we dance here. You are in France, so you learn to dance our way, *oui?*" She laid her head on his chest. "Relax, Jack. I won't bite you."

Jack began to relax as the wine from dinner took effect. "You're a good dancer, Michelle." She smelled like lilacs. He closed his eyes and tightened his embrace.

"That feels good, you know? It's been a long time since I

was held in the arms of a man."

"Shh. Don't talk. Just dance."

Monsieur Martin opened the door to the parlor. He said something to Michelle in French, and she left the room in a snit. "I think it's time for you to leave," he said to Jack, leaving no room for argument. "Your ride is waiting outside."

"Yes, sir. Did I do something wrong? We were just dancing. Nothing else."

"It's been a long, miserable war. You did nothing wrong, but it is time for you to leave."

"Yes, sir, it is time for me to leave. I gotta get ready to go home. I gotta get well."

52

Headquarters Company
Garmisch, Germany

Jack walked into the barracks. A tall, skinny kid lay sprawled across Grotsky's cot, reading a book. Unaware of Jack's presence, he ran his hands through his thick black hair and turned the page. Jack cleared his throat. The kid held up his hand, not saying a word, and continued reading. When he finished the page, he looked up from the bed and stared at Jack for a moment before speaking: "You must be Smitty. I'm Ray. I'm taking the other guy's place."

"The *other* guy? You mean Grotsky? He's not just some *guy*." Jack threw his duffel bag onto his cot with such force that it almost collapsed. His anger startled him. He had no idea that his feigned recovery was so thinly veiled.

"Sorry. I didn't mean to be disrespectful, sir."

"And don't call me sir. I'm a private, just like you, kid. And by the way, my name is Jack—just Jack."

"Jack. I thought you weren't coming back for another week. They kick you out early?"

"No, I decided it was time to get back to bein' useful again. The malaria's gone. No sense wallowing in all that other shit. I just told 'em I was leavin' and there was nothin' they could do about it."

"So, you're okay now?"

"Don't look so scared kid, I'm fine. I'm not bonkers. I promise."

Two weeks passed and Jack was surprised at how easily he fell back into the routine of army life. He felt good. He spent his days making plans for what would happen when the war was over and he returned to his darling Dorothy.

The sound of mandolin music wafting into his room brought him up short. "Grotsky," he murmured, "He's back." He ran across the hall in the direction of the music, fully expecting to find Grotsky sprawled across a cot, plucking away at the mandolin. Instead, he saw a soldier strumming the strings as though the instrument belonged to him. Jack snatched the mandolin. "Where'd you get this?" he demanded, irate that someone had stolen Grotsky's pride and joy.

"I bought it off a Kraut last week. It ain't Grotsky's, if that's what you're wonderin'. Jesus, Smitty, ease up."

Image after confusing image raced through Jack's mind: Grotsky in the truck playing "Lili Marlene," Grotsky sitting across from him in the little French house, Grotsky running for cover with the mandolin held close to his chest. "Don't call me Smitty! I'm *Jack*! he screamed."

"Cool down, man! Here, have a little schnapps and relax."

Smitty threw the mandolin on the soldier's cot, stormed out of the room, and slammed the door. Ray stood motionless, stunned by Jack's outburst. "You OK, sir?"

"No, I'm *not* OK. Go have some schnapps with the jerks next door or something. Just leave me the fuck alone."

"Yes, sir!" Ray closed the door behind him. Jack collapsed onto his cot.

You should be here, buddy, not me. Why did you have to go get blown up anyway, you stupid son of a bitch? It shoulda been me. He lay on his bed, holding his knees to his chest, rocking himself in a soothing back and forth motion, imprisoned in his own grief.

Shoulda been me.

53

May 7, 1945

"It's over."

Jack continued to shine his shoes. "What's over?"

"The war."

"You mean the Krauts are retreating again? Where're they goin' this time?"

"Jack, the goddamned war is over."

Jack's mind numbed. "Over. Ya mean we're goin' home?"

Ray began to laugh. "Yes, sir. We're goin' home."

Jack tried to stand, but his legs gave way, and he fell back onto his cot. "Over!" He sprang from his bed and tackled Ray, who fell into the hallway with Jack on top of him.

"Hey, take it easy, man!" Ray said. "I wanna go home in one piece."

Jack gave out a loud whoop and headed for the front door. Soldiers were milling around, shaking hands, hugging, crying. Fifteen minutes passed before silence fell over the group.

"What now?" Jack asked Ray.

"How the hell do I know? I guess we just keep doin' what we're doin' until they come and tell us different."

Jack walked back into the barracks, climbed the stairs two at a time, and then flopped down onto his cot. He picked up his shoe brush and started buffing his boots. An imperceptible easing of the heaviness in his gut began. Tears dripped onto his boots. "I'm goin' home; I'm goin' home," he repeated in rhythm with the shoe brush swishing across his boots. "I'm goin' home!"

Beaver City

May 7, 1945

Dorothy put her planimeter down and looked out the office window. People were running out of Warton's Department Store, the post office, and the bank. She heard cheering. Strangers were hugging each other. "What's going on?"

Mr. Anderson opened his office door and rushed into the room. He cleared his throat three times. "The war in Europe is over, ladies." He stopped, clearing his throat a fourth time. "The war is over. You have the rest of the day off. Go celebrate!"

"The war is over." Dorothy repeated his words as they seeped into her thoughts. She blinked her eyes. "It's over?"

Carol headed for the front door. "That's what he said! It's

over! Come on, let's join the party!"

Dorothy blinked her eyes rapidly, trying to make sense of the words. "The war is over! It's over! He's coming home! My husband is coming home! I have to go home and get ready. I need to get the bedroom set out of the storage shed and make the bed up, and I need a new dress. What do you think he would like? I don't even remember. I'm going to be a wife, a real wife!"

"Dottie! You'll have plenty of time for that later. Let's just go celebrate."

Dorothy went back to her desk to grab her purse and saw Betty with her forehead pressed against her desk. "Come on, Betty. It's over. Your husband is coming home. I know we've had our differences, but it's all over now. Come join the party!"

Betty didn't move. Her lips trembled. "It's not over. It's just beginning. I'm pregnant."

54

Germany

Ray sat on his bed with a pencil and pad on his lap. "So, how many points do you have?" Jack scribbled something on a pad of paper. "Eighty, as best as I can guess. I need at least five more. If they don't give credit for that last battle in Austria, I'm screwed. I'll be stuck here with the occupation force for God only knows how long. I gotta write my wife and explain how this thing works, and I don't wanna get her hopes up. I don't know what to do." He tore the sheet of paper off the pad, crumpled it up, and threw it across the room.

"Hey, man, take it easy. They'll give you credit for it. Why wouldn't they? It just takes some time."

"But there are guys with ninety and a hundred points, and they aren't going home either. How am I supposed to get home, even if I do have eighty-five points?"

DOROTHY READ THROUGH Jack's letter:

My Darling Dorothy,

How's my Honey doing these days? Are you working hard? To my estimation you always work hard. Honey, I can't blame you for getting impatient with me for not writing. I know I'm plenty slack in writing but it's so hard for me to settle down and write a letter.

They're sure not sending many home anymore. There still lots of guys with 9Ø to 1ØØ points. No, I hardly think I'll have to go to the Pacific, but one never knows what might happen when you're in the Army.

Well, here's hoping I make it home soon. I love you, darling and I think of you everyday.

All My Love

Jack G.

Pad and pencil in hand, Dorothy wrote 'Jack's Advanced Service Rating Score' at the top of the page. "He entered the army in February of '42, so that's 39 points. He's been overseas since April of '43, so that's another 25 points. That's a total of 64 points." She frowned. "He's 21 points short of making 85." She stopped to reread the newspaper article she had found about the rating system. "It says he gets five points for every battle he was in. He needs five battles to get enough points. I wonder if he has enough."

Resisting the desire to give way to tears, she picked up the newspaper and scanned the article once again. "There *has* to be a way."

"Sure there's a w-way, Sis. H-how does this point system w-w-work, anyway?"

"They use a system to determine who comes home and when, and, as near as I can figure, he's short by twenty-five points. There has to be a way to make up those points."

"Well, we c-c-can try telling them he needs to come home and help me farm."

"You're right! He mentioned a friend of his, Grotsky, who was trying to do that. I wonder if it worked. Walter, you're a genius! I'll write him right now and ask."

JACK SAT MOTIONLESS on his bed, staring at the letter.

> Darling,
>
> I have been adding up the points it's going to take to get you home, and, as near as I can figure, you are short about twenty-five points. How many battles were you in? You need at least five battles. Were you in that many? Seems safer to do what you were doing, just driving around in a truck. Anyway, Walter and I were talking about it, and we were wondering what happened to that friend of yours, Grotsky, and getting them to let him go home to help farm. Maybe we can do something like that, at least for a while, until we're ready to go to Washington and grow apples. What do you think, Honey? Now that the war is officially over, I am finding it harder and harder to be

without you. I want you home, Honey. I want to start our life together.

Write me soon, and let me know what you think about the idea.

All my love,

Dorothy

The last words that Grotsky had spoken now emerged from the murky shadows of Jack's mind and into the stark reality of the present moment:

"I'm goin' home, man. They gave me the deferment. I'm goin' home in a couple of days."

How could he tell her the truth? Grotsky's memory tormented him day and night. He saw him in every Deuce and a Half that rumbled past, and heard his mandolin playing every time "Lili Marlene" came on the radio. One question kept him in continual agony, a question he would grapple with for the rest of his life, one with no answer that could assuage his sorrow: "Why him and not me?"

55

Beaver City

Dorothy read Jack's letter again, trying to make sense of it all.

> Dearest Dorothy,
>
> Honey, I have been in battles over here.
> What did you think I was doing in that truck,
> just driving around the countryside? You or
> anyone else don't realize the circumstances
> that we're under over here. I have 2Ø points
> from battles I've been in. I am waiting to hear
> about my last one. Then I'll have the 25 points.
>
> Honey, I know it's hard for both of us
> being apart for so long. I still have hopes of

being home sometime in December, but it don't pay to get our hopes up too high cause there's so damned many disappointments in this Army.

I probably should have told you sooner, but my friend, Grotsky died. He got all the papers signed to go home early, but he died. That's how it is over here. One day you're here and the next day you're gone. But, don't you worry. I'm coming home.

What a day it will be when we can start living a normal life together. We can try to get the early out deal, but even if we don't, I want to settle down and start farming right there in good ol' Beaver City. Forget Washington. What do you say, darlin'? Home sounds pretty good to me right now.

I'll let you know about the points from the last battle but don't get your hopes up.

All My Love,
Jack G.

One emotion collided with another. Relief that he had more of the necessary points than she thought clashed with the news that his best friend died; confusion that he didn't say how Grotsky died quickly led to fear that Jack might suffer the same fate; sorrow that she wasn't there in person to console him butted up against total bewilderment at the changes she sensed in him. He signed all his letters "Jack," not "Smitty." He spoke of farming close to Beaver City and giving up their dreams about Washington. What happened to living life to the fullest, and why did he keep saying not to get her hopes up? That sounded more like her pa than the man she married.

Dorothy studied the map on her wall and the route she had charted. She consoled herself, as she often did, by drifting into a much-loved daydream.

DOROTHY STOOD IN the door of their Airstream trailer. "Honey, don't forget to stamp that fire out. We don't want to burn down any forests."

"I got it out real good, darlin'. Now, what's for breakfast?"

Dorothy loosened her robe so her breasts lay exposed. "Me." She threw her robe to the floor. "Come here and give your apple grower some lovin'."

Jack picked her up and carried her into the trailer. "You sweet woman, you." He laid her on the pullout bed as though she were made of glass.

Two hours passed. The afternoon sun beat through the window. Dorothy opened her eyes, turned over, and ran her hands across Jack's bare chest. "Honey, we missed breakfast. I think it's time for lunch."

Jack grabbed her. "I want the same thing for lunch that I had for breakfast."

Dorothy giggled and jumped out of bed. "Honey, when will we be in Washington?"

"It all depends on when you get tired of stopping to see everything there is to see."

"I'll get tired of that about the same time you get tired of getting the same thing for breakfast every morning."

DOROTHY STUCK A thumbtack on the map over the spot for Rocky Mountain National Park.

"Stop number one. He's just homesick; that's all," she said out loud in an attempt to appease her growing uneasiness. "Once he's home with me, he'll change his mind."

56

August 1945

Germany

Jack walked into the makeshift dance hall. WACs lined the wall. "One for every ten soldiers, I'd say. Well, let's see what we can do."

Ray smelled Jack's breath. "Jesus, man, you've been drinkin' straight since you got that letter from your old lady. That was two weeks ago. I'm not even sure you were sober on guard duty the other night. What the hell did she say? She foolin' around on ya?"

Jack took a swing at Ray. "Shut the fuck up. Peaches would never do that. You don't know her. She's perfect. She loves me no matter what."

"Sorry, it's just hard to see you like this. You gotta shape up, man. We'll be goin' home pretty damned soon."

"I don't know where you get off bein' so damned optimistic all the time. It's cuz yer just a kid. You didn't even have to leave headquarters. Anything can happen at any time; we have no control, and that's the truth."

"Yer talkin' about Grotsky, ain't ya?"

"Fuck you, Ray. Now, get outta my way. There's a WAC with my name written all over her, and I'm gonna find her, right now."

Ray kept a close eye on Jack, who meandered toward the wall of WACs. "Be careful, buddy. That's all I'm sayin'. Remember that perfect little wife of yours back home."

Jack perused his choices and headed toward the first brunette in the line. "Hi, doll. Wanna dance?"

"Sure solider, but I'm not your doll. My name is Sarah."

"Sarah! Damned. I knew a Sarah in Boston. Now *that* girl could dance. As a matter of fact, she was good at a lotta things." He winked at her.

"Well, there are a lot of Sarahs in the world. Do you wanna dance, or don't you?"

"Come on, honey. I'll show you how a real man dances." He grabbed her around the waist.

Sarah turned her head. "How much have you had to drink, soldier? Maybe you better go get some coffee."

"Look, honey, how much I drink is none of your damned business. Now, let's just dance." He took a step forward and his foot landed squarely on Sarah's toes.

She pushed him away. "That's enough, buddy! Go back to your barracks and sober up."

Ray put Jack's arm around his shoulder. "She's right. Let's go."

"Let go of me, you little punk! I'm just tryin' to blow off some steam. I don't wanna end up with a Section Eight. Just let me go!"

"All right, Jack, let's go 'blow off some steam.' " Ray headed toward the door with Jack in tow. Jack swung, hitting Ray across the jaw. Ray pushed him to the ground and then straddled him. "Look, old man, I've had about enough outta you. You make it real hard to be a friend. What got into you anyway? You're actin' crazy!"

"I am crazy. I can't go home like this. I can't tell her the truth about Grotsky, how he died, that it shoulda been me. She's got all these ideas about movin' to Washington, risking everything, and I just can't do it. Life's a crapshoot. You gotta play it safe."

RAY HANDED JACK a cup of coffee. "Good morning!"

Jack crouched on the edge of his cot, holding his head up with his hands. He lit a cigarette and took the coffee from Ray. "Thanks, kid." He looked at a red mark across Ray's jaw. "Oh, shit, I thought maybe that was a dream."

"No such luck, sir, but it's over now. From your looks this morning, I'd say you've suffered enough."

"What's that package?"

"I don't know. It showed up this morning. I told them to leave it at the foot of your bed so you didn't stumble over it."

Jack picked up the package and read the return address: "Mrs. Daniel Grotsky." He stopped reading. "What the hell?" he murmured. With great care he began to remove the outer wrapping. He warily pulled back the flap of the box. On top of Grotsky's mandolin lay a letter:

Dear Smitty,

I feel like I know you. Daniel talked about you in almost every letter. He thought the world of you.

He told me how the two of you used to play tunes together when you drove around in your truck delivering stuff. I want you to have his mandolin. I know that's what he would have wanted me to do.

God bless you, and I pray you make it home safely and very soon, and that you and your wife have a wonderful life together. I know that's what Daniel would have wanted for you.

All The Best,

Doris

Jack eased the mandolin out of the box and sat it in the corner by his bed. He waited, sure that Grotsky would walk through the door at any minute, pick it up, and start playing.

He wants only the best for me. That's what she said. Only the best, he thought. He picked up the mandolin, ran his hand along the smooth wood, fiddled with the tuning keys, and began to strum the strings. All the heartache remained, and the unanswered question persisted, but a subtle shift moved through him like a gentle breeze on an early May morning back home.

57

Beaver City

Darling Dorothy,

How's my Honey this nice bright morning? At least it's nice and bright here. I got that August 10th letter yesterday. I love you for writing as often as you do. I'll have to admit that your GI has it coming for not writing any oftener. I just have trouble settling down enough to write, but I'll do better from now on, I promise.

Honey, if I didn't have you waiting for me back home, well I'd been in the Sec 8 ward long before now. I'll assure you that I'm okay and will be even better when I am home and in your arms.

We're going into a shuffle again. We're leaving this outfit pretty soon and going to the 14th ordinance which is scheduled to go home at the end of October. So, maybe I'll be home sooner than I had planned, but don't get your hopes up. Honey, don't be too mad at me, cause really I love you more than anything else in the world.

All my love and kisses,

Jack G.

Carol put her purse in her desk drawer. "Don't tell me you're still reading that same letter from the first of July."

"No, I just got this one. He's coming home in October. That's only six weeks from now! I'm gonna be a *real* wife in six weeks."

"Well, you better rest up. Story has it that when those GIs get home they have big needs, and they don't waste any time getting it."

"Carol! I've never heard you talk like that!" Dorothy began to blush.

"Oh, come on. You *are* a wife now. You know how men can be anyway. Can you imagine what they're like when they haven't done anything for a while? It's gonna be fast and furious— mark my words."

"Well, Missy, I have news for you. Those GIs aren't the only ones going a long time without anything. We'll just see who is faster and furiouser."

Carol leaned back in her chair, laughing. "Dorothy Smith! Well, there's a side of you I've never seen before. You little sharecropper, you."

"I'm no sharecropper! I'm a married woman. I'm just saying women have needs, just like men.

"*Just* like men?"

"Well, close anyway. Oh, never mind. How did we get onto this subject anyway? You're making me all flustered."

JACK RUBBED THE chamois across the fender of the jeep until he could almost see his reflection. He slapped the chamois against the fender, satisfied with his work, and walked into headquarters. "Reporting for duty, sir. I have the colonel's jeep out front, all ready to go, sir." He saluted the sergeant and waited for his orders.

"Well, son, this is your lucky day. How would you like to go home?"

"Oh, sure, sir. I'd love to have the afternoon off, sir. Thank you." He saluted the sergeant and prepared to leave.

"No, soldier, I mean home as in the US of A home."

"Well, we're scheduled to go at the end of October, sir. Is that what you mean?"

"Now, private, right now! Go get your duffel bag packed and report back here in one hour. Do I make myself clear?"

"But..."

"Look, private, we have an opening on a ship that's leaving this afternoon. Private James came down with appendicitis, poor bastard, and he can't go. I just found out, and you walked through the door. Do you wanna go or not?"

"Yes, sir. I'm leaving right now, sir. Thank you so much. Do I have time to write my wife?"

"You are dismissed, private! Now!"

Jack ran out the door. He whooped and hollered all the way back to his barracks.

RAY WALKED INTO their room where Jack stood, stuffing things into his duffel bag. "What's goin' on? Where you goin'?"

"I'm goin' home. I'm goin' right now. The sergeant said so, in one hour. It's over. I'm leavin'. Look, Ray, you stood by me and saw me through some hard times. I don't know what I would've done..."

"That's enough. I know. I can't believe you're leavin'."

"It'll be your turn soon enough. Hey, maybe we can look each other up back in the States. Deal?"

Ray gripped Jack's hand. They stood there for a moment longer before Jack picked up his duffel bag and ran out the door.

Ray stared at the empty doorway. "Deal, sir."

LESTER, THE WESTERN Union man, opened the door to the Triple-A office. Everyone stopped working. A telegram meant one of two things: a message filled with great news or a message filled with sorrow. He approached the counter, and everyone waited for the fates to tip one way or the other.

"Good news!" Enlightened by experience, Lester knew the need for a quick answer to the question that hung in the air. "Mrs. Jack Smith? Is she here? Oh, there you are, Dorothy. It's from your husband."

Dorothy exhaled, realizing she hadn't breathed since Lester walked through the door. She rushed to the counter, tore the envelope out of his hand, and ripped it open. "Thank you!" she blurted out as an afterthought on her way back to her desk.

"He's on his way home!" Lester blurted out, unable to hold back the news any longer.

Dorothy read the telegram:

CAMP PATRICK HENRY: HAVE ARRIVED
HERE SAFELY. EXPECT TO SEE YOU SOON.
DON'T ATTEMPT TO WRITE OR CONTACT
ME HERE. LOVE, JACK

"He's here in the US, and he's coming home!" Dorothy took an envelope from her desk drawer and headed to Mr. Anderson's office. She knocked on his open door as she entered. "Mr. Anderson..."

"I heard, Mrs. Smith." He nodded toward the envelope. "I assume that's your resignation?"

Dorothy blushed. "How did you—uh, yes, it is, sir. I'll give you two weeks notice, but when he arrives, I need..."

"No need to explain. You have things to do. We'll manage. Why don't you take the rest of the day off and clear your head? Get things in order."

"Thank you, sir, from the bottom of my heart. You are so generous."

"That will be all, Mrs. Smith. I'll see you bright and early tomorrow morning."

Dorothy ran to her desk, hugged Carol good-bye, left the office, and returned a minute later for her purse and the telegram. She ran the four blocks to her house, telling everyone along the way of Jack's imminent return.

Climbing the stairs to her front porch two at a time, she banged open the front door and made a beeline to the phone.

"Number, please."

Dorothy shuffled through a pile of notes beside the phone.

"Number, please."

"Just a minute, Grace. I can't find the number."

"Oh, hi, Dorothy. I just heard the news. Smitty is on his way, huh?"

"Yes, and I want to call Mr. Linder in Oxford about that Airstream trailer he has for sale."

She recovered a small slip of paper from the pile. "Here it is! It's 2564."

"Gonna buy it as a surprise?"

"Believe me, I would like to, but I at least want him to hold it for me until Jack gets here. I know he'll love it once he sees it."

58

Train to Fort Leavenworth

The rocking of the train and the tic-a-tac of the wheels on the tracks calmed Jack. Question after question flashed through his mind:

My wife. I have a wife. I'm a married man. How can I support us?

Last time I farmed was a disaster. What if the same thing happens again?

Maybe Walter and I can be partners. Can I truly work with Walter?

What if the attacks come back, and I start shaking and puking?

"Where you from?"

Jack jumped, startled at the sound of another voice—this one outside his head. "What?"

"Where you from? Where you goin'?"

"I'm from Nebraska—Beaver City, to be exact. I'm goin' home to my wife."

"Lucky bastard. I got a 'Dear John' from my wife. She wants a divorce."

"Sorry. Don't seem fair. I'm Jack." He extended his hand to the tall, skinny kid peering at him over the top of the seat in front of him. "You don't look old enough to be married, let alone fight a war."

"Well, I lied. I'm twenty now, though, and plenty old to start my life all over again." He shook Jack's hand. "Name's Sam, by the way. Nice to meet ya."

"Where you goin'?"

"Kansas. I'm goin' back to farmin'. It's the only thing I know how to do. How 'bout you?"

"Farmin' for me too. My wife wants to move to Washington and grow apples, but I don't know—sounds awful risky."

"Hell, why not? You ain't so old yourself. Why not take a chance?"

"Takin' chances ain't paid off for me. Even when people try to take a chance, make things happen, it don't work, more times than not. People get killed for nothin'."

"Well, have ya ever even been to Washington?"

"Yeah, I worked there for a while, but I don't know nothin' about growin' apples."

"So farmin' it is, huh?"

"Guess so. If you could make a livin' ridin' a motorcycle or drivin' a fast car, I might consider takin' a risk. That might just be worth it."

"Can you fix 'em?"

"Hell, yes. I drove a Deuce and a Half during the war. That's half what we did. Drive 'em and fix 'em, drive 'em and fix 'em."

"Why would you choose farmin' over bein' a mechanic? There's real money to be had doin' that."

"Nah, too risky."

Sam moved to the seat beside Jack. "I'd say you gotta lot of thinkin' to do, mister. Hell, you lived through a war, and ya didn't die. That's a risk that paid off, ain't it?"

"I know, but some people—a lot of people—died. You have to be careful to make it. That's what I think. Anything can happen outta the blue by no fault of yer own. Ya just gotta be careful; that's all I'm sayin'."

Outside the train window, a hawk flew over a plowed field. It began to dive toward the earth and plucked up something with its beak. Jack looked on. "You just gotta be careful," he mumbled as the hawk flew away with its prey. His thoughts turned to home.

> "BABY, I'M HOME!" He grabbed Dorothy from behind and wrapped his arms around her waist. "I'm home, Dottie. It's you and me now."
>
> Dorothy said nothing. She stood motionless in his arms. He turned her around and then pushed her away. "You're not my wife!"
>
> "Yes, I am. Don't you recognize me?" Her face blurred.
>
> "No! You're not my wife!"

JACK SHUDDERED. THE train slowed to a stop at a depot in a small town in Missouri. Sam rubbed his hands together. "I'm starvin'. Let's get off and get a hamburger with all the trimmin's. After goin' without for two years, I been eatin' one every chance I get."

KETCHUP MIXED WITH dill pickle juice ran down Jack's chin. "This has to be the best burger I've ever tasted."

Sam nodded in agreement. "Everything tastes so damned good, don't it?"

"Yeah, no more B-rations for us!"

"Is your wife a good cook?"

"The best. She's gonna make me fried chicken dinner when I get there. Man, I can taste it now, with mashed potatoes, and she makes the best gravy ya ever tasted, and her green beans—"

"Stop, will ya? I get the picture. Yer killin' me here. We better get back on the train, or we'll be eatin' hash at the depot till the next train comes through."

Sam and Jack ran the distance to the train, jumping on just as the conductor announced, "All aboard!"

"JACK, I BEEN thinkin' 'bout you and yer not wantin' to take a risk. You can't live like that. Life is meant to take risks. Look at me. I joined the army underage, got to see the world, and now I'm ready to take on a new adventure."

"Yeah, look at you: divorced. You forgot to mention that! If ya hadn't run off, maybe you'd still be married. And seein' the world? You call fightin' a war, watchin' people die, haulin' dead bodies—you call that seein' the world? Your best friend gettin' blowed up?" Jack winced as the painful memories exploded in his head once more. "Never mind, kid—yer too damned young to get it." He walked down the aisle toward the door.

"Hey, man, I didn't know! I'm sorry!"

"Shut up, kid, and mind yer own business!"

Jack opened the door and moved onto the platform of the Pullman coach. The scenery whizzed by. It took him several attempts to still his hands so he could light a cigarette. "Damned, I gotta get ahold of myself," he said out loud. "This has gotta stop."

Beaver City

"Walter, do we still have that old trailer of Pa's? You know, the one he used to haul milk to the store?"

"Yeah, it's out b-b-back in that old shed. I don't know what k-kinda shape it's in. Why?"

"I—uh, *we* might need it. You know, Jack and I are moving to Washington—well, maybe. We're going to travel first, see the whole western US: Colorado, Wyoming, Idaho—"

"I know, Sis. I l-l-live here, remember? I saw the map in your room, and it's all you been t-t-talkin' about fer a month."

"Sorry, I'm just excited! I have an Airstream trailer all lined up for us to see about buying when he gets home. But once we decide on where we're going to live, we'll be back to pick up our things and move 'em, so that's why I need that old trailer. Think you can make it work?"

"Sure, Sis, you know I'll d-d-do it for ya."

"I know, honey. You're the best. We also need to talk about the farm. Are you ready to buy my half?"

"Almost. If you c-c-can wait till the corn is harvested, I can give you a better idea. I hate to see you sell your half before Jack g-g-gets home, Sis. He may have other ideas."

"No! He won't. Once he sees the Airstream, he'll be his old self again—you watch and see."

59

Beaver City

The train began to slow, and Jack's heart raced. He stood up, duffel bag in hand, peering out the window at the familiar landscape. The conductor moved sideways to maneuver around Jack. "It's a few more miles before we stop, son. You might as well sit awhile."

"If you don't mind, sir, I'll stand."

"You GIs are all the same." He smiled, shook his head, and continued down the aisle.

Jack gripped the back of a seat as the train jerked and its brakes screeched. The depot came into view. He leaned over, looking from one end of the station to the other. *Where is she?* He rubbed his sweaty palms on his pants. He walked to the front of the car, waiting for the train to stop and for the conductor to open the door. He stood motionless, trying to collect himself. *How the hell long can it take to stop a goddamned train?* He opened the door and stepped onto the platform as the train continued to roll into the station. He looked left, then right, and then left again.

"Welcome home, honey."

He spun around at the sound of her voice, dropping his duffel bag in the process. He held her at arm's length. "Just let me drink you in," he said as he touched her face, buried his nose in her hair, and ran his hands over her dress. He kissed her forehead. "It's you. You're here, standin' right in front of me." He wrapped his arms around her and held her, rocking back and forth. "I'm home; I'm home," he repeated, with no attempt to stop his tears.

She had never seen him cry. "Yes, you are; you're home," she cried, holding him even closer.

Jack picked up his bag, threw it over his shoulder, and wrapped his other arm around Dorothy. "Where to, darlin'?"

"My house. Walter is staying out at the farm now. We have the house to ourselves."

"You mean I'm sleepin' in your old bed?"

"It's our bed now. Think you can handle it?"

They walked the four blocks to the house, stopping every few yards as people welcomed Jack home.

"Here we are." Dorothy began to climb the steps to the porch. She opened the front door and waited for Jack to enter first. He dropped his duffel bag.

"What are you doing?" she asked in total surprise. In one graceful sweep, he picked her up and carried her across the threshold, down the hall and up the stairs. "Jack! Put me down! You can't carry me up these stairs. I'm too heavy."

"Watch me." He continued up the stairs and on to her bedroom. He began to unbutton her dress. She removed his belt with one sweep of her hand. He slid her up onto the middle of the bed and lay down on top of her. "Is this a dream?" He kissed her neck, her cheeks, her lips.

She closed her eyes and threw her arms open, allowing him complete freedom to explore her body. She expected him to be in a hurry, just as Carol had described. Instead, he took his time, removing her dress, her slip, her bra, touching her with great care and a gentleness she hadn't experienced with him three years earlier.

He moved his hands over her naked body. Unable to wait any longer, she wrapped her legs around his hips.

DOROTHY AWOKE WITH a start, rolled over, and smiled. "It wasn't a dream." She watched him sleep for a while before slipping out of bed and into her dress.

An hour later, Jack awoke to a familiar smell. Confused in the darkened room, he reached out to turn on a lamp beside the bed. He breathed in the aroma wafting up the stairs from the kitchen. "Fried chicken." He jumped out of bed, stopped long enough to don a pair of pants, and then ran down the stairs, two steps at a time.

Dorothy moved the chicken around the skillet, whistling as she worked. He tiptoed up behind her, kissed her neck, and cradled her breasts in his hands.

She shrieked. "Jack G. Smith, you bad boy! I could have knocked the whole skillet of chicken onto the—"

He swirled her around and stopped her chatter with a kiss. "Wanna try some French kissin'?" He pushed his tongue into her mouth.

"That's disgusting!" She giggled and then touched his lips with her tongue. "Well, maybe it isn't so bad." She paused. "The chicken! I won't have my first meal for you burnt over learning to kiss French. Now, go sit down and let me finish."

"Are you sure?" He wrapped his arms around her from behind and began to kiss her neck. "Absolutely sure?"

She continued to fry the chicken, and he started walking away. "Wait. I can finish with you here, close to me," she said. "Come back."

Jack began to sing "Tennessee Waltz" in a whisper into her ear. He moved her around the kitchen in a one-two-three motion.

They stopped by the stove. Dorothy placed the chicken pieces on a plate and began to stir flour into the drippings left in the skillet. "Get me some milk, would ya, hon?"

Jack danced his way to the icebox and back to her with milk in hand. She poured some in the skillet and began to stir it into the flour. "Keep singing." He slipped the spoon out of her hand, turned off the burner under the skillet, and danced her around the kitchen, through the dining room, and into the living room, stopping in front of the couch.

"I thought you wanted fried chicken," she pouted.

"There's only one thing I want more," he said as he lowered her to the couch.

60

Three Days Later

Dorothy jerked the covers off Jack. "Get up, honey."

"What the hell?" He reached for her hand. "Hey, you, come here."

"Oh, no ya don't. I need a little rest. Three days, honey, that's a lot of lovin' after three long, dry years."

"I know, so come here, come on, just once, and then I'll do anything you ask."

"You said that yesterday, and where did it get us? On the couch, on the stairs. I swear I never thought I would ever—"

"Oh, come on, Peaches. You love it just as much as I do, don't ya?"

"That's why I'm standing over here, fully dressed and ready to go." She walked out the bedroom door. "Come on, honey. I'll make you a nice *real* breakfast."

"How about some more of that fried chicken? Let's make it just like we did a couple nights ago."

"Stop!" she yelled from the stairs. "Now, get up, get dressed, and come on. I have a surprise for you."

Jack sat up and began to dress. For the first time he noticed the maps on the wall. He traced the route across the map from Beaver City to Denver, up to Cheyenne and Laramie, and on through Idaho. His finger stopped at the end of the route. "Washington. Damn." The clod in his belly returned for the first time in three days. He took the stairs one at a time, trying to compose his thoughts. He entered the kitchen and walked past Dorothy.

"Do you want your eggs sunny-side up again? Hey, what's wrong? Oh come on, honey. We can play some more when we get home. Don't pout like that."

"We need to talk."

"I know we do. Me first. I have something to show you, but it's in Oxford, and it's just killing me to not tell you all about it. I want it to be a surprise, and I know you'll just love it. Not another word. Now, it's your turn."

"I saw your maps."

"Oh, so what do you think? I mean, nothing is written in stone. They're just ideas. We don't *have* to go through Denver. I just thought it would be fun. Who knows where we'll end up, right? We'll just close our eyes and throw a dart at the map, and wherever it lands, that's where we'll start. Honey, what's wrong? What's going on?"

"I told you in a letter, remember? I wanna stay right here and farm, not in Washington or any other place, but right here."

Dorothy put up her hand. "Stop. Here, eat your breakfast, and then we'll drive to Oxford, and you'll see. Everything'll be just fine."

JACK SPREAD HIS arms out in front of him. "I feel like a damned fool with this scarf wrapped around my eyes. Where are you?" He stopped in midstride.

Dorothy took his hand. "I'm right here. We're almost there. Just ten more steps. I'll guide you. Now, stand right here and take off the scarf."

Jack jerked the scarf off and threw it to the ground. A 1938 forty-foot Airstream trailer met his gaze. Its silver color reflected the sun so that he had to shade his eyes to see.

"What do you think, honey? Isn't it gorgeous? It's just perfect. Come on. I'll show you the inside." Dorothy began climbing the stairs of the trailer.

"No! Stop right there! Dottie, I ain't changin' my mind! You didn't do something stupid, did you? You haven't bought this damned thing, have you?" She walked through the door of the trailer. "Dottie! Come down from there, right now!" He approached it and began to climb its steps. He peered into the trailer and saw Dorothy with her back to him, her hands covering her face, her body shaking with each sob. "Damned, honey, don't cry." He put his hand on her shoulder.

"Don't touch me! You yelled at me!"

"Stop, honey. I'm sorry, but you aren't listening to me. This is where we belong. It's too risky to go off running around all over the country. This whole cockamamie idea is crazy."

"You're calling my ideas, my dreams for us, crazy? I thought you wanted fun and adventure."

"Honey, please listen to me."

"No, *you* listen, Jack Smith, and you listen good. I have loved you since the moment I set eyes on you when I was in high school. You left me high and dry and moved to Washington without so much as a good-bye or 'see ya later.' I thought you were gone forever, and I made myself believe I could love somebody else, but all the while I knew it wasn't true. Then you came back into my life and swept me off my feet all over again. You even married me, and then you left again. I wrote you every day, and I worried myself sick day and night when you didn't write. I never knew if you were dead or with some French whore."

Jack's eyes widened. "I never—"

"I'm not finished!" Dorothy yelled, pacing up and down the trailer. "Now you come home, and all of a sudden you've lost your nerve. You used to be such a daredevil. The very thing that drove you away from me attracted me to you all the more. What happened to Smitty? Where did he go?"

Jack walked toward the door. "He went to war."

Stunned by his words, Dorothy ran to the door. "Jack! Wait!" He started the car and backed it up as she ran down the stairs. "Wait, honey! I'm sorry! I'm so sorry!"

He slammed his foot down on the accelerator. The tires spun. Gravel and dirt filled the air.

Dorothy collapsed to the ground, watching her dreams dissolve in a cloud of dust. She meandered back to the trailer and sat on the steps, holding her head in her hands. Twenty minutes passed. Someone walked up beside her, but the sun blocked her view.

"I'm sorry, Mr. Linder. I guess we aren't going to buy the trailer."

Jack knelt in front of her. "Honey, I'm sorry too. There's so much you don't know that I never shared." He stared at the ground, clenching his jaw, willing himself to speak. "I think I should—" He stopped. He tightened his fists and began again. "I think I should tell you at least some of it."

He began to speak, choosing each word with great care. Long pauses followed each new thought. He continued to talk, and the clod loosened. Words came with less hesitation as he told her about hiding in the cellar while shells whistled overhead, never knowing if he would make it through the night, and the clod crumbled. He told her the complete story about Grotsky, but he remained silent about the dead bodies he transported. They lived on in the remnants of the clod now buried deep within his soul.

She held him as he talked. He embraced her as she wept.

EPILOGUE

November 6, 2009

Dorothy lay in bed, her breathing rapid and labored. Three of her four children surrounded the bed with their spouses. Everyone hovered around her in silence, hypnotized by her breathing, worried that it would stop, yet worried that it would continue.

Dorothy's youngest son, David, spoke first. "Is she in pain?"

Jo, Dorothy's only daughter, responded, "No, she's comfortable. She may be able to hear us, though, so don't be afraid to talk to her."

Paul, the middle son, grinned. "She can't hear worth a damn when she's awake. I doubt she can hear us, now that she's in a coma."

Jo cocked her head. "Maybe, but you never know. I've seen stranger things happen over my thirty years in nursing." She looked around the room at her brothers and their wives. "OK, everybody, time for dinner. I'll stay with Mom and catch a bite to eat in the cafeteria. It's not bad—for nursing home food. We can talk more in the morning about"—she hesitated—"about things."

Everyone left, and Jo dipped a small sponge in some water. "Mom, I'm going to clean your mouth a little. It looks awfully dry." She wiped her mother's lips and then swabbed the inside of her mouth with expert care. Dorothy stirred and then lapsed back into a deep sleep.

Jo held her mother's hand. "I have your hands, Mom. Look at that. We have the same knobby knuckles, same double-jointed thumbs. It's gone by so fast. How can you be ninety-two years old? How can I be sixty-two?"

December 1945
Beaver City

Jack drove the motorcycle over the curb and onto the sidewalk that led to the front door of the house. He revved the motor. Dorothy ran out the front door, stopping on her tiptoes when she saw Jack on the motorcycle.

"You wanted Smitty back. Well, here he is. Hop on—I have a surprise for you."

"On the motorcycle? But I have on a dress."

"So? Pull up your skirt, wrap your legs around me, hold on tight, and off we go. Come on!"

"I can't. It's too risky."

Jack threw his hands up. "Too risky? Now who's the fuddy-duddy?"

"I know it doesn't make sense, but I can't. Where are we going?"

"Holdrege."

"That's over forty miles from here. Besides, it's December! We can't go that far on a motorcycle."

"I thought maybe we'd go see the world on it."

"Now you're just making fun of me. I'll get my coat, but we're taking the car. I have a surprise for you too."

"Wow. I'm home two months, and you're gonna try to surprise me again? What's next?"

Dorothy threw her coat over her shoulders. "One surprise at a time. You first."

"Not till we get to Holdrege."

JACK STEERED THE car to the side of the road and stopped. He took a scarf out of the glove box. Dorothy frowned. "What's that for?"

"Turnabout's fair play. Cover your eyes tight and don't peek."

Dorothy placed the scarf over her eyes. "You didn't do something foolish, did you?"

"Like I said, turnabout's fair play. Make fun of me if you want. We'll be there soon."

A mile later, Jack stopped the car and turned off the engine. "I'll come open your door and guide you, so don't peek."

"I won't, but hurry up. I'm so excited I'm about to pee my pants."

Jack opened the passenger door and took Dorothy's arm. "There's a curb here, so step up. Now, just walk forward about ten steps, and I'll take off the scarf."

Dorothy giggled, stepping forward with trepidation.

Jack removed the scarf from Dorothy's head. In front of her she saw a small house, which she was certain had been painted white at some point in time. Its black shutters glistened in the afternoon sun. A crumbling sidewalk led up to a porch, which was missing several slats.

"I know it needs paint, but I didn't have time to paint all of it. I did get the shutters done, and I can fix the front porch easy. Do you like it? Come on. I'll show you the inside."

"You bought it? It's ours?"

"You ain't mad, are ya? It came with the station."

"What station? What are you talking about?"

Jack sat down on the porch and motioned for Dorothy to sit beside him.

"I got to thinkin' about everything you said when we were lookin' at the Airstream trailer, about the old Smitty bein' lost, and I got ta thinkin' about this kid Sam that I met on the train. Dottie, you know I love cars and motorcycles, and I'm real good at fixin' 'em. This gas station came up for sale. I saw it in the paper. So I came up here last week and checked it out, and I just knew it was the right thing for us. It ain't perfect, but it's ours, honey. We can make it into our home."

Dorothy took Jack's hands in hers. "Maybe this is the perfect time to tell you my news." She paused. "I'm pregnant."

November 7, 2009

"Mom, I'm here!"

Dorothy opened her eyes wide. "Jack? Is that you?"

"No, Mom, it's me, Daniel." He knelt beside her bed.

"Daniel! Well, where's your dad?"

Daniel mouthed, "What do I say?"

"Mom, it's Daniel. He just got here from Illinois," Jo yelled in her mother's good ear. "Now all your kids are here."

Dorothy furrowed her brow. "But where's Jack?"

"You'll see him soon enough," Jo whispered. She shrugged her shoulders and turned to give her big brother a hug. "Nine years and she still can't remember he died. She used to ask me where he was every time I came to visit. She mimicked her mother's voice, 'Where's your dad?' I'd tell her, and then an hour later she'd ask me again."

DANIEL AND JO thumbed through the photo album, eternally present at the side of their Mother's bed. Daniel pointed to a photo of him and Jack on a beach. "There it is."

"Do you remember that vacation?"

"A little, but I was only four. It's more of a family legend than anything. I've heard the story so many times, it sorta feels like I remember it."

"I was only two, so I have no recollection of it except what Mom and Dad used to tell us. What an adventure, taking two little kids clear across country to Yellowstone and on to California. Think about how long it must have taken to get anywhere back then: no interstate, and what was the speed limit—fifty-five or something?"

Summer 1949

Dorothy squinted at the clear California sky. "No clouds to look at today," she said to Jo, who lay beside her, sucking her thumb.

The waves pounded the beach. Jack yelled at Daniel, "Get away from there! Yer gonna get drowned if yer not careful!"

Daniel squealed and ran back to his father, jumping into his open arms. "Let's build a sandcastle, Daddy."

"OK, buddy, let's go get our shovels."

Dorothy patted Jo on the back and listened to the rhythmic sound of the waves. Jo relaxed into her mother's soothing touch.

Jack ran up the beach toward her with Daniel on his shoulders.

Dorothy stood and brushed the sand off her swimsuit. "I can't believe we're here. How did you make it happen?"

Jack put Daniel down. "Go find our shovels, buddy."

"Remember how we always wanted to travel? I figured we better do it now." He leaned over and touched her belly. "Before this one is born, or it would never happen."

"It's a dream come true, and I love you for it." She nodded her head toward Daniel. "Better go make that sandcastle before he decides to take another swim."

Jack kissed her forehead. Daniel began running toward the shoreline with Jack following close behind. "Daniel, wait for me!"

November 7, 2009

Paul and David entered the room, greeting their older brother, talking, telling jokes, laughing louder than usual. Jo sat beside her mother's bed, holding her hand. Dorothy's breathing slowed. Her skin became cold and clammy. "Jack?" she murmured.

DOROTHY SAT AT a table next to the dance floor. She folded her hands on the table, straightened her hair, took a sip of water, and moved her chair so that she faced the door. "Where is he? He said he'd be here." She searched the dance floor for the fifth time.

The front door opened. A tall figure stood in the doorway, silhouetted by the street light behind him.

"Jack, is that you?"

DANIEL HEADED TOWARD the door. "I think I'll go check in at the motel and change my clothes."

"No, not now. It's time." The tone of Jo's voice left no doubt what was about to happen. They gathered around Dorothy's bed, each reaching out to touch their mother one last time.

"JACK, IS THAT you?" The figure entered the dance hall. Dorothy's body relaxed into a deep peace. She shaded her eyes with her arm, hoping for a better view of the person who now stood before her. "Jack?"

The strains of "Tennessee Waltz" played in the background. He reached out and took her into his arms.

"Wanna dance, darlin'?"

Acknowledgments

My first readers were ten friends who agreed to read my novel and critique my work. Most importantly, they also provided continual encouragement and support during the process of rewrites, delays, and procrastination. They are Jan Cox, Jan Gugeler, Kathleen Gibboney, Linda Dale Jennings, Jean Maas, Sandy Paul, Dolores Rowland, Tony Rowland, Julie Villia, and Leah Witherow.

Two of my oldest and dearest friends went above and beyond my expectations in reading and critiquing my work. They provided the first real copyediting and proofreading of the novel. My sincerest gratitude goes to Mark and Martha Hoover. Thank you especially for your comment about missing the characters after finishing the book and wishing they would stick around for a while longer.

I also owe a debt of gratitude to Tom Locke, my copyeditor and proofreader, who is a stickler for detail as well as grammar and spelling. Polly Letofsky, my consultant and coach from My Word! Publishing, is the reason the novel is actually in print. She kept me motivated throughout the entire publishing process, took care of multiple details, and provided referrals to top-notch professionals. Thanks go to Victoria Wolf at Red Wolf Marketing for the beautiful book cover, to Andrea Constantine for the excellent layout design, and to James Hallman at WriteWorks for his editing skills.

Last, but far from least, I need to thank my developmental editor, Bill Virden. He kept me inspired through five years of reading letters, of getting me over the idea that I couldn't really write a novel, of answering endless historical question and grammatical questions, and of reassuring me over and over that it was, indeed, a novel worth publishing. He has read and reread every word, every sentence, and every rewrite without so much as a heavy sigh. The fact that he is also my beloved husband, lifelong friend, and confidant is an added perk.

I extend my deepest appreciation to each and every one of you!

Lyrics used in the novel:

About the Author

Jo Virden is the author of *A Passion For Life: Ruth Marie Colville.* Her first love is writing short stories. *My Darling Dorothy,* which started as a short story, evolved into Jo's first novel. She is passionate about promoting childhood literacy and spends many hours volunteering in reading programs throughout the Denver Metro area. She lives in Arvada, Colorado with her husband, Bill, and she enjoys outdoor photography, long walks in the Rocky Mountains and spending time with her grandson, Cyrus.

CPSIA information can be obtained
at www.ICGtesting.com
Printed in the USA
LVOW12s2227140716
496396LV00001B/22/P

9 780997 430806